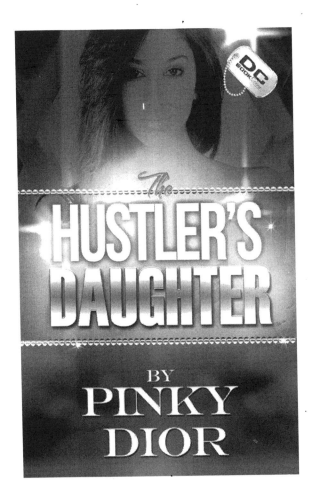

The HUSTLER'S DAUGHTER

BY PINKY DIOR

Published by DC Bookdiva Publications

Copyright © 2013 by DC Bookdiva Publications

Author Pinky Dior

ISBN-10:0-9887621-4-5
ISBN-13:978-0-9887621-4-5
LCCN: On File

Publisher's Note

This is a work of fiction. Any names historical events, real people, living and dead, or the locales are intended only to give the fiction a setting in historic reality. Other names, characters, places, businesses and incidents are either the product of the author's imagination or are used fictiously, and their resemblance, if any, to real life counterparts is entirely coincidental.

DC Bookdiva Publications

#245 4401-A Connecticut Ave

NW, Washington, DC 20008

In loving memory of my Nana,
Lela Williams

Acknowledgements

In Loving Memory of Lela Williams, I love you and miss you so much, Nana. I just wish you could have held in there a little longer. I know you would be extremely proud of me. I always told you about my books and showed you my book covers, and I know you're a woman of God and loved going to church. I knew they weren't the type of books you would read, but at the end of the day, I knew you were still proud. I wish you could just be here to receive a paperback book of mines because that's what we both were waiting on for so long. I know what you would do with it. You would probably carry it around in your purse all the time and say, "This is my grandbaby Ricketta's book", lol. I miss your voice, your love, I just miss your presence. You were that woman, like my second mother. My life changed completely when you passed away; I stopped writing. I just had, and still do have, a lot going on. But I know you wouldn't want me being stressed out, depressed, crying so much for you and my family. I'm making a step to change and work on getting my life the way it was. Around the time you passed, I was blessed with becoming pregnant. I felt like that was you; my baby girl will have your soul. Thank you, Nana. I love you and I will make you proud. This book is dedicated to you. I know you're in heaven smiling down now.

To my beautiful daughter Mercedes, I love you so much. You are so smart and I just can't wait until you get older to see how much of a good mother I am. I know you will be proud of me when you get older and I have to be the lead role model in your life. I don't want you to ever go through what I went through. I want you to live the life I never had, and what I promise, I will deliver. You and my unborn baby girl deserve the world, and Mommy's going to give it to y'all. Love y'all.

I want to give a special shout out to my mother Tonya for being there for me through any and everything. Although we have never really had the closest relationship, I still love you. And I love you more now that our mother and daughter relationship is getting better. We are much closer than we were way before. I know your mother isn't here anymore, but she's still with you, and now I have to be your best friend. I appreciate everything that you do and have done for me. Thank you for keeping a roof over my head, food on the table, and clothes on my back. I owe you, and I want to be able to do what you've done for your children and me. I have to work my butt off so when you get older, you will live comfortably and won't have any worries except your health. I love you, and once again, thank you.

I want to give a special shout out to my older brother Ronnie, aka TEFLON! I've had *The Hustler's Daughter* title in my head for many years when I was in high school. I posted it on the bottom of my pictures and I'm like, this would be a good title for a book. I remember us talking about it one day, and the ideas kept flowing, an idea just clicked, and I ran with it. I wrote every day, all day. I had to stop because my hands hurt, and I wrote part one in less than three months. Thank God you helped me, because this book wouldn't be a book without you. This book is a CLASSIC! No other book like it, and I truly thank you for helping me come up with an amazing concept! Love you, bro.

To my other siblings, Richard, I know we don't get along, but at the end of the day, you're still my brother and I still love you. Maybe one day we can be closer. To my little sister Rayonna, I know we don't have a close relationship, but we still have our sister bond our way, and I love you. Shout out to my niece Sienna, my nephew Adonis, and their mother Jackie, I love ya'll and miss y'all so much!!! Shout out to Stakkz, the father of my daughter Mercedes and unborn child. I know we've been through a lot. It's been a long three years. Our relationship was never perfect, but we had good times. But I appreciate the good, and I appreciate what you have done. I still have love for you, and I wish you nothing but the best.

I also want to give a special shout out to my two cousins, who I call my sisters, Shania and Shacora. I know we all had our ups and downs, but we been down with each other since diapers. So you know I had to give y'all a separate shout out. We used to wear the same clothes sometimes and people say we looked like triplets. We had our fun. And at the end of the day we all have grown into beautiful women and I love y'all forever, my sisters! Rest in peace to your mother, my favorite Auntie Satori Williams. She bought me my first laptop and I appreciate her more than ever for that, because if it wasn't for her buying me that laptop...I don't know if I would even be writer. Thanks, Auntie. Rest in peace.

Shout out to my God sister, Shavornya. We've had our ups and downs, you know. But at the end of the day, I love you from the bottom of my heart and we do have a good bond. We spent so much time together, laughing, chilling. We even worked at the same hotel. You're just a good person in general, and I love telling you what I'm going through and my problems because you're always there and give good advice. Thanks to you, I'm starting to realize a lot and take control of what I deserve. Love you.

Shout out to my home girl Sequaia, author of *Model Behavior.* We met on Twitter, and then we started talking on the phone, and then we wrote our first anthology together, entitled *Bitches Ain't Loyal.* She's real cool peoples. I can talk to her about anything and I'm glad we met. Although she's all the way on the west coast and I'm on the east coast, I know our friendship will be a forever lasting one, despite the distance.

Shout out to my entire family. There are so many cousins, uncles, and extended family to write all of your names. But I love you all, and stay strong!

Special shout out to DC Bookdiva. I know it's been a long three years and *The Hustler's Daughter* is finally coming to life, to print. In 2010 my life changed forever and you helped me become a published author. If Eyone Williams didn't write me a message on Facebook that day, believing in me, I don't even know if I would be published right now. Within a couple of days of reading *The Hustler's Daughter,* I got a three book deal contract and I was excited and in tears because I've waited so long to get published and it was really hard and I was just about to give up and try to self-publish. So I thank you for giving me the opportunity to live my dreams, which was to be a published author. Shout out to the entire DCB team and the people who support us, thank you all!

Last but not least, I want to give a shout out to my readers and supporters. Even way before I was published, people and teachers I went to school with had so much faith in me. They couldn't wait until my books dropped. I appreciate y'all waiting so long to actually be able to read something from me in print or online on Amazon and Barnes & Noble. Thanks to everyone who has rocked with me since my first short story "Hazel Eyes" and is still rocking with your girl. I know I have been M.I.A. for a while since my nana died, but I'm back on the scene, and I may be down but I won't be down forever. I'm back and Pinky Dior is here to stay, forever!

Thanks for your support, feedback, your reviews, and most of all, your love. Shout out to my Facebook family. Y'all show me so much love besides my books, and that's real!

www.pinkydior.com

Ace of Spades

Don reclined in his broad leather seat smoking a thick Cuban cigar. It hung on the side of his mouth as he effortlessly inhale the tasty smoke. He slowly exhaled the smoke from his full curvy lips. Smoke seductively filled the air, as if he were posing for a Playgirl photo shoot. He wore a long, thick, diamond-encrusted necklace. It complimented the studded Rolex on his left arm. Glancing over at the window, he noticed they were minutes away from touching down in Cuba. Don always flew in style in his multi-million dollar private jet. His entourage was deep. He was accompanied by his right-hand man and brother Roy Carter, his left-hand ace Frank Cilliaco and several body guards. He even brought along a few street workers, his food attendant Milan, and of course his designated jet driver Alberto. This group had the benefit of traveling with him exclusively. Don always enjoyed the beautiful cerulean waters of the Cuban coastline. While looking out of the window, he could see the beautiful palm trees at a distance. The jet began its descent and Alberto's voice announced that they would be landing in just a few minutes. Don sighed in relief. He was finally about to touch Cuban soil again and begin his mission. He slept throughout most of the flight, but Roy woke him up when he began talking to him.

As the plane landed and he heard the wheels rumbling, Don gazed at Havana through the small window. He smiled at the sight of the beautiful city and the wonderful memories it contained. Although he only came to Cuba for business, he always felt safe and relaxed when he was here. The Cubans showed Don major love. Back home in New York, however, the game was totally different. Of course he was well-known and respected, but he always had to watch his back. Don had to stay ten steps ahead of the game, just in case a nigga tried to make a move.

"Ya'll nigga's ready?" Don asked with a smirk on his face.

"We ready," everyone said in unison. That response was all he needed to hear in order to move forward. Stepping off the jet, Don took a deep breath of Cuban air. The crisp air filled his lungs giving him a boost of momentum.

A black stretch limo pulled up seconds after they landed. The driver hopped out and grabbed their luggage placing it in the trunk. Along the ride, they admired the trees that gave Cuba an exquisite look. They were complimented by the waters of the Atlantic Ocean cascading along the right side of the street.

Of course, all the beautiful females walking around in their bathing suits could not be ignored. Their breasts billowed over the tops of their bikinis and drew attention from everyone that passed.

The limo pulled up to Blau Arenal Club, located in the eastern section of Havana, in the Playas Del Este area.

Don gazed from his window and noticed a brown haired female standing in front of the hotel. She was wearing a white button-down shirt with a navy blue pencil skirt. She was young and very attractive, but not his type. He was in Cuba to handle his business; he didn't come for a vacation. He knew she was a worker sent by his new connect. He was told she would be wearing a white collared shirt.

The limo came to a sudden stop, and everyone grabbed their Louis Vuitton duffle bags and suitcases out of the trunk. The entourage slowly walked toward the hotel. They were stopped by the young woman and she spoke to Don.

"You must be Mr. Carter?" The young woman inquired as she approached him and his crew.

"Yes, I'm Mr. Carter, and you are?" he extended his hand.

"My name is Alana," she smiled as they shook hands. He kissed it before releasing it and she smiled.

"I'm just helping you with your hotel service and setting everything up for tomorrow."

Don thanked her, as she continued on.

"Manny will take your things and escort you to your rooms," Alana informed them.

She continued to tell them that everyone had their own individual rooms. Don was kind of impressed; the last connect had two people sharing a suite. He had a good feeling about this new connect. He had to kill his old one when they tried to rob him. He and his goons thought Don was a rookie, but Mr. Carter and his crew were more experienced than they realized. As they were escorted up to their rooms, Alana pulled Mr. Carter to the side so she could talk with him privately about the meeting with her boss.

"Tomorrow, be ready at 8 AM. The limo will pick you guys up promptly at that time and not a minute later. From there you will go to the designated area," Alana spoke with her eyes and made sure she was specific about everything. She didn't need any problems on her end.

"Where are we meeting?" Don inquired taking a cigar out of his jacket pocket.

"The car will take you along with the person of your choosing to the docks.

"We'll all meet you there, and proceed to making the deal so we can make this money." Alana smirked when she noticed Mr. Carter's million dollar smile.

"Yes, let's get down to business," Don rubbed his hands together. Alana began to walk off, but forgot to say something. She stopped in her tracks and turned around to say, "Hey, Mr. Carter don't forget to bring your $50,000 security deposit."

"Do I get it back?" Don joked.

"No," Alana half-smiled as she continued to walk down the corridor, purposely trying to switch her hips. Alana was a pretty young girl, but she was not what Don looked for in his women. She had a caramel skin complexion, long brown hair that reached her mid-back, small lips, and her body was petite-yet curvaceous.

She definitely wasn't ugly, but she wasn't spectacular either. He preferred a woman that was had the beauty and style of Marilyn Monroe. Don shook his head as he turned around and pressed the button for the elevator.

Don opened the door to his immaculate room and inhaled the fresh aroma of vanilla-scented candles. He tugged on his goatee, and smiled at himself in the mirror. He was full of confidence; he loved the man he had become. These days, he feared no one but God. In the past, there were times when he feared the man in the mirror as well.

Don began settling into his room and putting away his clothes. He sprawled across the bed and decided to take a quick nap before the meeting. Three hours passed and he awoke after looking at the clock. He noticed it was time to meet his crew in the lobby.

Don got up and grabbed his hotel room key and slid it into his pants pocket. He departed the room and headed down to the lobby for the meeting. As he neared the hotel lobby, he saw everyone sitting there. They were patiently awaiting his arrival.

"Alright people...tomorrow is the big day," Don assured them. "Tomorrow we wake up early to be ready at 8 AM sharp. I don't want any late comers because I don't have slackers on my team. The limo will be here on time, so we need to be in the lobby by at least 7:45," Don informed them. He then took a short pause and said, "This is a big day for me, for you...for us," Don pointed to each of them as their eyes met his. "Dress appropriately, wear your game faces; we're money makers and we are here to make money. Let's get this shit on and poppin," Don chanted as his crew joined in unison. "Go get some sleep; we got a long day ahead of us." Don stated before turning his back to them and walking out of the lobby.

Back in his room, Don removed his slacks and button down and hopped in the shower. After he showered, he kept it simple with a fresh wife beater and Polo boxers. He emerged from the bathroom and walked over to the doors across the room. They led to a well-maintained round balcony. Stepping out onto the balcony, he placed his hands on the black banister. He leaned forward and looked out into the distance observing the magnificent view of Havana. The skies were dark, but the lights of the houses lit up the terrain as far as his eyes could see. It was breathtaking, and Don stood there and soaked in all in. He felt the city of Havana sparkling in his eyes. As he sat down in the Lazy Boy chair on the balcony, he pulled out a fresh Cuban cigar and lit it. He puffed on the cigar and blew the smoke through his nose. He thought about the big day that was rapidly approaching. It was the day in which he was going to meet his new connect. This was vital in getting his product sold and his money made. This day was slated to be one of the most important in years. It would make Don Carter a richer and much wiser man.

Meeting of the Minds

The sun silently rose over the palm trees, peeking through the balcony's curtains. Don set his alarm for 5:30 AM. He immediately jumped up when he heard the annoying beeping screaming in his ears. He yawned as he stretched his muscular arms over his head and arched his back. He definitely needed a massage later today; he'd been having back pains lately.

Don quickly jumped in the shower for fifteen minutes and got dressed. He stood in the mirror and gave his face a quick shave, just to shape it up. Don admired his smooth dark mocha skin, nice fade, and his chiseled face. It was all complemented by his goatee, which gave him a real grown man look. He had full lips that many women craved and thick eyebrows.

Don's face was the epitome of a handsome hustler. He threw on a pair of Armani black slacks, his 2 carat diamond earrings, and his platinum Rolex. He wore an all white Armani button-up shirt. On his feet were a pair of $2500 Gucci all-black alligator shoes.

Don grabbed his cell phone and headed downstairs to the lobby where his crew was waiting around. It was seven forty-five on the dot. He loved his people because they listened; as instructed they'd arrived on time. He exchanged words with everyone before they walked outside to wait for the limo to arrive.

Don looked down at his Rolex, it read 7:55. He thought that the limo would already be there by now. He and his crew were right on time. The limo cruised up to the curb five minutes later at promptly 8 AM. The driver got out of the car and greeted them with a smile as he opened the door. He patiently waited until they were all inside to close it. Don inhaled deeply as they rode to the docks.

Alana and the other workers greeted them at the docks. She introduced Mr. Carter and his crew to the workers who represented the connection. They exchanged handshakes before boarding the expensive and immaculate yacht. '*You know this cat got money,*' Don thought while looking at his brother. Roy Carter knew exactly what he was thinking.

Feeling the yacht come to a complete stop, Don looked around at his crew and nodded, "Let's do it." He smiled as he got up. He followed Alana from the yacht and was blown away at the sight of a beautiful multi-million dollar estate before his eyes.

The Conglomerate

Maria stood in the living room with her French manicured nails pressed against the chair. She was gazing through the window, waiting for her father's yacht to arrive. She could see the waves crashing up against the shore as the yacht got closer to her father's estate. Maria couldn't wait to see her father's new customer.

All of her father's customers were old and lame. She knew this one had a lot of money and was coming from New York. She had a feeling he would be different from the others. She could tell by the way her father talked to him over the phone. The yacht pulled up slowly to the dock and came to a rest. Maria turned around in her 4 inch stiletto heels. She clicked across the marble floor on her way to her father's office. Usually she would have to knock, but this time the door was wide open.

"They've arrived," Maria informed him.

Her father, Vicente, was one of the largest drug suppliers in Cuba. He was seated in his chair behind a beautiful mahogany desk with his arms folded and a smile across his face.

"Bring them in," Vicente said as he slowly got up. Maria exited the office and headed down the corridor to open the front door. Alana was already walking up the brick path with the entourage trailing behind. Maria's eyes met with the guy who had his head down, but quickly lifted it up high when he realized someone's gaze was upon him. She gave him a warm smile to ensure him that he was welcomed along with the others.

"Good morning everyone, I hope you enjoyed your ride here."

"The food was excellent, thank you," Roy Carter chuckled rubbing his stomach.

"Yeah it was, and the ride was outstanding. Cuba is beautiful, and so are you." Don said as he stepped in front of Alana to grab Maria's hand and kiss it. Maria's face instantly turned red as she blushed and could no longer hide it.

"Well I'm glad you love it out here and thanks." She nodded her head and tried to regain her composure.

"It's nice to meet you...my name is Don, Don Carter. What's your name?" Don asked.

"My name is Maria and you can follow me straight through here." Maria said as she turned around.

She walked them down the corridor of the mansion and led them to a huge room that was nearly empty. It only held a black sectional sofa in the center of the room and a huge TV sitting directly in front of it.

"You may be seated," Maria informed them as she stepped out of the room. A few minutes later she returned with a guy who stood about 5'2". He had grey hair with traces of black and wore it slicked back. He had a thick mustache that complimented his grey bushy eyebrows. His skin tone was a dull yellow. He definitely had some years of experience in the game; his name was Vicente.

"I'm glad you all made it," Vicente smiled as he greeted each of them. He walked around and gave everyone handshakes. When he reached Don, he immediately stood up and gave Vicente a hand shake and a hug. Maria smirked, '*my kind of papi,*' she thought to herself about Don's gesture.

"Alright Maria, start the tape sweetie," Vicente told his daughter as he took a seat in his chair that was wheeled in behind him by one of his workers. Maria grabbed the remote and hit the play button. She began her speech about her father. It was the normal routine with new clients.

Throughout the entire presentation Maria couldn't keep her eyes off Don Carter. She noticed he was checking her out as well. Don stared at her the entire time she was talking. Maria was getting hot due to his intense stare and had to take off her blazer and loosen her shirt collar.

"Let's get this deal started," Maria finished her lecture and smiled as everyone clapped in unison. She bowed her head a little, showing appreciation for the applause. Vicente smiled at his daughter's performance.

"So, are we ready to get down to business?" Vicente asked.

"Yes, Vicente," Don spoke loudly.

"Maria, get the deposit. Let's go into the dining room for drinks." Vicente instructed her and got up. Everyone except Don followed him into the dining room while Maria gathered her things. Don sat across from her meticulously watching her every move.

"Let's go." Maria said as she walked past him with her heels clicking. She walked down the corridor and stopped at a large oak door. She had to unlock it by pressing her hand onto a brightly lit green pad.

The pad made a chirping noise to let them know the door was open. Don followed behind her in awe. Maria made sure she strutted when she walked and put a little extra into each step. Don was instantly mesmerized by her hips and the way her plump ass jiggled. He didn't want to disrespect his new business partner's daughter by staring, but he couldn't help it. Maria's body was curvaceous and her face was immaculate. She was stunningly beautiful.

The short-sleeved white blouse she wore revealed just the right amount of cleavage. Her 34 C breasts were nice and full. Her hair was long, thick, and jet black. It hung down to just below her waist and swayed when she walked. Her pink full lips were topped off by a mole that stood above them. Don was already in love. Maria was the most gorgeous woman he had ever laid eyes upon, she was definitely a keeper.

"Do you have the security deposit?" Maria asked as she extended her hand. Don placed the duffle bag he was carrying on the table. Maria grabbed the bag and dumped the contents on the table. Her father told her to count the money to make sure it was all there. As she sat down to begin counting the money, Don chuckled.

"It's all there Ma, I wouldn't even come to Cuba and play ya'll like that." Don said smiling as he rubbed his chin hairs. Maria shot him a glare; she looked down at the money and back up at him. She knew he wasn't stupid, and she didn't want to count the money anyway. She was just testing him.

If she would have counted it by hand, she would have been there for hours. Instead, she turned and walked over to the money counting machine and placed a stack of bills in. As she placed the last stack of bills in the machine, she realized that the amount greatly exceeded what her father asked for. It was the entire $100,000. '*Damn this dude must be swimming in pools of money,*' Maria thought to herself as she turned back around and stuffed the money back in the bag. There was a light knock on the door and Alana came in with Roy by her side. They both had grandiose smiles on their faces as if they've had a great conversation. She grabbed the duffle bag with the money from the table.

"It's all there," Maria assured her as she watched Alana exit the room with the duffle bag hung over her shoulders. Roy stood with a toothpick hanging from the right side of his mouth and smiled as he watched Alana exit the room.

Don watched Maria pull several surgical masks from a small cabinet. "Put these on." Maria was quite adamant about this request.

She handed everyone a mask to cover their faces. They placed the masks on and followed Maria into the next room. They could not believe their eyes upon seeing so many kilos of cocaine. This room held more product than any of them had ever seen at one time. Don was just as captivated with this sight as he was with Maria's beauty.

"What's the problem?" Maria asked curiously, looking back at their astonished faces.

"Nothing at all," Don replied, quickly switching up his facial expression.

"Alright, let me get these duffle bags out." Maria grabbed some bags and started putting kilos of cocaine inside them. Vicente had already set aside the correct amount; all she had to do was supply them with their product. The first order was one hundred kilos. Don knew Vicente's shit was legit. If there were any problems, he would be coming for Vicente's head. Don didn't care how much power and respect he had in Cuba.

After Maria was done, Alana walked into the room and helped her place the bag on a cart. Alana rolled the cart down the hallway and put the product in the back of a snack food delivery truck. Vicente walked into the room holding a cup of Patron in his hand while smiling widely at Don.

"Now we have to go to the man above me." Vicente said.

"And who is that?" Don was eager to know.

"Lieutenant Coffins." Don didn't know how to react at the mention of a lieutenant. He wasn't sure if a lieutenant would pull a stunt like this and put his career in jeopardy. Don quickly realized that he didn't give a shit. They were all getting paid.

"Okay, that's what I'm talking about then." Mr. Carter smiled as he shook hands with Vicente. Maria stood at a distance staring at Don while he conducted business with her father. She had to bite down on her lip to control her rising passion. Don was a tall, dark and handsome businessman. She was falling in love with him already.

Maria was never attracted to black men before, but there was something about him that captivated her spirit. She could tell that there was something different about him. His swagger was dangerous, impeccable and couldn't be mistaken. He was a man in control of his own destiny. When he walked past her, she could smell the intoxicating aroma of success. Maria wanted Don Carter all to herself.

The Set Up

Don was set to be introduced to Lieutenant Coffins later that evening. He and Vicente sat in his limo getting acquainted and having a few drinks. Don couldn't wait until his opportunity to meet the man above Vicente. He had been anticipating this meeting all day. Don left his crew back at the mansion, bringing only Roy with him. Vicente, Don and Roy sat behind the tinted windows drinking and having small talk. Vicente gingerly puffed on a Cuban cigar. He tasted the full flavor of the smoke and blew it into the air, fish bowling the limo.

"Are you ready to meet the Lieutenant?" Vicente asked with his hand on the door handle.

"I was born ready." Mr. Carter smirked as they all exited the limo. Don and Roy followed Vicente. Don made sure to keep his brother with him during his drug transactions. He knew that if anything ever happened to him, his brother Roy would take over the business. He also knew that Roy would annihilate the culprits involved in his downfall. Don threw his heavy duffle bag across his shoulder; it was filled to the brim with dead presidents.

Once they made it through the front door, they were escorted down the corridor of Lieutenant Coffins' mansion. They noticed that the mansion had armed guards stationed at each door. They walked down a spiral staircase, as Vicente led

Don and Roy into a room where Lieutenant Coffins was sitting. The Lieutenant was comfortably sitting at his desk and reclining in his chair with four guards standing behind him. The guards were mean mugging and they were all armed with AK-47's.

Don and Roy Carter were not intimidated by their stares, they shot nasty glares right back at them. A simple look in their eyes put everyone on notice that they were not to be fucked with either.

"Good afternoon, Vice." Lieutenant Coffins shook hands with Vicente. Vicente only allowed the lieutenant to call him 'Vice.' "Afternoon Lieutenant." Vicente nodded his head and looked over at Don and Roy to begin the introductions.

"This is Mr. Don Carter and he's the one who runs the business, along with his brother Roy who is next in line." Vicente smiled as he patted Roy's shoulder. The lieutenant immediately stood up and walked over to shake both of their hands.

"It's nice to meet you, Mr. Carter." Lieutenant Coffins stared him in the eyes and wouldn't look away until he walked back over to his chair to sit down.

"So what brings you to Cuba?" he asked.

"Business," Don simply stated. "I need a favor."

"And what may that be, Mr. Carter?" The lieutenant asked him while he reclined back in his chair and massaged his chin.

"I have kilos of coke that I need to transport back into the U.S. and I heard you're the guy I need to talk to in order to make that happen."

"You think it's just that easy huh?" Lieutenant Coffins smirked and sat upright with a serious look on his face.

Don shook his head and said,

"Well with your power and status, I know you have the authority to make it happen."

"And what do I get out of this?" Don didn't have to speak to answer the lieutenant's question. He grabbed the duffle bag from his shoulder, unzipped it, and dumped the stacks of cash on the table in front of the lieutenant and everyone else. He definitely had the lieutenant's full attention after that move.

"How much is this?" Lieutenant Coffins asked. He picked up a couple of stacks and smelled it as he fanned the money across his nose.

"Dirty money," he nodded his head in approval.

"It's fifty thousand." Don spoke with confidence. "Half of what I gave my supplier." Lieutenant Coffins looked at the money, placed it back in the bag, and handed it to one of the security guards. He then stood up and looked at Don.

He pointed to him and said, "Right this way."

They followed the lieutenant onto the elevator and rode it down into the basement. It reeked of death and destruction. Don covered his nose and pursed his lips together as he inhaled the smell of people who perished under the lieutenant's command. The room was filled with large marble coffins. There had to be at least one hundred coffins filled with dead bodies.

"What's this?" Don was puzzled. He looked around wondering what the hell was going on. Lieutenant Coffins pointed and motioned with his hand for them to come over. Don and Roy slowly walked toward the coffins. They watched closely as the lieutenant opened one. The coffin contained a   decomposing dead body. Don had a baffled look on his face. He looked back at Roy who just shook his head.

"I know this looks crazy, but if you want your fucking product to get to its' destination-then you're going to have to do it this way." Lieutenant Coffins said with a harsh tone. Don wasn't intimidated by his tone and didn't bother reacting. The only thing he cared about at this point was getting his product on the streets of New York.

"Mata bring me the knife." The lieutenant said to one of his security guards. Mata walked off and returned with a knife, he carefully handed it to his boss. Don watched as the lieutenant removed the dead person's jacket and cut his body down the middle. Don grimaced, but he kept watching; he was curious about this process. He focused on what the lieutenant was going to do next.

"...the product?" the Lieutenant held his hand out. One of Vice's workers grabbed the duffle bags, opened one up, and handed the lieutenant one kilo. He placed the coke inside the dead person's body. Mr. Carter was truly fascinated as he watched the Lieutenant perform his magic.

Don was impressed after the initial demonstration; he was pleased that the lieutenant was the person helping him. Vicente called a few of his workers in. They grabbed the duffle bags and began to work, filling up a few more bodies with the kilos of coke.

"Now after this is done, I will give you a call to let you know when the drop is made. From here on out, I have everything under control." Lieutenant Coffins assured Don.

"Thank you Lieutenant. It was nice doing business with you." Don shook the lieutenant's hand. Don walked out of the mansion feeling like a mastermind. He couldn't wait to get back to New York. He had just secured a better connection, which led to another connection that would easily net him tens of millions of dollars-maybe even more.

Forbidden Love

The night life was beautiful in Santiago de Cuba. The palm trees danced to the rhythm of the beautiful breeze. The waves clung together and crashed against the shore. Cuban music filled the air and people filled the streets dancing and lingering around.

Don and Roy Carter stood at the bar at Casa de la Trova, the area's hottest night spot. Don leaned his back against the bar and his eyes focused on Vicente's daughter, Maria. Her long straight hair was now done into a deep wavy style that flowed flawlessly down her back. She rocked a pink tube top that accentuated her succulent breasts. He gazed at her diamond navel ring, which glistened from across the room as she moved her body to the beat of the music.

The white Hawaiian skirt she wore gave her a classy look. To set it all off, she wore 3 inch white stilettos with strings crawling up her legs. Her ears were accessorized with huge diamond earrings which were hidden by her thick hair. They occasionally made appearances when her hair swayed side to side as she danced. She wore a Tiffany diamond bracelet on her left arm and a Tiffany diamond necklace hung high on her neck.

Don's eyes were glued to her. He needed Maria in his life. She was a very beautiful woman, and he was too smart to pass her by.

"Don, you know you can't have her." Roy told his brother, as he noticed him keeping tabs on Maria. "You can't mix business with pleasure," Roy warned. Don paid him no attention; he was in a zone. He grabbed his glass of Patron, took a sip, and walked across the floor. He took a seat next to Maria and continued to admire her beauty.

"Can I have a Cuban Mojito please?" Maria asked the bartender as she placed her hand under her chin. She glanced over with a sly look on her face when she noticed Don slide onto the stool next to her.

"May I help you?" she asked kindly.

"Yes you can...I want to get to know you." Don said bluntly with no need to beat around the bush.

"My father would kill you." Maria's heavy Cuban accent came out.

"Excuse me?" Don asked with a bewildered look on his face. The bartender came back over and placed her drink on the table. Maria grabbed her drink and continued..."My father would kill you if he found out that we talked." She casually stated.

Don stared at her as he eyed her lips wrapped around the tiny straw; they were full and glistening. He desperately wanted to reach over and give her a seductive kiss.

"He doesn't have to find out." Don smirked.

"My father knows everything." Maria assured him as she finished her drink and got up, "Everything." She said with an intense look in her eyes and with a serious tone.

"Sorry, but I have to go." Maria walked away and Don followed after her. He caught up to her and gently pulled her arm. Maria turned to face him with eyes full of lust. Don returned the gaze. They both knew what they wanted, and that was each other.

"Just dance with me," Don smiled at Maria giving her his best puppy dog eyes. Maria grinned while shaking her head side to side, but she reluctantly gave in.

A popular very Cuban song came on, and Maria loved it. She had to dance to this one. She was about to put her hips to work. She hadn't been out in a while; Vicente didn't allow her and Alana to do much. They spent the majority of their time working around the house.

"Alright," Maria smiled, "You're lucky this is my song." She said as she clapped her hands together several times, "Let's go." Don stood behind her and grabbed her gyrating hips. They began dancing to the beat. He was impressed with her dance moves, but he was a little embarrassed because he could hardly keep up with her. Don was a gangster and he didn't have to dance. When he went to a party he would just stand off to the side with his burner on his waist and a bottle in his hand.

Maria sang the song as she seductively danced with Don. All eyes were on them tonight. Not only was she a pretty and very intelligent woman, she could also dance with the best of them.

Throughout the night, Maria and Don drank heavily. In between drinks, they were on the floor grinding their bodies together as they laughed and chatted. Maria even took the time to show him some moves, she was trying to help him keep up with her.

"Let's get out of here." Maria leaned in and whispered in his ear. Without hesitation, Don quickly grabbed her hand and led her to the door. Maria stopped in her tracks and looked both ways before stepping out into the street.

They walked across the street to the Casa Granda hotel. Maria stayed out of sight while Don secured a room. Once he was given the key, they both hopped on the elevator. She pressed her back against the elevator wall and bit down on the bottom of her lip, staring at Don. He felt her gaze and turned to her; their lustful eyes met.

They stepped out of the elevator and Maria walked in front of him and slid the hotel room card into the lock, opening up the door. Once inside the room, their lips quickly met each other's. The hotel key fell from her fingers and onto the carpet. Maria wrapped her arms around his neck as Don ran his fingers through her long hair. They fell back onto the king-sized bed.

Don started placing kisses on her neck. Maria let out soft moans as he removed her tube top. He made his way down to her chest and began passionately licking around her nipples. He pulled down her skirt and was happy to find out that she wasn't wearing any panties. He smiled as he put his tongue to work. He licked her clit up and down until she was dripping wet. Maria grabbed the white linen sheets and balled up her fists as she let out loud seductive moans. She loved the way Mr. Carter was pleasing her, and she grabbed his head and moved her hips in circular motions. She was swept away by his touch and lost in a state of euphoria.

"Fuck me Don." She yelled, getting impatient. Don pulled down his pants and rummaged through his pocket for a condom, but he didn't have any. He came to Cuba for business; he didn't know he would be fucking.

"Shit, I don't have a rubber Ma." Don told her. She didn't care and covered his mouth with passionate kisses. Don took that as a yes and continued on his mission.

He took off his shirt and tossed it to the floor. He grabbed his dick and slid inside of her. She passionately held onto him as he slowly gave it to her.

Stroke after stroke, Maria grabbed his back and dug her French manicured nails into it tearing into Don's flesh. She couldn't keep her composure, her legs started shaking hysterically. She loved the way he was pounding her; she had never felt this good.

As she lay on her back enjoying every second of orgasmic bliss, Don leaned forward as he took her nipples into his mouth and sucked on them slowly. Maria wasn't done yet, and wanted to show him what she was working with. She motioned for him to go on the bottom as they rolled over and switched positions. Maria was now on top and she slowly went to work. She masterfully rode his dick up and down. Don moaned loudly as he looked up at her. He grabbed her hips and watched her titties bounce up and down in his face.

Maria groaned as they continued to make love. This didn't feel like just sex; there were some emotions attached. Don released his juices inside of her walls and within seconds she climaxed again. It was almost as if it was planned. After they were done, Maria collapsed onto his chest as Don held her in his arms. They fell asleep in each other's firm grasp like they were husband and wife.

The next morning at 7:45 AM the sun started creeping through the hotel window. Don lay beside Maria still holding her while they slept. His cell phone started vibrating on the table. He carefully removed his arm from around her waist trying not to wake Maria up. He turned around and retrieved his cell phone from the night stand along with his Rolex. Don answered his phone and it was his brother Roy.

"What's good wit' cha bro?" Roy asked as Don answered the phone. "Yo bro, I'm at the hotel that was across from the bar...chill the fuck out...I'm on the way." Don closed his phone while his brother was still talking. He got up quietly and stepped into his pants and slid on his shirt. He watched as Maria silently slept like an infant. Her long hair flowed down her back, and the white linen sheets were wrapped around her curvaceous body.

After he got dressed, he wrote his phone number on a piece of paper and placed it on the nightstand. He bent down and kissed her on her forehead, after he gently brushed her hair back to remove the pieces of hair that were in her face. Before exiting the room, Don looked over his shoulder and saw she was still resting like a sleeping beauty. He didn't want to leave like this, but his flight was scheduled to depart at 9:00 AM. He had to go back to New York City to make his money.

XXXXXXXXXX

Maria woke up and rolled over in the bed to find Don absent. She slowly got up and ran her fingers through her thick hair as she looked around the room searching for Don. She sucked her teeth as she snatched the sheets from her nude body and tossed her legs across the bed. Maria got up still naked and walked across the room. She headed straight into the bathroom.

She used the bathroom, took a shower, and rinsed her mouth out using the mouthwash the hotel gave her. After finishing up in the bathroom, she emerged and walked over to the bed. She looked over at the clock and it read 8:00 AM.

"Shit!" Maria yelled as she quickly grabbed her clothes from the floor and put them on, "Dad's gonna kill me!" Maria mumbled as she slipped on her skirt and sat on the bed to put on her heels. She placed a stray piece of hair behind her ear, and from the corner of her eye she noticed a white piece of paper sticking out from the night stand. Maria turned her head, reached her hand over and grabbed the piece of paper.

A gracious smile appeared across her face as she read the paper. On it, Don wrote his phone number and the comment, 'one day I will make you my wife.'

Maria could only blush; she had the time of her life with Don Carter. She got up from the bed and called a cab to take her home. She hoped that her father wasn't awake when she got there. She knew he would definitely be pissed and start asking questions about where she was and what she was doing while she was absent from his presence.

As the car pulled up to Vicente's estate, Maria was extremely nervous. The entire ride she was practicing excuses to explain why she was just getting home. She hopped from the car and headed towards the house. She quickly fixed her pink tube top and made sure her hair didn't look messy. She slid her key into the front door and bit down on her lip, hoping she would not have to face Vicente. She slowly crept in, closing the door behind her. She tried to sneak across the marble floor but it was hard not to hear her since her heels clicked loudly on the floor. She stopped to remove them.

As soon as she passed her father's office, she overheard him on the phone. She dashed up the spiral stair case and rushed into her room. She looked over and noticed her sister Alana sound asleep in her bed. She slipped out of her clothes and into something more comfortable. Maria sat down on her chair and she grabbed the brush. She brushed her thick hair down to the back of her head.

"Where are you coming from?" Alana asked. Maria looked in the mirror and eyed Alana, who was stretching her arms and yawning.

"I went out last night." Maria said bluntly.

"I'm aware of that." Alana said sarcastically as she sat up looking at the clock, "It's almost... nine o'clock and you're just coming in the house...where were you?" Alana asked eagerly.

"At the hotel across from the bar with Mr. Carter," she cooed.

"Oh my God Maria, what were you thinking?" Alana covered her hand over her mouth, "You didn't sleep with him right?"

Maria stopped brushing her hair and turned around smiling, "Of course I didn't." Maria said sarcastically while rolling her eyes, "What else would we go to a hotel for?"

"If Daddy finds out, he's going to kill you." Alana assured her.

"Well he won't find out, unless you say something." Maria shot her a nasty glare.

"I'm not going to say anything Maria." Alana said with sincerity, "You just better hope he doesn't find out, because if he does he will kill..." Maria cut her off.

"He's not going to find out!" Maria barked, as she got up and flicked her hair back and exited the room. She walked down the spiral stair case and over to the living room. She stood and stared from the window. A slight smile appeared across her face when she watched the waves crash up against the shore. She was reminiscing about the first day that she met Don. She was into her day dream and didn't realize her father was behind her. She only noticed when she felt him breathing down her neck. Maria closed her eyes as she felt his hand caressing the side of her neck.

"I see the way that you look at him." Vicente said with a tone dripping with jealously, "And I see the way that he was looking at you." He said referring to Don, "And I promise you Maria, if you ever think about..."

"Father, I have no interest in Mr. Carter." Maria was lying straight through her teeth.

"Good, you better keep it that way." Vicente hissed as he drunk the last sip of whiskey.

"There will never be you and a Mr. Carter because if you go against my rule, the both of you will end up dead!" He slammed down his glass of whiskey on the window sill and walked away.

Maria jumped back; she was startled from the sound of the glass when he slammed it down. Those words repeatedly echoed in her head. She knew Vicente wasn't joking; he was a man of his word. If he found out about their secret love, both of them would suffer the same fate-DEATH!

xxxxxxxxxx

Don sat on his private jet and gazed out the window. Maria was on his mind during the entire flight. She was such a woman: she was beautiful, smart, classy, stylish, sophisticated, and could dance and fuck all night. She was everything he'd ever wanted in a female. He didn't want to leave her behind, but business always came first. He sincerely hoped that one day they would get the chance to meet again. Roy noticed his brother was quiet and decided to ask him what was up.

"Damn bro, you good?"

"Yeah, I'm just thinking." Don scratched his chin.

"That chick got you wide open, huh?" Roy laughed.

"Nah yo, she's different. Yo...I think she gon' be wifey." Don smirked as pictures flashed through his mind of the two of them getting married.

"You just met her bro'...and she just gave it up to you." Roy chuckled.

"I don't give a fuck about that..." Don started getting upset. He didn't even want to talk with Roy about this; he was so negative sometimes.

"You got bigger and better problems to be worried about besides some chick that lives way across the world from us." Roy said as he sipped on his drink. Don knew there was some truth in his brother's last statement. "Yeah, whatever you say bro." Don said dismissively. He still couldn't take his mind off Maria completely.

For the next few days, it felt good to be back in New York. When the drop was made as promised within the week, Don was the happiest hustler in the city. He stood in his workroom watching his soldiers unload kilos of coke. The money was already starting to come in, but this time it was coming ten times harder.

The Other Woman

Meringue music and cigarette smoke filled the living room of Carmen's Spanish Harlem apartment. The late night breeze entered through the half open window. Carmen stood with a lit cigarette in her mouth as she moved her hips side to side. She wore skin tight black leggings and a white t-shirt with ruffles on the shoulder. Her golden blonde hair was cut into a short bob that shaped her face and brought out her perfectly tattooed eye brows. She took a long drag on her Virginia Slim cigarette, as she closed her eyes and grabbed a Corona from the fridge. She popped off the top and began to sip on it.

There was a loud banging on her door, but she couldn't hear it due to the loud music. She danced around in the living room and when the song finally changed, the knocking continued growing louder.

"Who the hell is it?" Carmen yelled with the cigarette still dangling on the side of her mouth. She turned her head towards the door and started slowly walking over to it.

"Come open the fucking door!" Carmen smiled and rushed over to the door and unlocked the two locks. On the other side she saw her boo, Don Carter standing there. She reached in for a kiss, but he rushed past her and immediately started talking shit. Carmen just rolled her eyes as she closed the door behind him and locked it.

"You didn't fucking hear me knocking?" He yelled over the merengue music. She looked at him wide-eyed with no response.

"You need to turn that shit down." He barked. Carmen walked over and turned down the music, "What you having a party in here or something?" he playfully asked, as he took off his jacket and threw it on the couch.

"Yeah, still celebrating when you left." she sarcastically joked as she gulped down the rest of her Corona and slammed the empty bottle down on the coffee table. She bent down and placed her burning cigarette in the ashtray and seductively walked over to him.

"I missed you Baby, did you miss me?"

"Of course I missed you." Don said as he smiled and he picked her up. Carmen wrapped her legs around him and they exchanged a long sensual kiss.

"How was the trip? Did you meet any new girls?" she asked, and she quickly resented asking when he said yeah. She knew Don wasn't with long talking and he didn't have to explain shit to her. She wasn't his girl; she was just someone he would fuck with here and there. He also used her to cook up his crack.

"How much did you miss Daddy?"

"Daddy?" she cocked her head back as she playfully rolled her eyes, "You know I missed my Papi." She smiled and winked at him.

Don had to admit that he did miss her too. He only missed her because she was the only one he fucked on the regular, and she kept her pussy nice and tight for him. As he walked down the hall with her in his embrace, they clumsily kissed while he groped her thick ass. He gently pushed the door open with her back and aggressively threw her down on the bed. He began unbuttoning his pants and didn't stop until he was naked. Watching him undress, Carmen was growing more aroused. She hurriedly removed her clothes as well.

The nipples on her perky breasts grew erect from visual stimulation. Don looked down and noticed her pussy was neatly shaven, just the way he liked it. He climbed on the bed and on top of Carmen. He kissed her neck and traveled down her chest focusing on her breasts. He hungrily sucked on each of them. She moaned with pleasure; she loved when he flicked his warm tongue across her hard nipples. It made her pussy drip like a broken faucet. He abruptly stopped licking her breast and stood up on his knees. He stroked his manhood to full attention.

"Put it in, I need you Papi." Carmen groaned.

"Oh you missed Daddy's dick?" he laughed as he saw the lustful gleam in her hazel eyes.

"Stop playing with me, I want it now." She whined. He could tell she was extremely horny. He obliged her requests and slid his dick inside of her. He slowly thrust in and out of the pussy. Carmen bit on the bottom of her lip as she watched him. Every time he went in he hit her with the slow pumps, he knew that drove her crazy. She couldn't take much slow fucking, it felt too good.

"Faster Papi, faster!" she yelled out loud. "You want it fast? You want me to go faster?" he asked, as he started speeding up the pace.

"Hell yeah! Give it to me Papi!" she said between gritted teeth.

"Turn that ass around."

He got up, and she quickly turned around and placed her ass in the air and buried her face on her champagne colored silk pillow. Don grabbed his dick, slipped it right into her wetness and went to work. He grabbed her short hair, but kept losing his grip. Then he grabbed onto her hips as he rapidly pumped her back and forth on his dick. He grunted as he neared climax, and sweat poured down the side of his face. Carmen moaned and screamed out in ecstasy.

"Ohhh, Don Carter, Mhmmmm"

"Damn Maria, you feel so good Ma." Don didn't even realize he had called her the wrong name and neither did Carmen. "MARIA!" He said again as he exploded inside of her sugary walls. '*Fuck,*' he said to himself, as he realized he was calling Carmen the wrong name.

Since he left Cuba, Maria was all he could think about. Even when he and Carmen had sex, all he thought about was him and Maria making love. Carmen cocked her head back as she turned to him and moved away. She forced his still leaking dick out of her pussy.

"So who the fuck is Maria?" Carmen's New York accent was thick and heavy combined with her Dominican accent. She folded her arms across her breasts as she waited for a response.

"What you talking about?" He asked while wiping remnants of cum off the tip of his still erect dick.

"You know what the fuck I'm talking about! You just called me another bitch's name!"

"Man, you tripping!" Don said with a harsh tone, he quickly slipped on his boxers, "I'm out."

Don put the rest of his clothes on and quickly walked towards the door.

"Oh so you just gon' come over here, hit it, call me another chicks name and expect me not to be mad? What the fuck is your problem nigga?" Carmen retorted.

"First of all Carmen, you need to fucking relax." He pointed his finger in her face, "Last time I checked you weren't my fucking girl." He retorted and grabbed his car keys off the nightstand.

"Well you know what, fuck you and that bitch MARIA!" Carmen shouted, "That bitch is all the way in Cuba, you think she's calling your name when she's fucking another guy?" Carmen laughed at her comment, "Don't come to me when you feel like fucking some reliable pussy! You can afford to go to Cuba whenever you want, right?" She said with her head tilted and a devilish smirk on her face. She did have a point, but Don wasn't about to agree with her. He simply turned his back and headed out the door as she rushed down the hall and said, "Run, run that's what you always do!" Carmen screamed, as he slammed the door in her face.

She turned around with her back against the door and slowly slid down to the ground and cried. She held onto her knees and sobbed uncontrollably. She loved Don and would do anything for him. This was the first time he'd ever called her another female's name. That was just unacceptable.

She didn't hear from Don for months after that night. However, one day he got a new shipment and needed her to cook the work. Of course they had sex again. It started to go back to their regular relationship until he stopped calling her out of the blue. He never returned her phone calls and she had know idea why.

Seeds of Love

Nine months passed and Maria had not seen or heard from Don Carter. She sincerely missed him and wished she could see him again. She was currently living in a different Cuban city, Santiago de Cuba. Maria had been staying with her aunt since she found out she was pregnant. She was too afraid to tell her father, so she moved out. She knew Vicente was a man of his word; he wouldn't hesitate to kill her and Don.

Vicente would be outraged if he knew her and Don had sex and created a baby. He always reminded her of Rule #1- never get involved with his customers. She had always obeyed his rules, until now. However, there was no turning back. She found out that she was pregnant six weeks after Don left Cuba to return to New York. She knew it was his child; she wasn't sexually involved with anyone else.

One day Maria woke up with heavy pains in her stomach. She rubbed her protruding belly and bit her bottom lip. She rocked back and forth trying to bear the pain of the rapidly increasing contractions. Maria screamed out in pain causing her aunt Maleese and the maid Edella to rush up the stairs and into her bedroom. They found her screaming in agony and tears excessively streaming down the side of her cheeks.

Maria threw the blanket from her body. Despite the pain she was in, she searched for Don's phone number. She found it in her night stand next to the bed.

"Oh my God, let's get her to a hospital!" Maleese insisted while watching her niece struggle. Maria sat back down on the bed as the pains resurfaced.

"Maria, calm down, you're moving too much." Edella said as she helped Maria to her feet. Maleese ran over and grabbed Maria's coat from the closet and placed it around her shoulders. Maria could barely walk. Her legs felt like they were made of rubber and she was extremely woozy. The three of them slowly walked down the stairs, when Maria felt a warm sensation running down her leg. She slowly put her head down and watched as the clear fluid oozed from her vagina and down her leg. She was leaking onto the marble floored stairs.

"My water just broke!" Maria automatically assumed. They rushed her to the front door where one of their drivers picked Maria up. They were off to the hospital in a flash.

Maria was sweating profusely throughout the entire ride. Her mind was overwhelmed with the thought that she was already having the baby. They arrived at the hospital in enough time to get her on a stretcher.

Maria passed out several times due to the pain before she officially made it into the room where she would deliver her baby. When she was finally conscious, she turned on the radio and listened to some Cuban music. The doctors told her that she wasn't ready to have her baby just yet; she was just having a little leak. Maria lay in the hospital bed and stared up at the ceiling. She was in deep thought about what she would tell Don, when and if she finally spoke to him.

Several minutes later, she had the urge to pee. She sat up in the bed and looked around for a way to call for help. She found the call button on the side of the bed to call for assistance. She seriously had to pee, and it had already begun to trickle down her leg. Finally the nurse came to Maria's aide.

"Are you okay Maria?"

"Yes, I'm fine." Maria smiled as she tried to get up, "I just have to use the bathroom."

"Hold on, let me help you." The nurse moved in closer to Maria and pulled back the sheets. Both of their jaws dropped as they stared at each other in amazement.

"You already had your baby." The nurse was astonished. She called for the doctors to come cut the cord and assist with anything medically that she could not.

"What?" Maria started crying with tears of joy streaming down her cheeks. She couldn't believe that her baby was already here. It amazed her that she didn't have to push or endure hours of painful labor. Tears flooded her eyes as she gazed at her beautiful baby. She had a new baby girl. The baby was wide awake and didn't cry at all. Once she was cleaned off, she was handed to Maria. Maria lovingly gazed into her daughter's eyes.

"That was the easiest birth I've ever seen." The nurse chuckled.

"I had no idea." Maria shook her head side to side, "I thought I had to use the bathroom or something." They all laughed. Maleese and Edella rushed into the room.

"Maria, she's so beautiful." Her aunt smiled as she sat on the side of the bed.

"Thank you." Maria held her baby girl in her arms. She took in all her beautiful features including her slanted eyes. She was surprised to see that they looked to be grayish-green in color. Her small pink lips had a mole on the top right corner. It resembled Maria's; she had one near her lip on the same side. Her baby had thick neatly shaped eye brows and a round petite nose. She looked almost exactly like her Maria, but she was a little darker. She had a light complexion with a hint of caramel. Her head was full of curly black hair. Maria and Don brought a beautiful baby girl into the world.

"What are you going to name her?" Edella asked. Maria didn't have to think twice. One name rolled off the tip of her tongue. "Mercedes," she blurted out, with a big smile across her face. "Mercedes Carter." Maria nodded her head up and down and smiled from ear to ear.

"Can you two excuse me for a moment?" Maria asked. Her aunt and the maid exited the room and patiently waited in the lobby. Maria grabbed the number that was on the table and placed a piece of her hair behind her ear. She picked up the hospital phone and dialed Don Carter's number. She nervously placed the phone to her ear and waited for him to answer. Many different thoughts ran through her head. She didn't know how he would take the news. He probably wouldn't believe her when she told him. He would probably deny it and say Mercedes wasn't his child.

Tears gathered in her eyes as the thoughts ran through her head. She didn't want her daughter to grow up without a father. She wanted her to have a wealthy life, and she knew Mr. Carter could provide that. She bit on her bottom lip while waiting for him to pick up. Sadly, she only got through to his voicemail. She ended the call and looked through her room's window. Her future would hinge on Don Carter's response, when and if he found out about Mercedes.

xxxxxxxxxx

Don cruised down the streets of New York bumping LL Cool J's "I Need Love". He wore his blue New York fitted cap pulled low over his eyes. His car windows had limo tint, so no one could see inside. Although people knew when he hit the corner; everyone knew he was driving a gold Lexus with 22 inch chrome rims. He had just returned from replenishing his product with his brother Roy. The next order of business was to collect some paper that was owed to him. Things had been going smoothly for them since they got back from Cuba. Their money game stepped up tremendously.

Everyone in the Carter family was eating and had cake. Don's cell phone was in his pocket and he could feel it vibrating. He reached into his pocket and realized that it was a weird number, but he recognized the Cuban area code. He thought it was Vicente calling from another number, but when he answered he got a pleasant surprise.

"Yo?" Don flipped up his phone and put it up to his ear. "Don?"

"Who's this?" The voice sounded familiar, but he couldn't put a finger on it.

"Maria."

When he heard her name, Don almost dropped the phone. He had been thinking of her since he left, but became very focused on making his money. He loved the connection between the two of them and wanted more.

"Oh my God, Maria-how have you been?" Don was happy to hear from her. He was wondering what took her so long to call him. He started thinking that she wasn't interested in him and what they had was just a one night stand.

"I've been good. I mean, I'm happy." Maria smiled. She looked down at her newborn baby girl that she held in her arms, "Umm... I have something to tell you."

"Go on. I'm listening. We have a lot to catch up on." Don couldn't wait to pick up where they left off.

"I was pregnant with your child, and today I gave birth." She informed him. The words were like music to his ears. Don couldn't believe what he was hearing. He had to look at his cell phone again to see if this was really happening and not a prank call.

"Are you there?" Maria asked.

"Yeah, my bad, I was just thinking." Don shook his head and chuckled. "I'll be down there soon." He smiled from ear to ear at the news.

They exchanged words and she gave him the address to where she was staying. "Hold on," he held the phone up to his ear and drove with one hand. He grabbed a piece of paper and a pen from between the seats and wrote the info on a piece of paper as he managed to drive. After all the important information was exchanged, he hung up the phone. This was going to change things for everyone.

"Who the hell was that?" Roy asked noticing a change in his brother's demeanor.

"Call Ms. Price and let her know I will be going out of town for a couple of days. I need a ticket to Cuba, no make that two round trip tickets." Don informed his brother.

"Yo, what the fuck Don, we're not supposed to go to Cuba until next month to re-up. So why the change of plans bro?"

"That was Maria, Vicente's daughter." Don smiled, "Something came up that just can't wait bro."

"Aww man, what happened?" Roy laughed, he was eager to know.

"She just gave birth to my daughter." Don couldn't help smiling. His dimples were in full view, and he was elated. Roy was just as surprised as Don; he couldn't get any words out.

"I have a daughter, a lovely baby girl. Mercedes Carter," Don whispered to himself.

Denial

Don stood near the bed as he bent down and tickled his daughter's stomach. She wore a pink onesie and had on a pink headband. Her curly hair was already starting to grow, enhancing her beauty. He loved the way her bright green eyes popped out at him. She was the prettiest baby he'd ever seen; she was a Carter baby.

Don loved his life, but he loved it even more when he was blessed with a beautiful baby girl. She and Maria were the missing links to absolute happiness. As he kept giggling and tickling Mercedes, a cute smile came across her face. Her gums were in full sight. She was only three months and fifteen days old. He loved making his daughter smile; it gave him great joy to be her father. Every time he had a long hard day of hustling, he would come home and Mercedes knew how to put a smile on his face and warm up his heart.

Don could hear his wife walking up the steps. Within seconds Maria emerged into their master bedroom. She was dressed in a pair of grey sweatpants and a wife beater. Her long hair was pulled back into a ponytail in the center of her head. She carried the baby's bottle in her hand along with a pink pacifier. He looked up and lustfully stared at Maria. He had to admit that she looked amazing for a woman who just had a baby.

He knew other chicks who had babies and lost their perfect bodies. He shook the sexual thoughts out of his head as he picked Mercedes up and held her in his arms. He looked into her green eyes. With every passing day, he learned to love her more and was prouder to be her father.

"Is her bottle ready?" Don asked.

"Yeah, I have it right here." Maria said sarcastically as she held up the bottle and waved it around. Don screwed up his nose as an awful stench crept into his nostrils. He turned Mercedes around, she was giggling and full of joy. He lowered his head next to the back of her diaper.

"Whew, I think she pooped." Don said turning his lips up to his nose, "You need to change her." He said in a kind but demanding tone.

"Why can't you change her?"

Maria's eye brows shot up in defiance. Suddenly Don was saved when his phone started ringing.

"Come on Ma, next time." Don smiled, "My phone ringing, take her." He handed Mercedes over to Maria. Maria's piercing eyes stayed glued to him.

"You're not off the hook." Maria said. Don rushed over to his jacket and pulled out his phone.

"Hey beautiful, you ready for mami to change your stinky butt?" Maria smiled as her daughter giggled at her.

Maria laid her down on the bed and began changing her, but not without keeping an ear to what was going on with her husband. She turned her head and watched as Don answered the phone. He spoke in a low tone. His voice was agitated, demonstrating that the phone call made him angry. He left the bedroom and disappeared into the hallway. Maria tried to eavesdrop, but his voice quickly faded away.

xxxxxxxxxx

It was a year later, January 15th 1991. Carmen lie on the hospital bed as she held her new born baby in her arms and stared down into her beautiful hazel eyes. She had a caramel skin complexion with a head full of light brown hair. Carmen decided to call Don and tell him the news. Although she had a feeling that if he saw her daughter, he would deny her.

Carmen was adamant that Don was the father. However, after he stopped messing with her, she did have a dude on the side. She held the hospital phone in her hand and slowly dialed his number. She really didn't want to go through with it, but she told herself she had to do it for her child. She named her daughter Hazel, after looking into her eyes for the first time. She finished dialing his number and held the phone up to her ear. It rung a few times before he picked up.

"Yo?" He answered.

"Hey Don, what's up?" Carmen asked, trying to gauge the mood and strike up a conversation. She realized she had to ease into it because they hadn't spoken in a year. That was also the last time they had sex.

"What do you want?" He whispered in an agitated tone. He was seemingly annoyed and knew this call would bring about problems.

"I have something to tell you." Carmen stammered for fear of his response.

"What is it?" He questioned, taking in a deep breath.

"I'm at the hospital and I just gave birth to your daughter." Carmen smiled, but it quickly turned into a frown and tears. Don's heart dropped and he couldn't believe what she was saying to him.

"You know what Carmen? I don't know what type of shit you're on, but I stopped fucking with you for a grip, that isn't my baby!" He denied.

"How could you say that?" Tears filled her eyes at his response. She almost thought he would be happy, but clearly she was mistaken.

"You know you're the only dude that I fucked with." Carmen shook her head as she couldn't believe the words that came from his mouth.

"You know what, what hospital are you in?" He asked angrily. She gave him the information and room number.

Don hung up the phone and slid it into his pocket. He headed up the spiral staircase. When he entered the room, Maria was just finishing changing Mercedes' diaper. She held Mercedes in her arm as she fed her milk from the bottle.

"Babe, I got to dip for a second." Don said grabbing his jacket.

"Who was that on the phone?" Maria asked as she eyed Don suspiciously.

"It was my brother; I got to collect some dough from him."

"What time you coming back?" Maria sleepily moaned, Don walked over and kissed her on the forehead.

"I don't know, but I should be back in less than an hour." Don said as he bent down and kissed Mercedes on the top of her curly hair.

"Alright, love you." Maria said as she puckered out her lips for him to kiss her.

"Love you too baby."

He could feel Maria's eyes watching him as he grabbed his car keys and headed out the bedroom door. Once Don hopped in his Lexus, he quickly made his way to the hospital to see if what Carmen said was true.

Fifteen minutes later, he pulled up onto Lenox Street in front of the Harlem Hospital Medical Center. He parked the car and got out. He headed inside as the double doors slid open. He walked up to the receptionist and asked for Carmen Diaz. The nurse pointed down the hall and he quickly followed her directions. As he walked through the door, he looked as cool as ever. Carmen held her composure as she lay in the bed, but soon old feelings started to resurface.

She wished she could just wrap her arms around his neck, tongue him down and make love to him. She knew that since he went to Cuba, he had changed. She knew that things would be different after he called her another female's name. "So what's up?" he asked looking around the room, "Where's the baby?"

"She's in the bassinet sleeping." Carmen pointed to where her baby was. She silently prayed that once he saw her, his feelings would change. Don walked over to the baby with his hands in his pocket. He looked over and stared into the baby's hazel eyes, she was staring straight back into his.

He compared Carmen's daughter to Mercedes and he didn't see any similarities. Although his daughter Mercedes looked more like her mother, she shared a few resemblances of his. She was definitely a Carter. To him, Carmen's baby looked straight Dominican and just like her. The baby didn't share any of the Carter family traits. He turned around silently and coldly stared into her eyes.

"You ready to sign the birth certificate?" Carmen excitedly asked.

"She's not mine." Don nonchalantly answered. "And I don't want you to ever call me again. I have a beautiful wife and a gorgeous daughter. I'm not going to let you come between us and break up my happy home." He said. "Good luck finding the baby's father."

Don walked out and turned around to see tears forming in Carmen's eyes. She was shaking her head in disbelief. Her blood boiled.

"Don't call me ever again Carmen, have a good life." With that he exited her room hoping to close a chapter in his life. He thought he had already done so one year ago.

Carmen sat in her bed and cried. She worried about the day she would have to explain to her daughter that her father denied her. It was a lesson everyone would learn severely.

The Princess has Arrived

Mercedes grew up to be drop dead gorgeous by the age of fifteen. She matured to be a beautiful girl with a voluptuous figure. Over the last couple of years, everything about her changed drastically. Mercedes had that perfect skin tone, which was the result of being mixed with African-American after her father Don and Cuban descent after her mother Maria. She stood 5'2" in height and full pink lips with a tiny beauty mark on her top lip. Her lips always glistened with pink lemonade MAC lip gloss.

Her long and thick jet black hair flowed down her back; she was petite, but thick in all the right areas. Her perfectly waxed eye brows brought out her beautiful green eyes. Mercedes always giggled when people confused her natural eye color for contacts. Basically, Mercedes Carter had it all.

Don Carter moved his family into a luxurious mansion in New York. He owned expensive paintings and exclusive custom made furniture. The Carter house could be on a TV show or used for a huge movie. Whatever his family wanted, he supplied. The ability to provide made Don Carter a happy man. His first born daughter was his reason for living.

Who's That Girl

The month of September rolled around quickly. Just a month ago it was summer and the sun was beaming and everyone was outside. Now it was over and fall was settling in. Mercedes' birthday was approaching next month and she'd been planning to celebrate for a while.

She couldn't wait to party with her friends. Mercedes' father was planning to send her to one of the highest class, most expensive private schools in Long Island. She didn't want to go to a private school. She felt that she could do just as well at a public school. She also knew the boys in private school weren't her type, but she wouldn't dare tell her father that information.

Mercedes recalled walking into his office a few weeks ago with her mother by her side.

"Good morning Daddy." Mercedes greeted her father. He lifted his head up from the newspaper and pushed it aside, giving his daughter his undivided attention.

"Good morning Baby Girl," he smiled and responded. She was definitely a "Daddy's Girl". Mercedes moved closer towards his table.

"What's up?" Her father asked, knowing the look in her eyes when she needed or wanted something.

"Daddy you know how you want me to go to private school?" Mercedes asked. He nodded his head knowing what she was here for, Mercedes nervously bit down on her bottom lip as she continued to speak.

"And...I really want to go to a regular school Daddy. And plus it's closer to the house instead of in Manhattan." Mercedes exaggerated because Manhattan was also close to their home in Long Island.

"Daddy I don't want to go to that private school, I want to stay close to home ...where my heart is...where the Carter family heart is."

Mercedes used her eyes as a way of manipulating her father to get what she wanted. She had him right where she wanted him. Don let out a deep sigh and folded his hands together and placed them on the desk, reclining in his chair.

"You know I want the best for you Mercedes right?" Don said considering what she said. He loved her and would do whatever she asked.

Mercedes nodded her head up and down excitedly. Deep down she knew that's all her father ever wanted for her, nothing less.

"I'll let you go to the school of your choice, but under one condition." Don spoke in a demanding tone as he pointed his finger. Her eyes bulged with fear, hoping he didn't ask her to do something that she was unprepared for.

"Under what condition Daddy?" she asked inquisitively, as she nervously tapped her foot on the ground.

"That Mr. Gates will pick you up and drop you off at school." He wanted her to be as safe as possible within reason.

"Daddy, I can't get on the train?" Mercedes asked.

"Listen I'm doing you a favor here, either you get dropped off by the driver, me or your mom. Your other choice is to go to the private school in Long Island." Don smiled as he reclined in his office chair.

"What about a car for my birthday?" Mercedes was cheesing from ear to ear, as she knew she was pushing her luck.

"Don't push it." He father warned her, giving her the eye.

"Alright, alright, I guess I'll take the ride from Mr. Gates." Mercedes smirked, although she loved getting on the train. Even though they were always crowded, she couldn't help but to like that mode of travel. There was always lots of eye candy on the train, it was the place to see and be seen.

"Where's this school?" her father asked.

"Queens." Mercedes spoke loudly. She wanted to go to a school in Harlem, but she knew her father wasn't going to allow that. Don looked at his daughter with a look of dissatisfaction. He didn't want her going to a public high school at all, much less in Queens.

Don wanted her to go to school and get her education. He wanted her focused on a future outside of the game. He had never said no to her before, but he was seriously considering doing so in this instant. Those thoughts went out the window when his eyes met with her slanted almond shaped green eyes. Mercedes had him wrapped around her finger.

"You better get out of here before I change my mind." Mercedes ran behind her father's desk and firmly embraced him. She pulled back from the embrace and smiled from ear to ear.

"Thank you Daddy...thank you." She reached over and hugged him again as she chanted. Elated, she disappeared into the foyer floating on cloud nine. Don grinned as he noticed his wife in the background chuckling at him and shaking her head side to side.

"Now I don't know why you even bothered in the first place signing that girl up for private school. You knew damn well she didn't want to become one of them snobby white girls." She shook her head. "You know you don't even have the audacity to say no to her." She assured him.

"Just like I could never say no to you right?" Don smiled as he walked over towards Maria and wrapped his arms firmly around her waist planting soft kisses on her neck. She smelled like a succulent sweet pear.

"You're beautiful and you smell so good." Don planted a wet one on her neck. Maria moved around him and smiled.

"Better stop that's how we made the first one." Maria assured him as she walked from his office beaming.

"It was truly a blessing." Don smiled.

"Heaven sent." Maria smiled. Don loved his daughter. He wanted more children, but Maria didn't. Every time he brought it up she would remind him that Mercedes was his number one princess, his first daughter. If they chose to have another one, Maria knew all hell would break loose. Mercedes wanted all of the attention to be on her and wouldn't be able to adjust to the changes around the house if they ever decided to have another Carter running around.

XXXXXXXXXX

Queens High School was packed with students. Mercedes sat behind the tinted window of the black stretch limo as they pulled up in front of the high school. It was her first day of high school, and she was a little nervous. The school was comprised of blacks, whites, Latinos, and Asians. Everyone in front of the school curiously watched as the limo pulled up. They all wanted to know who was getting out.

Mercedes took a deep breath. The driver, Mr. Gates, got out the car to open the door for her. She swallowed hard and thanked Mr. Gates for the ride. He told her he would be waiting for her when she got out of school.

Mercedes was dressed to the nines as she entered the school. Everyone watched her as she strolled through the halls. The boys wondered who she was and how they could get her attention. Everyone was awestruck. She felt like she was Janet Jackson with paparazzi. Mercedes thanked them with a smile and continued walking down the hall. One of the girls became curious as to who Mercedes was and shot her an envious glare. She chuckled with her friends as they posted up against the lockers. She mumbled under her breath, "Who's that girl?"

"Mercedes Carter." Mercedes confidently answered.

The girl didn't realize Mercedes could hear her. She was embarrassed and her face turned red. The girl's name was India, and she was a junior. Mercedes thought she was pretty; however, she wasn't on her level. India didn't have shit on Mercedes. She was thicker than Mercedes and had huge titties that were busting out of her white t-shirt. She had on some tight blue Fashionista's from Wet Seal and the usual blue and white Jordan's that everyone rocked. *'Typical Bitch,'* Mercedes thought to herself as she eyed the girl up and down.

India stood about 5'6". Her hair was dyed red and it reached her mid back, but wasn't longer than Mercedes. She had her chin pierced and she clearly had a nasty attitude.

"Did I ask you?" India retorted and rolled her eyes, as her girls started laughing. Mercedes chuckled at the girl's sense of humor, but never once was she intimidated by her. Although India was taller and bigger than her, Mercedes knew that didn't mean shit.

"I'm just telling you because I heard you wanted to know." Mercedes smiled as she began walking away. She quickly did a 360 when she heard her yell, "Aye, anyone knows who the fuck is a Mercedes Carter?" The hall filled with laughter.

"A girl whose shoes you can't dare walk in, bitch." Mercedes said clearly and calmly, letting her and her little friends know she wasn't some girl they could walk all over.

'These bitches must have me confused, I'm really the wrong bitch to fuck with,' Mercedes thought to herself.

India stared angrily at Mercedes. She wondered who she thought she was with her attitude and rich girl persona, trying to act like she was the shit. Oohs and Ahhs filled the hallway because Mercedes' come back had India at a loss for words. "Punta!" was all India could come up with.

Mercedes loved the attention. She made sure she switched her ass down the hall. She definitely had all eyes on her after the verbal altercation.

After two classes, it was lunch time. Mercedes refused to eat the lunch that the school was serving. She spotted a vending machine and purchased a bag of Lay's chips, an Almond Joy, and a bottle of Dasani water.

The cafeteria was full of students and filled with laughter, chatting, and yelling. She noticed the girls from earlier sitting in the back grilling her; Mercedes rolled her eyes as she looked away for another seat. She spotted a table with four girls, so she swallowed her pride and walked over to the table and smiled.

"Hey, Um, is this seat taken?"

"No it's not, you can sit here." One of the girls politely said.

"Thank you." Mercedes removed her bag from her shoulder and placed it beside her.

"Hi, my name is Candice, but they call me Candy for short what's your name?"

"Mercedes, Mercedes Carter." She spoke her name with pride.

"It's nice to meet you." Mercedes nodded her head up and down in agreement.

"And these are my good friends Chamari, Hazel, and Shateeya." Candy introduced the rest of the girls. They all greeted one another. These girls were the first ones to make Mercedes feel welcomed in her new school.

Mercedes opened up the bag of chips and started eating. She then felt someone staring at her and looked up to see Candy all in her grill. "Is there a problem?" Mercedes spoke up.

"No, no, no." Candy chuckled. "You just...look familiar. Do I know you from somewhere?" Candy asked, as she narrowed her eyes. She was in deep thought trying to remember where she knew Mercedes from.

"No, not that I know of." Mercedes looked at the girl just as hard as she was looking at her. She also felt in her heart that this girl looked familiar too; she couldn't put a finger on it.

"Wait...didn't you use to go to the private elementary school in Long Island?" Candy asked.

"Yeah, I did."

"You don't remember me Mercedes?" She asked smiling ear to ear.

"I remember when we use to be in the gym and all the boys would chase after us and we would scream you got the cooties...you got the cooties....Ha Ha Ha."

That brought up so many memories when she sang that song. Candice turned out to be her best friend from an elementary school in Long Island that she attended until she transferred.

Mercedes covered her mouth with her French manicured nails as tears welled up in her eyes. Candy was her best friend all the way from kindergarten. She couldn't believe how different she looked now. So much so, that she didn't recognize her. Finally she had one ally in this new school; she was happy to have an old friend by her side.

"Oh...my...goodness," Mercedes slowly said as they both stood up and reached across the lunch table giving each other a hug. They held onto each other for about one minute rocking side to side.

"I'm so sorry, you looked familiar but I just couldn't remember where I knew you from." Mercedes apologized as they took their seats.

"I can't believe it." Candy smiled.

"Do you still have that charm bracelet I gave you?" Candy threw up her arm and smiled. "Of course I wear this every day." She proclaimed proudly showing off her wrist.

"Wow, you look good Candy." Mercedes eyed her up and down.

Candy was not your typical girl; like Mercedes, she too was also a bad bitch. If there was one thing she and Mercedes had in common, it was their love for style and fashion. Never would you see them rocking shit from Old Navy or Forever 21. Candy had a caramel skin complexion and her hair was dirty blonde. It screamed it had been dyed too many times. She carried a small petite frame, but had big breasts and a nice little round butt.

Candy had pretty big brown eyes, a small pointy noise, and small lips. She was a definitely a beautiful girl. Candy was Mercedes' ride or die bitch from way back, and she was thrilled that they got reacquainted.

Hazel was pretty in her own way. She was half Dominican and African- American and had mahogany colored skin. Her body was curvaceous. She had long, thick, curly, light brown hair with blonde highlights. Her mother named her Hazel after looking into her eyes, but people in the hood called her Haze because she loved to smoke Purple.

Chamari stood 5'5", she was a chubby girl with a cute face. She wore appropriate clothes for her size. Mercedes loved the hair style she rocked. It was a short bob with spiral curls which brought out her eyes. It reminded Mercedes of Keyshia Cole's hair, red in the front and blonde in the back.

Last but not least, there was Shateeya. She was the gangsta of the crew. She was a tall dark skin girl, with the flawless skin of a model. She had black healthy hair stretching past her shoulder blades. She rocked a gold Marilyn Monroe piercing on top of her lip that Mercedes thought looked nice on her. She was a cool girl, but if anyone looked at her in the wrong way she would slice them with the quickness.

While the girls were sitting on the bench, they caught Mercedes staring at one of the sexiest dudes in the school. Chino was staring right back at her. He was Dominican, Puerto Rican, and half Korean. He stood about 5'8" and had a medium build. He had thick hair which was coifed into a pony tail and stretched down his back. His baby hairs lay down smoothly along his double line-up. His goatee was neatly shaven, giving him a grown and sexy appeal. His chinky hazel eyes brought out his flawless mocha colored skin complexion. His arms were completely covered with tattoos.

The only imperfection he had was a big scar that ran from the corner of his right eye and halfway down his cheek. In spite of that, he was still the cutest guy in school that she had seen thus far. All of the girls wanted him, but Mercedes knew she would get him.

She watched him as he looked at her while licking his full thick lips. He had Mercedes drooling. Her girls saw her and began cracking up; they could tell he had her open. He had all the chicks in the school open like that. She started twitching in her seat because she felt her panties getting wet. This was a new experience; no one had ever made her wet just by looking. She was coming into her womanhood, and she knew when she was aroused.

Mercedes looked at his gear and sized him up from head to toe. Chino rocked huge 14KT Gold pave` diamond earrings. They glistened from both sides of his ears. He had a nice sized Rolex on his left arm. He was exactly her style with his expensive gear and flamboyant colors; he could dress his ass off.

Chino wore a purple fitted Ed Hardy eagle rhinestone tee, with some Ed Hardy eagle strikes embroidered jeans. He had on a pair of customized purple Air Forces to match his shirt.

"Damn girl, you must be feeling home boy, huh?" Chamari asked.

"Hell yeah, he fly as shit." Mercedes smiled as she looked at her girls.

"You ain't got a chance with that." Shateeya assured her shaking her head side to side.

"And why is that?" Mercedes asked.

"Girl please, Mercedes is a bad bitch. She's beautiful and I think he's feeling her too." Candy chimed in. They all looked over and noticed he was still ice grilling their table. That's when the girl from earlier, India, walked over and tried to hug him. Chino gently pushed her way and turned his back towards her.

"Because of that!" Shateeya pointed her finger over to India.

"And she ain't got shit on Mercedes." Candy said, as Chamari and Hazel agreed.

"That was his ex, but she fucked around on him and he cut that bitch off." Hazel said.

"I know he's still fucking with her though." Shateeya acted as if she knew everything. Mercedes felt bad vibes from her, as if she was jealous.

"That bitch?" Mercedes laughed. All of them looked at her wondering why she was laughing. "How do you know her?" Candy asked.

"I bumped into her earlier and she rubbed me the wrong way, you feel me?" Mercedes said.

"So I had to let her know who I was...Mercedes Carter bitch, and don't forget it." Mercedes smirked as Candy screamed, "That's my bitch." They gave each other dap and started smiling.

"That's India. India Jones, the leader of the crew Queen Bee's." Hazel informed her. "She thinks she's ill because she's been bullying mad bitches in this school, but she knows not to fuck with me. I'll slice her ass up real quick. Her and her little Latina crew think they're what's up." Shateeya sounded like their spokesperson.

"Enough talk about that stupid bitch," Candy cut her off. Lunch time was over and they all went about their business for the remainder of the day. Mercedes knew she had some competition, but she wanted what she wanted. She was going to get it. That's just how she rolled.

As Mercedes ended her school day, she and the girls came across India and her girls. Chino stood at a distance from her with his boys, still focusing closely on Mercedes. India quickly noticed that her boo was giving Mercedes the eye and stepped in.

"What the fuck are you looking at her for?" India said as she stood there with her hands on her thick hips.

"Why the fuck are you tripping India?" Chino asked. "Get out my face." He warned her.

Mercedes looked at Chino and he quickly made her face blush. She was happy that he was defending her. She turned and walked down the hallway with her girls.

"Damn girl, he had his eye on you." Hazel smiled. Playfully nudging Mercedes in the shoulder and laughing. They made it outside and the front of the building was extremely crowded. Mercedes noticed her limo had just pulled up.

"Damn, whose ride is that?" Shateeya asked. She was eager to know who was getting picked up in a limo.

"That's my ride. Alright girls, I'll see ya'll later." Mercedes smirked and looked around for Chino and India. She made sure that everyone saw her and knew what she was rolling in.

Mercedes kissed each of her new friends on their cheeks and walked down the stairs. She noticed India still trying to talk to Chino, but he wasn't paying her any mind. All of his attention was on Mercedes. She sashayed to the car walking past India and Chino. She was trying to make her mad. Mercedes clutched on her bag; she could feel all eyes watching her as Mr. Gates opened the limo's door. Her fellow students stared as if she was Beyoncé or something.

XXXXXXXXXX

Mercedes loved her first day of school. She had all eyes on her for most of the day. She knew the name Mercedes Carter would ring bells.

When she got home, her mother and father were sitting on the leather sofa. They noticed she was glowing and smiling from ear to ear. "Hi." Mercedes smiled at them and headed to her room, but her mother stopped her.

"So, how was your first day of high school?" her mother asked.

"It was great, I loved it." Mercedes smiled. "All the attention was on me...I had girls hating on me already." Mercedes chuckled.

"See baby, that's why I didn't want her going there. Hatin ass little girls." Her father sucked his teeth.

"What else happened?" her mother asked inquisitively.

"I met some new friends." Mercedes plopped down on the couch between her mother and father. "And guess what Mami? I got reconnected with my best friend Candice from elementary school, remember her?" Mercedes asked.

"Oh yeah, Candice, I remember her she's a sweet girl." Maria nodded recalling the years that the two spent together as kids.

"How about you invite them over tomorrow after school and let them help you with your Quincenera invitations and outfit." her mother suggested.

"But Ma I don't want a Quincenera, why can't I just have a regular sweet sixteen?" Mercedes asked.

"Well you know what Mercedes, you can have your sweet sixteen-but it still will have a little of a Quincenera's style." her mother smiled.

"That would be a good idea." her father chimed in.

"I just don't want no hood rats or loud mouth girls up in here, you hear me?" Maria said and Mercedes chuckled agreeing with her mother.

"I'm starving mom, what did Claudia cook?" Mercedes asked.

"Didn't you eat at school baby?" Mercedes screwed up her face looking at her mother as if she had ten heads.

"That food looked disgusting, I will never eat that crap." Mercedes tried to describe the food but she couldn't. Her face said it all.

"I'll pack my own lunch." Mercedes assured them. Her father burst out laughing, knowing that would never happen because they spoiled her so much. He reached over and kissed his daughter on the head.

"Ya'll woman know ya'll are picky." Don smirked.

"Come on Daddy, if you would've seen that food, you wouldn't even pick it up." Mercedes said smiling.

"Alright go in the kitchen, your plate is on the table." Maria told her.

Mercedes got up and walked into the kitchen. Her stomach growled as she sat down at the table and dug into her plate. It was filled with fried chicken, Spanish rice with gravy, and fresh vegetables. She was famished and ate all of her dinner. After she was done, she called Candice and they reminisced all night. They caught up and promised to never lose touch again.

Class is in Session

Mercedes awoke on Friday morning overflowing with excitement. She began school on Wednesday and it was already the end of the week. She was happy that the weekend was here. She removed the covers from her face and pulled herself out of bed. She began her ritual of brushing her teeth and hopped in the shower. School started at 7:30 AM, and she usually took a long time to get ready. In anticipation, Mercedes picked out her outfit last night.

She wore a pair of black Rhinestone Skull skinny jeans with a design of an embellished skull and heart on the right leg. Along with a pink Ed Hardy shirt; roses and spiders covered the front. She knew she was looking fly as usual. As she got dressed, she looked at herself in the mirror and grinned from ear to ear. She put on her pink love cross hat, also from Ed Hardy. It was embroidered with flamboyant colors. Her hat was pulled low, but positioned so that you could still see her eyes. Her long pretty hair flowed down the sides of her face.

Mercedes grabbed a pen and a note book and threw it in her Farrah Satchel Ed Hardy bag. She walked down the spiral staircase and into the kitchen. She noticed a bag on the table and there was a note attached to the bag that read,

"Baby Girl don't starve yourself -Love Daddy"

She cheerfully grabbed the bag. She was definitely a Daddy's Girl. She loved every moment of his attention, except when he was overprotective. She headed out the door and Mr. Gates was already outside waiting to take her to school.

"Thank you Mr. Gates." Mercedes said as she got into the car. They pulled off and she anxiously waited to pull up at the school. As they arrived, Mercedes informed Mr. Gates that he didn't have to open the door. She didn't want to feel too privileged. She wanted to fit in with others, even though she knew she wasn't like them.

She reached for the latch and opened the door. She stepped out and noticed that everyone was grilling her. Her home girls were posted up on the side waving her down. As soon as Mr. Gates pulled off, Mercedes started walking towards them.

"Hey, what's up girls?" Mercedes greeted them. "Hey." They all said in unison.

"Shit, waiting for the bell to ring." Candy added in. "Class starts in five minutes and I don't feel like going," she sighed. Mercedes wasn't paying them any attention; she was trying to look around for Chino.

"Girl, you look cute." Chamari smiled. "You got that Ed Hardy on deck huh?" Chamari asked admiring her bag, "This shit's official."

"Yeah that's how my girl rolls." Candy gave Mercedes dap as they snickered. The bell rang and everyone started rushing into the building.

Shateeya looked Mercedes up and down, "Cute," she said with obvious envy. "I'm off to class." Everyone noticed Shateeya acting funny, but they didn't comment. They all headed up the stairs and off to their respective classrooms. They had arranged to meet up at lunch time.

In her French class, Mercedes almost fell asleep because the teacher was so boring. India's loud popping of her gum woke her up. She grilled Mercedes. Mercedes took it in stride and mean mugged her from head to toe.

Finally, class was over and Mercedes exited to meet the girls in the cafeteria. She passed the line and shook her head at the people who stood in line waiting for that nasty ass food. Mercedes took a seat and placed her bag on the table. She was happy that her father decided to prepare a lunch for her. She opened it and noticed it was one of her favorites. He had cooked this one, some chicken ziti with broccoli covered in alfredo sauce. She had a Sprite to drink.

"Damn girl, you got it made." Hazel said as she bit into her pizza.

"Nah, I'm just not fucking with that nasty ass shit." Mercedes screwed up her face from the thought of eating the food served in the cafeteria.

"I'll eat it with no damn problems." Chamari added in as she laughed.

"I know your fat ass will." Shateeya laughed, but no one else found her funny. She'd been saying some slick shit lately, but no one called her on it yet.

"She ain't fat Shateeya, don't say that shit." Hazel shook her head and tried to hide the smirk on her face.

"Anyway, what are you guys doing today?" Mercedes quickly changed the subject because she didn't want her girls beefing over stupid shit.

"Nothing," Candy said as she looked at the girls and they nodded their heads in agreement.

"Well, Um, how about you all stay at my crib for the weekend?" Mercedes asked wanting to further build a relationship with her new crew.

"We don't even know you like that." Shateeya barked.

"Well, I know her like that." Candy looked at Shateeya and rolled her eyes. "How about ya'll, are ya'll down too?" Candy asked looking over at Chamari and Hazel.

"I'm down." Hazel agreed.

"As long as you got some food, I'm down too." Chamari laughed, as she rubbed her belly.

"You ain't got to worry about that, I have a maid named Claudia who cooks three meals a day and dessert too." Mercedes assured her.

"So are you coming with us or not Shateeya?" Mercedes looked in her direction.

"Come on, don't be like that Shi." Candy chimed in.

"Yeah, I guess I'll go." A smile appeared across her face.

"Cool, I'm having a sweet 16 next month for my birthday and need help with my invitations and shit." Mercedes informed them as she began digging into her food. All this conversation was holding her up from eating.

"Damn, you're only fifteen?" Hazel asked. "You look at least seventeen or so." Hazel was amazed that Mercedes was so young and beautiful. She stayed in the flyest gear and had everything that the others wanted.

"Yup," Mercedes ate her food, "How old are you?"

"I'm fifteen too." Hazel said. Mercedes finished her meal and lead the way for them to go back into the gym. Today was Friday and the teachers didn't feel like doing anything, so they allowed everyone to mingle. They had popcorn, music, sodas, and little games to entertain the students as a 'Welcome Back' ceremony.

Mercedes and the crew walked in. Chino sat with his eyes on her as soon as she entered. He walked towards her; Mercedes began panicking inside. She didn't know if she should walk away with her friends as if she didn't see him coming, or to stay and talk to him.

"Hey, how you doin Ma?" Chino greeted her with a kiss on the cheek.

"I'm fine and you?" Mercedes smiled internally feeling his warm lip on her face.

"I'm aight, just chilling you know." Chino nodded his head, "What's your name?"

"My name's Mercedes." He extended his arm and shook her hand as he stared into her eyes. "Mercedes Carter...what's your name?" She already had the scoop on him, but she didn't want him to think he had her open, or that she was already stalking him.

"My real name is Chanito, but my peoples call me Chino."

Mercedes stood there and didn't know what to say. His swag was on point, and she swore she was already falling in love. His voice was deep, but was soft and sexy. When he spoke, his New York accent became more prominent and she admired it. She looked over to her girls and spied them being nosey trying to overhear her conversation. Candice waved to her. Mercedes chuckled.

"So, where are you from Ma?" He asked.

"I was born in Cuba, but raised out here; I live in Long Island now."

"Oh word, why did you come to Queens for school?"

"My pops was trying to send me away to a private school and I didn't want to go. I wanted to come here." Mercedes replied and was rudely interrupted by India. She walked over and stood between the two of them, blocking Mercedes vision of Chino.

"Why you all up in her face?" India barked as she looked back and rolled her eyes at Mercedes.

"I told you about that shit India, you're not my fucking girl." Chino barked back. Mercedes didn't have time for the girl drama. She walked off, went over to her friends, and watched from a distance as the two of them argued.

"What happened?" Candy had to know.

"Hating ass bitch came over trying to cock block." Mercedes waved her hand in the air.

"Yeah he's definitely feeling you, and that bitch trying to get in the way." Candy added for effect.

The day in the gym quickly flew by and the girls were making their way outside. Mercedes saw Chino in her peripheral sitting down and leaning forward with his hands folded. He looked like he was pissed. She and her friends bypassed Chino and India and made their way into the hallway. When Mercedes walked outside, Mr. Gates greeted them all. The girls all called their mothers and informed them where they would be staying with a friend for the weekend. Shateeya and Chamari had never been in a limo before and were having the time of their lives. Candy had experienced a limo ride a few times, so she wasn't as gassed as the other two. They rode in the car and bumped the hottest music. When they got to the Carter home, Mercedes introduced her mother to her friends. She couldn't wait until tomorrow; they had a big day ahead of them.

The following morning the girls woke up to the pleasant aroma of breakfast cooking in the kitchen. They made their way downstairs and sat around the large table located in the dining room. Claudia prepared a variety of food, French toast, scrambled eggs, hash browns, sausages and sweet biscuits. Everyone was grubbing like they hadn't eaten in days. After they finished eating, Mercedes led the girls back upstairs to her bedroom.

She opened her closet and let the girls pick out an outfit. She had more than enough to share and wanted everyone to match her style. She watched as they were all amped, fighting over who got what. There were plenty of fashionable selections, enough for all of them.

Mercedes felt bad because Chamari was the only one who felt left out; she couldn't fit any of her clothes. She walked over to her closet and pulled out a Juicy Couture bag and gave it to Chamari. She was so excited that she hugged Mercedes and almost squeezed the living life out of her.

After the girls finished their mini makeover, they headed out. The first place they went too was the spot to pick her Quincenera's. They arrived at the party planning store called Ante Up Entertainment. Maria knew the owner, so everything she wanted was discounted as a gift to Mercedes. The party planning process took a while, but they decided on all pink and white affair.

They all hopped into the car and headed to the Plaza Mall. The girls were excited entering the mall. They were in and out of stores looking for the perfect party dress. Parisha's Boutique was an obvious destination. It was also owned by one of her mother's good friends; she was a lady from Paris and was working her way up to compete with Chanel, Fendi, and Prada. As they walked through the door the girl's jaws dropped. They were surrounded by so many beautiful dresses and accessories.

"Hello Mercedes, how are you doing today?" Parisha asked.

"I'm doing fine and you." Mercedes shook her hand.

"I hear you're having a Quincenera's coming up soon." Mercedes nodded her head and smiled as she looked over at her mother. '*It's my sweet sixteen not a Quincenera.*' Mercedes said to herself.

"Well, I have a few selections you may like." Parisha assured her. "Come this way." Mercedes and the girls followed her towards the back of the boutique. The girls sat on the couch, as Mercedes went into the fitting room to try on the dresses which Parisha picked out. As she walked in and out of the fitting room, the girls lent their approval or disapproval of the dresses. The last dress that Mercedes tried was sure to be a crowd pleaser. It wasn't too fancy; it was just perfect. It was a short pink cocktail dress with a demure strapless bodice top. Mercedes loved it, but she needed something to jazz it up.

"That dress looks beautiful on you Mercedes." Maria complimented.

"Yeah, it's really pretty." Candy added, and the other girls nodded in approval.

"Turn around." Maria said. Mercedes danced and twirled around showing off her dress. The girls chuckled as she danced.

"I love it mom, but I want the big puffy stuff that makes the dress look all pretty." Mercedes frowned.

"Baby don't worry about that. Claudia will take care of it."

"I'll take this one." Mercedes grinned as she walked back into the fitting room to change back into her clothes. She came back out and picked out the perfect shoes to match her dress. She wanted to make sure that everyone would envy her.

"Girls, you can get something too." Maria told them.

"Oh no Miss Maria, we can't." Candy spoke out loud.

"Shoooooot, I'll take you up on that offer." Hazel smiled as she was already looking through the dresses. Candy shot her a dangerous look. If looks could kill, Hazel would have died on the spot.

"It's okay Candice, if you're going to my daughters Quincenera. No problem. We want everyone to look as good as her on her special day." Maria smiled and waved her hands to the girls to go pick out something. They got up and Parisha showed them to her finest dresses. Mercedes helped the girls pick out their dresses. They all had style, but she didn't want them coming to her party looking too plain.

Candy picked out a pretty, short, cream and pink dress with a pink bow in the back. Hazel got a white strapless ruffle dress. It was hard for Chamari to find a dress in her size; all of the ones she tried on were too tight. Paris disappeared into the back and pulled out an all pink dress that she believed might fit. Chamari smiled as she put on the dress and it hugged her body perfectly, detailing all of her curves. Shateeya picked out a plain all white strapless cocktail dress.

After the girls picked out their dresses and shoes, they went to grab some ice cream from Baskin Robbins. They talked and giggled over the ice cream, then headed home with all of their shopping bags. They were truly enjoying themselves and Mercedes could tell by all the laughter.

For the entire weekend, Mercedes, Candy, Hazel, Chamari and Shateeya had loads of fun. They went out to the mall, movies, and the arcade. They did everything they could during the weekend and it brought them much closer. They all got along really well. They even told each other secrets that they would never tell anyone.

Late Sunday evening, as they sat in Mercedes' room, they began to share deeper secrets about each other.

"You still a virgin Mercedes?" Shateeya quizzed her. "Yeah," Mercedes shook her head, "Why you not?"

"Hell no girl, I lost my shit when I was thirteen." Shateeya proudly said.

"She's going to lose hers to Chino." Candy cooed as she playfully nudged Mercedes in the arm with her elbow. The girls burst into laughter. Mercedes blushed because she secretly wanted that to be true. She was excited about the chance to see Chino the next day when she would be handing out invitations. The fun would really begin and everyone would remember who she was, if they didn't already know. The haters were sure to come out in full force now.

You're Invited

Mercedes was excited. Today she would be officially passing out her invitations. People crowded the cafeteria because Candy made an earlier announcement about Mercedes' Quincenera. Everyone anxiously anticipated their invitation to her birthday party. Mercedes stood on top of a chair, with her girls standing next to her, as they called out people's names and handed them their invitations. The ones who didn't get invitations would be highly upset.

They were all aware that this was going to be the biggest party of the year, especially since it was Mercedes'. She called Chino's name out first, but he wasn't in the cafeteria at the time. She was a little sad at first, but she knew that he would get his invitation. His presence was vital.

After they were done passing out invitations, everyone who received one was excited. They were dancing around and chatting about what to wear. It seemed like everyone except for the Queen Bee's was invited.

They were livid. They sat at the table mean mugging the other happy students. India looked as if she wanted to kill Mercedes. She had her arms folded across her breasts and watched Mercedes laugh with her girls. Mercedes saw Chino walk in the cafeteria. He was looking better than she remembered. His hair was straightened and he had it pulled back into a sleek ponytail. She immediately grabbed her pink Louis Vuitton bag and made her way over to him.

"Hey Chino," Mercedes smiled. She made sure she sprayed on some of her Ralph Lauren perfume before she made it over to him. She wanted him to smell her when she wasn't around.

"Hey Ma," Chino kissed her on the cheek. Mercedes pulled out an invitation from her purse and handed it to him.

"What's this?" he asked, shaking the invitation.

"Open it," Mercedes urged.

"What a beautiful picture." Chino complimented. Mercedes blushed and watched him open the invitation. He read it aloud, "You are invited to Mercedes Carter's Sweet 16, a Pink and white affair- Leave the drama at home." Chino laughed as he rubbed his chin.

"So are you coming or what?" Mercedes wasn't amused, but she hid her annoyance.

"Of course I'll be there, why wouldn't I?" Chino asked.

"Maybe your little girlfriend won't let you come." Mercedes joked, but noticed he had a serious look on his face.

"Nah Ma it ain't even like that, that's my ex and she be tripping." He assured her, as he shook his head and chuckled at India's crazy ass.

"Alright that's cool." Mercedes nodded and turned to leave, but he stopped her with a question she never thought she would hear.

"So when are you gonna let me take you out and get to know you?" Chino asked while staring into her pretty eyes. Mercedes' heart dropped while he was asking her to take her out on a date. She wanted to scream, but she held her composure. Mercedes caught India grilling her and talking shit to her crew about her, but she didn't care.

"Whenever you want Chino." Mercedes stated as if she had it like that.

"How about I take you out Saturday, if you don't mind?

"Sure."

"I'll pick you up around 7:30?" He asked, but it was more like a demand.

"That sounds good," Mercedes smiled.

"What's your number Ma? So I can lock it in my jack." Chino reached into his Pepe jeans and pulled out his Blackberry. Mercedes grabbed her Sidekick out of her purse and they exchanged numbers. She could feel piercing eyes on the back of her neck, but she didn't care. She always got what she wanted; Chino was next on the to-do list.

"Alright Ma, I'm 'bout to meet back up with my boys. We gon' head to the gym, they having some career shit in there." Chino told her. "So check you later, aight." Chino kissed her on the cheek.

"Alright, see ya." Mercedes replied shyly as she watched Chino walk away. She looked around the cafeteria and found her girls walking toward her. She was beaming inside and couldn't wait until her party. Before she could even get her mouth open, her friends began grilling her.

"Yo Cedes, please tell me you got Papi's phone number?" Hazel questioned. Mercedes couldn't even respond, her smile answered her question.

"So did you?" Chamari added in.

"You can tell she did, look at her cheesing from ear to ear." Candy added.

"Yeah, I did. Guess what? He's coming to pick me up around 7:30 on Saturday." Mercedes smiled.

"Look at this bitch! He got her panties all wet." Shateeya laughed. Mercedes snickered along with her.

"Anyway let's head to the gym, I heard they are having a career fair in there." Mercedes informed the crew, and they headed to the gym. The girls walked around collecting information for different types of job openings and colleges. Mercedes told them she was going to the bathroom. When she emerged from the bathroom, India purposely gave her a hard bump to her shoulder.

"What the fuck?" India yelled out. "You need to watch yourself."

"No bitch, you need to watch yourself. You bumped into me." Mercedes responded.

"I know you not talking to me." India turned around and was now an inch away from Mercedes' face.

"I guess I am; you the only stupid bitch in here bumping into people."

"You know what, if you don't get this girl outta my face." India started yelling trying to get attention. She knew the look on Mercedes' face meant that she was ready for whatever.

"Bitch please! You just fucking hatin." Mercedes smirked.

"Hatin on what?" India laughed hysterically. "Chino don't want you."

"Well he damn sure don't want you." Mercedes blurted out, but she wasn't finished.

"Oh yeah, we exchanged numbers earlier. Don't you get it, he doesn't want your silly ass? Come on, you playing yourself."

That comment pissed India off even more, and she moved in closer. Within a few seconds, her girls were standing behind her like they were about to jump Mercedes.

"What the fuck, ya'll bitches gon' jump me?" Mercedes asked. "Come on, I'll take you bitches one by one. Square the fuck up." Mercedes may have looked like a pretty girl who only cared about how to dress, but her father taught her well. She feared no one. She pushed up her sleeves and was ready for anything India had planned.

Candy and the other girls heard all of the commotion. They made their way over to the bathroom, where the arguing was coming from. They stood behind their girl wondering what the hell was going on. They knew India was the cause; she was always starting shit, but could never finish it.

"What's the problem?" Candy questioned. She could feel the high level of tension.

"This stupid bitch just bumped into me on purpose. She don't know me, I'll fuck her up." Mercedes yelled as her nose flared in anger.

"Fuck that hoe!" Shateeya spat. "Don't make me get my razor." She carefully removed the razor from under her tongue and tried to pass it to Mercedes. India tried to jump at Mercedes as she turned towards Shateeya. Candy stood in between them trying to prevent them from fighting.

At this point everyone had run over to see what was going on. Chino's boy grabbed his shoulder and pointed out the situation to him. Chino couldn't believe it; he immediately ran over and jumped in between them. He pushed India away.

"Yo, what the fuck is your problem?" Chino yelled at India.

"This stupid bitch right here." India rolled her eyes at Mercedes with her arms folded across her breast.

"You always starting shit, one day you gon' get your ass whooped. Don't come fucking crying to me when you do." Chino spat as he turned around and looked at Mercedes. He apologized for India's actions.

"Nah it's all good, it's not your fault." Mercedes breathed heavily. "We still on for Saturday?" Mercedes smirked. She looked over Chino's shoulders making sure she was loud enough for India to hear.

India wanted to push Chino out the way and strangle Mercedes, but she knew that Chino would never fuck with her again if she did. She managed to keep her cool for the moment.

"Yeah, we still on." Chino smiled as Mercedes looked at him and said,

"Alright, call me." She reached over and kissed him on the cheek.

India was sweating bullets and her blood was boiling. Mercedes and her crew calmly walked out. They left the crowd speechless. India was already plotting revenge.

* * *

Mercedes was telling her mother about this boy she met at school for the entire week. Maria wasn't so sure if she wanted her daughter going out on a date with a boy; she wasn't even sixteen yet. Her mother couldn't say no to her. However, she told Mercedes that she would only be able to go if Don and Maria met him first. Mercedes reluctantly agreed. She secretly hoped that her father wouldn't be home; he probably wouldn't allow her to go.

Mercedes went upstairs and took a long shower. When she got out, she wrapped up in a pink beach towel. As she dried herself off, her phone started ringing. The ring tone was "Smile" by Lloyd Banks; she knew instantly that it was her boo Chino. She emerged from her private bathroom and skipped across the floor. She grabbed her phone from her dresser and quickly answered.

"Hello," she answered the phone while trying to sound sexy.

"Who you trying to sound all sexy for Ma?" Chino grinned. Mercedes covered her mouth, wondering how he knew. "Nah, I'm just fucking with you." Chino chuckled. Mercedes was a tad bit embarrassed.

"What you doing?" Chino questioned.

"Nada, just got out the shower."

"Oh, word up." Chino smirked with visions of a naked Mercedes running through his mind. "Well I was just calling to hear your sexy voice, but I'm gon' let you go do your thing. See you in a bit Ma."

"Alright see ya." Mercedes hung up the phone and pressed it against her chest. He gave her stomach butterflies. It was 5:30 PM; she had two hours to get ready. She rummaged around her closet looking for the perfect outfit. She eventually decided on an Apple Bottom pair of black skinny jeans, a black off the shoulder shirt with chain links hanging, and some black flats to match.

Mercedes brushed her hair up into a high pony tail and curled the bottom of her ends. She combed down her baby hair to give her an exotic look. She put on her bamboo earrings, which spelled out her name.

It was already 7:00 and Mercedes grew impatient as she waited downstairs for Chino to arrive. She decided to pour herself a glass of water. When she returned back to the living room, she noticed a car at the gate. The attendant called the house and Mercedes picked up the phone. "Yes...who? Chino...yes let him in." Mercedes informed the attendant as she gulped down her water. She ran into the bathroom to take one last look in the mirror. She checked her hair and made sure it was intact. She applied her lip gloss and smacked her lips together as she disappeared into the foyer.

"Mom, he's here." Mercedes yelled out to her mom from the foyer. Mercedes opened up the front door and noticed the blue L.E.D. lights from the gate. Chino was pulling up in a 2004 black Honda Accord coupe. It was dropped low, had no tint, and sitting on black and chrome 19" Racing Hart wheels. Chino got out of the car and clicked the car doors locked with his remote. He began walking up the stairs. He held two bouquets of red roses in his hand.

"Hey, you look beautiful." Chino greeted her with a kiss on the cheek.

"Thank you, come in." Mercedes closed the door behind him as he walked in. Chino looked at Mercedes in awe of how casual she looked, but still fly as ever.

"These are for you Ma." Chino said as he handed her the roses. "And the other ones are for your mother." Chino added.

"Aww, thank you." Mercedes smiled. "You're so sweet."

"No doubt Ma." Chino winked. Mercedes blushed and eyed him up and down. He was looking really sexy tonight. His hair was neatly slicked back looking smooth and wavy. He had the whole Sean John attire going. He wore a brown SJ premier vest with a fresh white t-shirt under it. He rocked some dark grey jeans with seamed back pockets. To top it off he rocked some all brown and white Dunks.

"Well you can sit down till my mom comes. I don't know what she's doing." Mercedes sat down on the sofa and admired her roses.

Maria came walking down the stairs with a big smile on her face. Her daughter looked extremely happy while talking to her male friend on the couch. Chino stood up and greeted Maria with a kiss on the cheek.

"How are you doing?" Chino asked.

"I'm fine and you, what's your name?" Maria asked.

"My name is Chanito." He introduced himself. Chino extended his arm out and handed Maria the roses, "And these are for you." Chino knew he had captured her heart.

"Aww, that's nice of you. Thanks," Maria smiled as she held them in her hand. "So what time are you guys going to be back?"

"Well the movie starts at 8:00, I will have her in here no later than eleven thirty." Maria swallowed hard and thought 11:30 seemed to be pushing it. She liked Chino already and thought he was a sweet and respectful guy, so she let it slide.

"Alright, you guys have fun and be safe." Maria smiled.

"Alright Ma, love you." Mercedes kissed her mom on the cheek and headed for the front door.

"It was nice meeting you Mrs. Carter."

"Please, call me Maria." She told him as she waved from the door. As Mercedes stepped outside, she felt relieved that her mother didn't talk too much. Chino respectfully opened the door and she slid into the leather seats. The car smelled like it was fresh off the showroom floor. Mercedes looked out the window and noticed Maria looking through the big windows in the living room. She shook her head at her mother. Chino started the car and pulled off; he circled around the path and zoomed down the smooth driveway. He put some music on as he drove, and Mercedes loved watching him shift gears.

Mercedes and Chino arrived at the drive-in movie theater. She always wanted to come to one of these and was thrilled with his selection. The parking lot was packed; everyone was running around and having fun. Of course some people were making out in their cars, while others were actually fucking.

He searched around for a parking spot. Finally they found one in the middle which gave them a perfect view of the huge screen. It was 7:45 and the previews were still on, so they decided to get something to drink. As Mercedes stepped out the car, the frigid air swiftly hit her face. She was freezing and folded her arms around her breasts. Chino walked around to her side.

"What's up Ma, you cold?" he asked.

"Yes I am." Mercedes chuckled. "I didn't know if I would need a jacket, so I left it." Mercedes explained. They stopped in their tracks as Chino went back to his car. He grabbed a Sean John jacket from the back seat and placed it over her shoulder.

"Thank you." Mercedes said as she removed a piece of hair that was flying in her face. He wrapped his arm around her neck as they walked to the food stand. Chino was happy that the line was short; he didn't feel like waiting in a long line and the movie was about to start.

He ordered a big bag of popcorn, two large Sprites and a box of chocolate covered peanuts. They headed back to the car and as Mercedes slipped into her seat, Chino passed her the popcorn and sodas to hold until he got settled.

It was perfect timing, the movie was just starting. They were about to see Denzel Washington's newest movie, *Déjà Vu.* Mercedes thought Chino must've read her mind; she really wanted to see this movie. She felt honored that he brought her with him and not India. Chino was gonna be her man, whether he knew it or not.

"You like Denzel Washington?" Mercedes inquired as she began eating her popcorn.

"Yeah he's one of my favorite actors, that's my nigga." Chino smiled.

"Yeah, he is a pretty good actor. I love Johnny Depp too."

"Let me guess because you think he look good." Chino looked at Mercedes with the 'don't lie' look. She couldn't help herself, she erupted into laughter.

"Yeah he is really handsome." Mercedes admitted. "But you look way better." Chino tried to hide his face, she had him blushing.

"Are you blushing?" Mercedes asked. She was trying to get a look at his face. Chino turned to face her and was smiling from ear to ear.

"Yeah you got me Ma." Chino smirked with his Colgate smile. "You're beautiful too. Actually, you're beyond it. I've never met a girl like you." He made Mercedes feel like a million dollars as he told her how beautiful she was.

"Thank you." Chino wasn't the only one who was blushing. Mercedes' cheeks were redder than a bowl of cherries, and her two pretty dimples were now exposed.

Chino loved everything about Mercedes from her head to her toes, she was the complete package. He watched as she silently ate her popcorn and enjoyed the movie. Her big bamboo earrings brought out her petite face. Her lips were glistening under the moonlight and he desperately wanted to kiss her.

"So what is it about me that you like?" Mercedes was eager to know.

"I like your beautiful eyes, I like your style, I like your body, I like the way you talk, I like your hair, and I could go on and on. I like everything about you." Chino caressed her chin.

"I like you too Chino. I've liked you from the first day that I saw you. I was like DAMMMMMNNNN." They both burst into laughter.

They had a full blown conversation about the first few days of school. They talked about their lives and really got to know one another. The movie was almost over, but neither of them was paying attention.

Chino gazed into her eyes and moved in for a kiss. Initially Mercedes was reluctant, but she soon puckered up. As their lips begin to lock, Mercedes realized that this was the first time she'd ever French-kissed a boy.

She wrapped her arms around his neck as they passionately kissed. Mercedes could feel her silk panties getting wet. They were interrupted by a loud knocking on Chino's window. India was outside banging; she was fuming.

Mercedes reclined in her seat and shook her head from side to side. She couldn't believe this bitch was trying to cock block.

"Excuse me Ma." Chino opened up the door and she heard them arguing back and forth. She walked over to Mercedes' window and grilled her; if looks could kill Mercedes would have been buried six feet deep. Mercedes didn't know how much more she could take from India. She promised herself that one day she would give her a serious beat down. Chino got back into the car and rubbed his hands against his face.

"Yo Ma, I truly apologize." Chino sighed. "I just don't know what the fuck is her problem. I cut her off and she still thinks that she own me or some shit."

"It's cool." Mercedes lied, as she looked out the window.

"You ready to go home Ma?" Chino inquired. "I don't want your mom's bugging out on me."

"Yeah, I'm ready." Mercedes yawned as her eyelids suddenly were heavy. As Chino exited the parking lot, he looked over and noticed Mercedes had already fallen asleep. He smiled to himself and thought she looked just as beautiful while sleeping. When he pulled up to her house, he gently shook her to wake her. Mercedes' eyes fluttered up and down and she finally sat up in the seat.

"You had a good nap?" Chino laughed.

"Whatever." Mercedes smiled as she looked around and noticed that she was in front of her house. "Thank you Chino, I had a really good time." Mercedes said as she reached over and gave him a kiss on the cheek.

"No doubt Ma." Chino smiled as he watched her exit the car.

"Night, Chino."

"Goodnight Ma."

Mercedes smiled as she sashayed to her door and unlocked it. The home was quiet and she knew her mom was asleep. Her father wasn't home; one of his cars was missing from the driveway. Mercedes dragged herself up the stairs.

As she got ready for bed, she received a text from Candy. She was too tired to get into all the details of her date. She told Candy she would call her and tell her everything in the morning. Mercedes didn't even manage to take off her clothes; she fell face first onto her bed and quickly dozed off to sleep.

October Breeze

October had finally arrived. Besides being Mercedes birth month, it was also her favorite month of the year. It wasn't too hot or cold, it was just right. The beautiful trees were a nice bright orange color and blew with the wind. The leaves fell freely from the trees and descended to the ground. She loved the beginning of autumn.

There was one week left until Mercedes big birthday party. Everyone at school was amped and couldn't wait. Mercedes became the most popular girl in school in a relatively short period of time. It was in part due to her style, her new boyfriend and her crew. Everyone clamored to be affiliated with her and her new crew. They called themselves "MOBB", which stood for Most Official Bad Bitches. Mercedes, Candy, Hazel, Chamari and Shateeya were of course all bad in their own ways.

Mercedes started schooling the rest of the girls about Prada, Chanel, and Fendi; any expensive brand that all girls dream about. She wanted her girls to step out in style, just because they were rocking with Mercedes Carter. She was always ten steps ahead of the game, just like her daddy, Don Carter. Of course, Mercedes was the leader of the crew. She represented herself as The Baddest Bitch.

After getting approval from her mother, she spent the majority of her time with the girls. They went into the city and did a little bit of shopping, went out to eat, went to the movies, and did what teenage girls like to do. They talked about boys and sex. Mercedes was anxious to lose her virginity. She was spending a lot of time with Chino and it was only a matter of time before she gave it up. Due to her father's traveling, he still hadn't had the chance to meet him.

She recalled one day when she and Chino were sitting in the sand on the beach and holding hands. They watched the sunset and the waves splash on the shore. They had the most perfect view into Manhattan, as the lights from the buildings reflected on the water. Mercedes loved looking at the stars that glistened in the sky.

"The water is so beautiful." Mercedes whispered, as she watched the waves. "And I love stars."

"Yeah, stars are beautiful things and they mean a lot to me." Chino said.

"And why is that?" Mercedes asked.

"My mother told me there are plenty of stars in the sky, but there's always one that catches your eye. When it does, you will never forget it. You will always see that star and it will forever be in your heart." Chino smiled, "And it's like I have a star that I see every night, it's my father. I always talk to it every night before I go to sleep. Stars are like scars."

"Aww, that's really sweet Chino." Mercedes responded.

"Yeah, I guess. I love coming here when I have to get something off my chest, or when I'm going thru something and just want to be alone." Chino admitted.

"So is there something you need to get off your chest?" Mercedes inquired.

Chino turned to her giving her his full attention while looking into her eyes, "I know I've only known you for like a month and some change, but it feels like I've known you forever."

Chino took a deep breath and Mercedes listened to the words that were charming her heart. "You're so beautiful, intelligent and smart. I mean look at you and look at me." Chino joked as they both laughed, "Nah, but you're everything that I ever wanted in a girl and more. The more time I spend with you, I can't help but think that you're my soulmate?" Chino smiled as he looked into her eyes. "All I want to know is, will you be my girl, my baby, my everything?" He sincerely asked.

Mercedes' eyes lit up with a wide smile. She had no idea he was going to ask her that question. She looked into his eyes and eagerly replied, "Yes Chino, I will"

Chino grinned and they started kissing. He ran his fingers through her soft and silky hair. Mercedes loved Chino's tongue game; he made her see stars when they kissed. After they made themselves an official couple, they took their time getting to know each other better. Mercedes was one of the luckiest and most hated girls in school because she was Chino's girl. India still couldn't get over the fact that they were dating. She envied Mercedes and wished she could be in her shoes. She knew that she could never walk in Mercedes Carter's shoes, but that didn't stop her from trying to put a wrench in the plans anytime it was possible.

Mercedes got home and found her mother sitting on the couch reading a magazine. She had the lamp on and a few vanilla scented candles lit. When she noticed Mercedes walking through the front doors, she put down the magazine and rested her elbow on the couch.

"How was your date?" Maria asked. She eagerly wanted to know the details.

"It was nice." Mercedes smiled as she walked over and sat down on the couch beside her mother. "He took me to the beach and we just sat and talked." Mercedes smiled, "It was really romantic Ma." Mercedes New York accent came out.

Maria had a smile on her face as she watched her daughter talk about Chino. She was really happy for her; she knew her daughter was falling in love. She was concerned about what Don would think of Chino, but didn't express her concerns to Mercedes.

"That's nice, and it is romantic. There aren't many young men who like to do things like that." Maria said. "All they want to do is have sex with you." She bluntly stated.

"MA!" Mercedes eyes widened.

"What? I'm just saying. Merccdes, are ya'll having sex?"

"No Ma, I'm still a virgin." She playfully rolled her eyes, "Now can we please change the subject?" Mercedes asked. She didn't feel comfortable talking to her mother about sex.

"Alright," Maria smiled, "If you ever do have sex, please use a condom. It's not that I want you to have sex now; I just want to let you know you can talk to me. I want you to be safe." Maria told her. She knew her daughter was getting aggravated, so she quickly changed the subject.

"So, how do you feel about turning the big 1-6 tomorrow?" Maria exaggerated.

"I mean, I don't know." Mercedes shrugged her shoulders, "I'm still not legal yet."

"I know that's right!" Maria said as she grabbed her drink from the coffee table.

"So just because your sixteen don't start thinking you're grown and will come in all wee hours of the night."

"Ma, I know. Tonight was special though, but it won't happen again." Mercedes rolled her eyes.

"Well goodnight Ma, I'm going to bed." Mercedes lied. She wasn't really tired; she just wanted to get away from her mother. She didn't want to have this conversation with her mother.

"Good night baby." They exchanged kisses on the cheek. Maria watched as Mercedes walked up the spiral stair case. When she got to her room, she took off her clothes and crawled into the bed. She couldn't wait until tomorrow; she would finally be the big sweet sixteen.

Super Sweet 16

Mercedes lay sound asleep in her canopy bed with the covers wrapped firmly around her body. She did not want to wake up just yet. As much as she wanted this day to come, she had mixed emotions that it was here. This was supposed to be her big day. She turned over, trying to avoid the sun light that peeked in through her pink sheer curtains.

After several moments of debating whether or not to get up, Mercedes heard a knock on her door. It was her mother; she walked into the room holding a small Carvel ice cream cake that had the number sixteen in the middle.

"Happy birthday to you, happy birthday to you, happy birthday to Mercedes, happy birthday to you baby." Maria sang. She placed the cake on the nightstand.

"Aww come on Mercedes it's your birthday, wake up." Her mother pulled the covers off of her daughter's body and playfully tickled her stomach. She knew that would wake her up.

"Alright Ma, I'm up...I'm up." Mercedes chuckled, as she held back the laughter. She sat up in her bed looking a hot mess. Her baby hair was all frazzled and pieces of her wavy hair were falling over in front of her face.

Maria chuckled at her.

"What's so funny?" She was curious.

"Your hair girl...looking like a damn lion, you need to go get your hair done." Maria smiled, knowing how to make Mercedes smile when she was cranky in the morning.

"Whatever Ma" Mercedes playfully rolled her eyes as she let out a chuckle.

"Make a wish." Maria smiled. She grabbed the ice cream cake off of the night stand and placed it in front of Mercedes. She closed her eyes for about ten seconds, made a wish, and then opened them back up.

"What did you wish for?" Maria jokingly asked.

"No, I can't tell you Ma. If I do, my wish won't come true."

"I'm going to put this back in the freezer and Claudia is making breakfast. Be ready in about a half an hour. It gives you enough time to get showered up and dressed." Mercedes watched as her mother walked out of her room and disappeared into the corridors of their home.

Mercedes quickly snatched up her Hello Kitty robe off the door and walked into her bathroom. She turned on her shower and wished she could just sit in the jacuzzi and relax. But today was her birthday, and she didn't have time to sit and lamp around.

When she was done in the shower, she threw on her robe and headed towards her walk-in closet. She quickly scanned over it to see what she was going to wear. It really didn't matter; she looked good in everything.

Today was her Sweet Sixteen party and she still had more items to purchase. She settled on an all pink Juicy Couture track suit and accessorized with some matching custom made Dunks. She chose a white velour Heritage tote to carry.

Mercedes finished getting ready and began descend the spiral stair case. Her stomach growled as she smelled the aroma of the food that the maid prepared. Mercedes walked into the kitchen and placed her purse on the empty chair so she could chow down.

"Good morning Claudia." Mercedes greeted her with a kiss on the cheek.

"Buenos dias." Claudia said in Spanish, as she finished up preparing breakfast.

"Good morning Mami." Mercedes kissed her mom on the cheek and hugged her. Maria wasn't really paying attention because she had her nose buried in the New York Times. She was sipping on a cup of hazelnut coffee.

"Mhmm, something smells good." Mercedes New York and Cuban accent kicked in heavily. She pulled out the stool and sat down, "What did you cook?" Mercedes inquired.

"Your favorite...I cooked some blueberry pancakes, scrambled eggs with cheese, bacon, sausages, hash browns and french toast. I cooked a whole feast." Mercedes and Claudia chuckled.

"Well thank God you did because I'm starving." Mercedes rubbed her stomach as she watched Claudia pile some food on her plate.

"Where's Papi, Mami?" Mercedes looked up at her mother. Maria took off her reading glasses and let out a sigh.

"Your father went out of town; you know that honey."

"But he said he would be back today." Mercedes barked.

"Sweetie I know, I know, but maybe he will be here tomorrow morning."

"He can't miss my birthday party! He never missed any of my birthday parties." Mercedes' entire mood changed. She knew she didn't want to wake up this morning for fear of bad news and now it was confirmed. She was mad that her father wouldn't be there for her first big official party.

"Mercedes I'm sorry Honey...your father had some business to take care of." Maria apologized, but Mercedes wasn't trying to hear it. She had heard it plenty of times before. She had hoped today, of all days, would be different.

"I have a surprise for you." Maria picked up her Gucci purse and started digging through it. Mercedes watched as she slid three different shaped black boxes across the kitchen table.

"What's this?" Mercedes asked as she looked at all three of the boxes wondering which one she wanted to open up first.

"You have to open it up to see." Her mother assured her with a sly look on her face. Mercedes quickly opened the smallest box; it was a 3 finger ring platinum diamond ring. The diamonds spelled the name Carter. She opened another box that held diamond earrings which said Mercedes; they were huge. Finally, she opened the last box from her father. It was a long diamond necklace with a key dangling. She wondered what the key was for, but she didn't think too much of it.

"And this is a present from me." Maria smiled as she picked up a pink gift bag off the floor. It had pink tissue covering the top. Mercedes snatched up the bag and it revealed a black and fuchsia goat Peakaboo bag from Fendi to match a pair of black and fuchsia Peakaboo shoes. Last but not least, there was a little box inside that contained some pink Baguette Fendi glasses. Mercedes absolutely adored them; she had wanted them for a long time.

"Thanks Mom." Mercedes reached her arms across the table and hugged her. She was almost squeezing the life out of her. "Okay." Maria said through gritted teeth, as she made a face and patted Mercedes on the back. Mercedes smiled as she pulled back from the embrace and sat down in her chair.

Mercedes ate her breakfast and was finally ready to get her special day started. She hoped her father would be there to complete it; that remained to be seen.

"Are you ready to go Mercedes?" Maria asked as she stood up.

"Yeah I'm ready." Mercedes washed her hands in the kitchen sink after placing her plate and utensils there.

"Alright let me grab my keys and we can leave okay?" Mercedes nodded as she grabbed her purse and her Juicy

Couture pink sun glasses. Her mother returned with the keys, they thanked Claudia for her wonderful breakfast and left their home.

The sun beamed down on them as they walked down the steps. Mercedes put on her glasses and swung her hair back as she walked towards her mother's 2006 BMW X5. They put on some Mary J. Blige and bumped it throughout the entire ride. They hit up the malls and brought some new shoes and clothes. This was a regular occasion for them. After they were done picking up her dress, they headed over in the city to the Dominican salon to get their hair done.

"I need to get my own salon." Maria said out loud as they got out the car and headed into the salon. It was always a dream of hers to have her own, but she didn't need to work or want for anything.

Mercedes decided to get it washed, pressed, and to have Shirley temple curls with a bang that hung a little bit below her eye brows. Mercedes was looking as gorgeous as ever for her birthday. After they got their hair done, they went next door to Lucy's to get manicures and pedicures.

It was now time to prepare for the party. She couldn't wait until later that night. She was about to have the biggest and most anticipated party of the year. This party would shut the city down, this was her night and it was all about Mercedes Carter.

Hours later...

Standing in front of the vanity mirror in her room, Mercedes finished putting spritz on her Shirley temple curls to keep them in place. She unloosened them to give them a fuller look. Her hair looked perfect. Her pink and white French manicure matched her dress and her pink eye shadow brought out her green eyes. Mercedes chuckled at herself as she played around in the mirror, pursing her lips together blowing kisses. She was indeed beautiful and nobody could tell her anything different.

She accessorized with a small Etoile four-row band ring from Tiffany's that brought out her long French manicured nails. Her small ears were glistening with Tiffany metro hoop earrings and she wore the necklace her father had brought her. She didn't care that her mother said she had too much jewelry on, she was so icy that Gucci Mane didn't have shit on her.

Mercedes grabbed several of her Tiffany metro bangles-each of them were worth almost $6,000 each. She slid them on her right arm.

She admired her beauty with her hands on her hips and gazed into the mirror. She eyed her voluptuous curves, which were perfect for the dress she was rocking. She looked and felt amazing in her two toned, white and pink strapless cocktail dress by Paris. The pink satin waist band was designed with faceted jewels that were replaced with real diamonds. It hugged tightly around the top of the dress making her breasts look plump and perfect.

Maria stood at the bottom of the spiral staircase beaming with the anticipation of seeing her daughter.

"Mercedes!!!!!!!!!!"

"I'm coming Ma", Mercedes said as she grabbed her white clutch and made her way down the spiral staircase. Maria began taking pictures with one of her professional cameras. Don bought them for her and Mercedes hated them because she was always snapping pictures like a paparazzi. She did it every year for her birthday and on other occasions as well. Mercedes smiled and her dimples were in full effect. Her girls sat on the couch laughing at Mercedes as her mother kept snapping.

"Mom you know how I feel about that camera." Mercedes chuckled as she was standing next to her mother.

"I know, I know, baby but this is your Sweet 16 girl. This only happens once and I must capture every moment. I remember when I was sixteen," her mother smiled.

"Ma!" Mercedes cut her off giving her a look that said-'this is not the time for that.'

"We have to go." Mercedes reminded her mother, as she saw the two toned pink and white limo entering the gates.

Mercedes smiled as she followed her mother through the front door and they got into the first limo. The other limo driver picked up her girlfriend's in a black limo.

As they pulled up to the banquet hall, Mercedes saw many people inside and outside. Some were still trying their best to get in. If you didn't have an invitation, you wouldn't be able to set foot into the party. There was a white carpet which rolled out to where the limo was parked. The driver got out and walked around to the passenger side. He opened the door for Mercedes and her mother.

Mercedes made a grand entrance. The onlookers envied her as her heels touched the ground showing off her dress. She loved to be the center of attention.

Entering the huge foyer, pink and white balloons bombarded the ceiling and every one screamed "HAPPY BIRTHDAY MERCEDES." There were more than a thousand people in the hall. Many people braved the crowd and tried to give her hugs, kisses and mostly gifts.

Inside there was a private lounge with tables filled with her father's workers. They provided the security and all of them greeted her. She thanked them as she looked for the one person who should have been there to greet her. He was nowhere to be found and she felt that he had let her down.

"Happy Birthday, Mercedes." The girls said in unison as they all walked up to her and gave her individual hugs.

"You look good." Candy complimented her.

"Thank you." she yelled over the music. Mary J. Blige's, "Family affair." pumped from the speakers as the bass thumped and the music spread throughout the entire hall. Everyone started wilin' out and showing off their dance moves.

Mercedes didn't waste any time, she started dancing and laughing with her girls. As they danced together on top of the stage, the music was interrupted and Mercedes looked up.

"What the fuck?" Mercedes blurted out, she was mad that the DJ had stopped the music. She looked up and was staring at the DJ who was now making an announcement.

"Are ya'll having a good time?" DJ Fat Scoop yelled. Her mother secured the well known New York DJ for her daughter's Sweet Sixteen party- nothing but the best for Mercedes.

"YEAHHH!" everyone screamed in unison.

"Happy 16ᵗʰ birthday Mercedes Carter...I hope you're out there enjoying yourself Mama. You look gorgeous tonight." The DJ smiled as he placed the spot light on Mercedes. She started blushing as she looked around and everybody was staring at her and clapping.

"Now are ya'll ready for an exclusive performance?" Everyone was wondering what he was talking about. "Well... ladies get ready to scream and fella's get ready to sing along as we bring you the best of the best....DIPSET...DIPSET...DIPSET." The DJ Announced. Everyone went bananas and screamed at the top of their lungs. Mercedes covered her mouth as The Diplomats were on stage. She didn't think that her father would come through on her special request, but she was wrong.

The Diplomats came out on stage, Juelz Santana, Cam'ron, Jim Jones and the whole crew. Juelz Santana came out and called Mercedes up to the stage, "Happy Birthday Mercedes, from the Dipset family Ma." Juelz gave her a hug.

"Now are ya'll ready?"

"DIPSET...DIPSET...DIPSET!" everyone chanted.

"Dipset, we in the motherfucking building get your hands up!" Cam'ron yelled into the mic. "Killa..Juelz...you on your own man. Let's go." Cam started throwing his hands up. "Dipset, Dipset, Dipset, Dipset." After The Diplomats were done performing, Mercedes and her crew kicked it with them in V.I.P. They were popping bottles, but Mercedes was way too young to drink. Mercedes decided to head back down the spiral staircase to the first level to search for her man, Chino. Her eyes scanned the hall as she searched for him and then Mercedes grabbed Candy off the floor and asked her if she had seen Chino. She told her no and kept dancing.

Mercedes was furious; he told her that he would be here but he wasn't anywhere to be found. She folded her arms across her breasts beginning to pout. She watched everyone enjoy themselves and the two people she wanted to spend the day with had abandoned her-her father and her man. She was disappointed with the day and how it was turning out. Her mother noticed and approached her with concern on her face.

"What's wrong baby?" Maria asked.

"It's nothing Ma." Mercedes lied.

"Alright, well go have some fun it's your birthday." Maria disappeared into the crowd as she sipped on her drink. Mercedes felt someone come up behind her and wrap their arms firmly around her waist.

"Hey Ma." She turned around with an attitude, wondering who had their hands on her. It was Chino and she couldn't be happier. Things were definitely looking up.

"Hey Baby." Mercedes smiled as she wrapped her arms around his neck.

"Happy Birthday Ma." Chino kissed her on the lips, she looked around hoping her mom didn't see that. "You look beautiful Ma." He spun her around gazing at her beautiful body.

"Thank you so much." Mercedes smiled as she looked him up and down. He rocked an all light pink tuxedo that had Mercedes emblazoned on the back. "You look good too baby, I love your outfit-it's cute." Mercedes said chuckling.

"Yeah, you know I had to come ten steps ahead of other niggas." Chino informed her while looking around. The song "Move Your Body" by Nina Sky pumped through the speakers. The ladies made their way to the dance floor and grabbed their dancing partners.

"Oooh, this is my shit." Mercedes cooed as she started bopping her head.

"Want to dance with me?" Chino asked. "Of course," Mercedes answered.

He grabbed her hand and led her to the dance floor and got behind her. Mercedes hips were now in full effect as she moved to the beat, "Move your body girl...Makes the fellas go...The way you ride it girl....Makes the fellas go."

Mercedes sang the song and looked back at Chino who winked at her, as she bounced her shoulders and winked back. After the song was over the DJ made another announcement.

"Everybody clear the dance floor please...Mercedes your father saved the last song for you...only for you." The DJ announced.

People started to clear the floor. He started playing the song by Beyonce Knowles, "Daddy." *Oh I wish my father was here right now, how could he not attend my birthday? He never missed any of my birthdays.* Mercedes thought to herself.

She noticed a man walking from the crowd and into the middle of the floor. Tears welled up in her eyes when she realized it was her father. A wide smile appeared across her face. Her father looked as handsome as ever. He had a fresh shape-up and huge 2 carat glistening diamond earrings. He wore a white tuxedo vest by Armani Exchange with a light pink collared shirt underneath. He accented his crisp white Armani tux dress pants with some light pink alligator shoes.

"Can I have this dance?" he asked with a smile, as he extended out his hand.

"You sure can." Mercedes smiled widely and grabbed her father's hand as they danced together. The crowd was silent and watched from the sidelines as Mercedes danced with her father. The dance floor was illuminated in pink and white with the spotlight focusing on Mercedes and Don.

Maria stood close by watching as Mercedes happily danced with her father. Watching him with his daughter reignited her feelings for him and how much she loved him. It was that Carter unconditional love.

Mercedes had her arms wrapped around her father's neck as he had his wrapped around her waist. She looked into his eyes with happiness, but questioned his absence earlier.

"Daddy, I thought you weren't coming."

"I can never miss one of your birthdays, no matter what." He promised as he kissed his daughter on the forehead.

Mercedes felt secure and safe when she was in her father's presence. The music softly pumped through the speakers. "I want my unborn son to be just like my Daddy, I want my husband to be just like my Daddy, there is no one else like you Daddy...And I thank you for loving me."

Mercedes smiled as she silently mouthed, "Love you Daddy" as a tear crept down her face. He wiped it away and said, "I love you too Baby Girl."

The Unordered Hit

Don walked up the spiral staircase and peeked into his daughter's room. She was sound asleep as her head lay against the soft pillows. Don thought she slept like the innocent angel she was.

Don was so overprotective over her; he wouldn't know what to do if anything ever happened to her. He crept into her bedroom and sat on the edge of the bed. He inched closer and gently rubbed her silky hair. He smiled as he gazed at his beautiful daughter. It had been a while since they spent father and daughter time together.

Today he would take her out and show her a big surprise that he'd been waiting to show her.

"Wake up Mercedes." Don gently pinched her cheeks.

"Ouch." Mercedes eyes fluttered open as she noticed her father was sitting beside her smiling ear to ear. "Why you do that Daddy?" Mercedes asked as she rubbed her cheeks.

"Are you ready?" He asked.

"Am I ready to go where?" Mercedes had a baffled look on her face.

"Well since I've been out of town and busy lately, I want to take you out today-just me and you." Don pointed to his daughter, lightly tapping her on her nose.

"What time?" Mercedes yawned, she was still sleepy.

"Whenever you get up and get dressed, but don't keep me waiting all day. I know how ya'll woman are, especially you and your Mama." He cracked a smile as he stood up and walked away.

"What's that supposed to mean?" Mercedes cocked her head to the side as her eye brows rose. Don turned around and stood in the door way.

"Ya'll take forever to get ready, I mean hours. Ya'll have to make sure ya'll hair, make up and nails look so fucking perfect." Don chuckled.

"Whatever Daddy, I'm about to get ready." Mercedes swung her legs over her bed and got up and did a quick stretch.

She rushed to get herself together as soon as possible. She couldn't wait to spend the day with the man who loved her the most. She didn't want to keep him waiting.

She threw on a white Supergirl track jacket with a pink tank top underneath. She wore the white matching Adidas track pants and a fresh pair of Adidas pink and white Superstars.

When she reached downstairs, her mother was sitting at the kitchen table reading *The New York Times*. Every morning she would read the paper and have a cup of hazelnut coffee from Dunkin Doughnuts.

"Where are you two going?" Maria asked as she looked up and noticed her husband walking down the steps fully dressed to meet Mercedes.

"Daddy said he wanted to take me out today." Mercedes smiled.

"Oh yeah, isn't that sweet." Her mother said as she sipped on her coffee.

"Yeah, I'm taking her out to a couple of places. I have a surprise to show her." Don smiled and winked at his wife. She already knew what the surprise was, but she wasn't going to spoil it for Mercedes.

"What is it Daddy?" Mercedes eagerly asked; she really wanted to know.

"You'll see, I don't want to spoil it for you." Don placed his hand over his lips and grabbed the keys out of his pocket. They walked towards the door.

Mercedes followed her father as he got into his Silver Range Rover Sport HST. It was equipped with 24 inch chrome rims. Mercedes reclined in her seat as she enjoyed the ride. She noticed her father pulling over and then he parked the car. She sat up in her seat and looked out the window.

They were at an expensive upscale restaurant called Bella's. It was an Italian restaurant located in the heart of Queens. Mercedes was last here on her 12th birthday, when she had an exquisite dinner with her father and mother.

As they arrived, the waitress immediately knew Mr. Carter and escorted them up the spiral staircase. It led to an upper-level of the restaurant, a more intimate area. Soft Italian music filled the restaurant and provided an ambiance of peace. The waitress handed them their menus and politely greeted them.

"Can I start you all off with anything to drink?" The waiter inquired.

"Yes, I'll have an iced tea with extra ice and a lemon." The waitress turned towards Mercedes and asked what she wanted. "I'll just have a glass of water, thank you." Mercedes smiled.

"This place is so beautiful." Mercedes said. "I haven't been here in so long."

"Yeah I know, they changed it up a bit." Mercedes scanned through her menu and had no idea what to order. Everything on it looked so delicious. She looked over it once more before coming to a conclusion.

The waitress came back to the table, "Are you all ready to order?" she asked.

"Yes." Don replied. He looked at his menu and looked up and placed his order. "I'll take the chicken parmesan with a side order of the Italian Famous soup."

"Okay, and what will you be having?" she asked Mercedes.

"I'm going to try the Shrimp Fra Diavolo with lemon sauce please, thank you." The waitress took their menus and told them the wait would be about a half an hour. Mercedes dug into the Italian bread.

"Mhmmm," This is really delicious." She licked her lips as her mouth watered for more. Don took a piece of the Italian bread and put it into his mouth.

"Yeah it is really good, but don't eat too much. It will make your ass full and you won't have room for your real meal." The two of them chuckled.

"So, how's school been going for you?" he asked.

"It's been going pretty good, you know, I'm focused on keeping my grades up. Other than that, I'm the most popular girl in school." Mercedes replied as she batted her thick eye lashes. Don burst into laughter.

"Girl you're a mess," her father chuckled. "I mean, look at you Mercedes. Your mother blessed me with one of the most gorgeous daughters in the world." Don knew he always made his daughter feel on top of the world when he told her that. "Just like your beautiful Mama." Don smiled as he chewed.

"Thank you," she shrugged her shoulders. The steam rose up from their food and tickled Mercedes' nose. She licked her lips; she couldn't wait until her food cooled off because it looked awesome. The shrimp were covered with perfectly sliced onions, fresh basil, Italian leaves, and lemon juice topped it off.

As they waited a few minutes to eat their food, they watched as an Italian female singer sang a beautiful song on the stage that was a few feet away. They clapped their hands in amazement as she walked off stage.

"She has a real beautiful voice." Don nodded his head in agreement and Mercedes turned around and began eating her food.

"So who's the new boy in your life?" he keenly asked. Mercedes almost choked on one of her shrimp when her father asked her that question out of the blue.

"Hmm?" Mercedes asked as she drank some of her water to help gulp down the shrimp caught in her throat. He repeated the question again, knowing that she heard what he said the first time.

"I mean...I have a new male friend, Chino." Mercedes hid the fact that he was her boyfriend. She knew that her father would disapprove, "He's a real cool guy. He's respectful and intelligent, a real sweet heart."

"Really, that's how they all are at first." Don informed her as he finished his food and wiped the sides of his mouth with the napkin.

"What do you mean Daddy?"

"I mean, I just want the best for you. I know how these silly New York nigga's get down. I just want you to go to school and finish college. Then get a nice job, and after that find a nice man like a lawyer or something. You don't need to settle for anything less."

Mercedes smiled and pretended to listen intently; she actually was, but she wasn't really hearing him.

"Daddy, I'm ready to go." Mercedes said as she finished her food and took one last bite of the Italian bread.

"Alright Baby Girl, let's roll." Don pulled out a crisp stack of money and peeled off two hundred dollar bills and tossed them onto the table. The bill only came up to one hundred and some change. He always left the waitress a nice tip. Mercedes got up and followed her father outside the restaurant and they got back into the Range.

Don then took her to one of the most expensive high class stores in the city, Fifth Avenue. Mercedes left carrying a lot of bags on both side of her arms. They were filled with Gucci, Prada, Versace and plenty of other brands. Today her father went all out splurging on her. He practically purchased everything that she wanted.

When they were done shopping, they loaded the trunk with their shopping bags and got into the car. Once Mercedes got situated in her seat, she saw her father reach behind the seat. He pulled out a bag and took out three gold boxes. He then placed them carefully on her lap.

"What's this Daddy?" Mercedes asked while picking up one of the boxes.

"Open it and see." Don informed her. Mercedes opened the smallest box; it contained a custom made diamond charm bracelet with a diamond heart on the end with the initials MC on it. The second box was a matching necklace with a diamond locket; it had the initials DC on it. When Mercedes opened it, she saw a picture of her and her father. A wide smile appeared on her face when she reminiscing on the day her and her father took professional pictures.

The final box contained a forty-two inch Diamond Cuban XL chain. Mercedes lifted up the chain with tears in her eyes as she gazed at the beautifully customized piece. It had the Carter family picture including Mercedes, her mother, and her father embedded into the plated pendant. The bottom read Carter Family in diamonds.

"Oh my God, thank you Daddy." Mercedes hugged him. "This is so beautiful...I'm definitely cherishing this and carrying this to the grave with me."

"You're welcome Baby Girl; I would give you the whole world if I could." He sincerely said. He had already given Mercedes everything that she wanted, needed, and even things that she didn't want or need. Mercedes was happy with what she thought was the surprise. However, she didn't know that she was in for a bigger surprise- something that she would least expect.

Mercedes noticed that they were in Long Island. She looked out the window and saw beautiful houses everywhere. Don told her to cover her eyes. She didn't know why, but she didn't ask questions.

"No peeking," he warned her. He pulled over and tied a blue bandana over her eyes. Mercedes chuckled at her dad's behavior.

He parked the car and walked over to her side to help her get out of the car. He held her hand and guided her. Mercedes walked up a few steps and heard her father unlock a door. She was getting impatient, yearning to know where she was.

Don took the bandana off and said, "You can open your eyes now." He watched Mercedes open her eyes and her heart skipped a beat. Don stood inside with a huge gracious smile on his face. Tears welled up in her eyes and a tear eventually crept down her cheek.

"Daddy, this can't be..." Mercedes looked at him shaking her head 'no' in disbelief. She had an astonished look on her face.

"Yes, this is for you Baby Girl." He cut her off, as Mercedes ran over to him and gave him the tightest hug she could muster. She hugged him for several seconds before pulling away. It was a beautiful two-story luxury condo. It had four bed rooms with three and a half bathrooms. When they walked into the condo, they were welcomed with a huge open foyer. A beautiful pink chandelier dangled overhead. The oversized living room had shiny wall to wall marble floors and an immaculate marble fire place. There were huge crystal clear windows that provided beautiful views of sunrises and sunsets. Every room had huge windows which gave you different views of the city.

As they walked up the suspended glass staircase, they entered the mid-level area. It overlooked the first level and provided a wonderful view of everything below. The master bedroom was the biggest room. It had its' own pristine bathroom with a walk in shower and a jacuzzi. It had wall to wall mirrors and two huge French doors. They walked through the doors and they lead to a different spiral staircase. It led to a flawless terrace, which had a beautiful view into the city. Mercedes couldn't ask for more. "You can't move in here until you turn eighteen." Don informed her. Mercedes was furious at that statement and she didn't understand why he showed it to her so soon.

"Why not Daddy?" Mercedes whined. "I thought that was the purpose of you showing it to me."

"You're only sixteen, your mother and I decided that when you turn eighteen you'll be off on your own and have your own place." Don informed her as they left the condo. He locked the door and headed to the car. Mercedes was a little upset, but she quickly realized that there was no reason to be. 'What sixteen-year-old in the hood gets their own crib?' Mercedes thought to herself as she sat in the car while they drove. She looked over and noticed her father looking in the rear view mirror; he kept looking in it every few seconds.

Mercedes glanced out of her window and noticed Candy and the girls. "Daddy pull over please, I want to holla at the girls for a minute!" Mercedes said as she looked at her father awaiting his approval.

"Aight, well make it quick I'm going to run to the barber shop. When I come back, be ready to go home."

"Ok Daddy," she happily said as she exited the car and ran towards her friends.

"Hey girls!" Mercedes yelled out.

"Hey." They all said in unison as they exchanged hugs and kisses on the cheek.

"Where are ya'll coming from, and without me I might add?"

"Oh please Cedes, we called you and you didn't answer your phone. We called your crib and your mother said you went out with your dad for Daddy-Daughter Day." Candy smiled as she playfully teased her. Mercedes looked down at her cell phone and noticed that she did have several missed calls from Candy.

"You're a Daddy's Girl." Shateeya laughed. "Aww, how cute is that." The girls laughed and Mercedes playfully hit Shateeya in the arm.

"Yeah, well we've been out since this morning. He took me out to Bella's..." Hazel cut her off, "Bella's, you talking about that Italian restaurant?"

"Yeah"

"Damn, I would love to go there one day. I heard their food is delicious." Hazel licked her lips at the thought of their food.

"Hell yeah, the shit *is* bomb-but listen he took me out shopping on Fifth Avenue and then guess what he brought me?" The girls looked at her wanting her to hurry up and spill the beans. "He bought me a condo." Mercedes chanted.

"No." Shateeya shook her head as the girls jaws dropped in amazement.

"Are you serious?" Candy asked, she couldn't believe her best friend.

"Yeah, I don't put on facades and Candy you should be the one to know that." Mercedes was highly upset that Candy didn't believe her. "But I can't move into the crib until I'm eighteen." She informed them.

"You're one lucky ass bitch." Chamari nodded her head. "You know how many bitches would kill to be in your shoes?" Mercedes had a devilish smirk on her face and simply replied, "I know."

Mercedes just happened to turn around and saw her father emerging from the barber shop holding a brown paper bag. He yelled out her name from across the street.

"Alright girlies, I got to go. I'll check ya'll later."

"Aight," they said in unison as they began to walk off.

When Mercedes reached the car, she heard tires loudly screeching.

"MERCEDES, GET DOWN!"

Don yelled. He had a gun pointed towards him and no time to draw his own. Mercedes' body froze for a moment and she began shaking hysterically. A dude in a cake delivery truck wearing a black ski mask had an AK-47 aimed out of the window. He began shooting wildly.

People scattered in different directions trying to dodge bullets. The bullets had no names, but they were meant for Don Carter. Don immediately hugged Mercedes tightly and dove to the ground. It was too late, Mercedes had already been hit. The blood soaked her white tracksuit as Don held her in his arms. He never imagined that he would one day hold his daughter in this situation. She was covered in blood and shaking uncontrollably.

* * * * *

The lobby was filled with silence as Don sat with his family and a few of his workers. They all were patiently waiting for the doctor to come out and provide them with information on Mercedes. Candy and the girls rushed down the hall and Maria got up as they hugged her.

"Is she going to be okay?" Candy asked with tears in her eyes.

"I'm praying to God." Maria sniffled as she wiped away her tears, "We're waiting on the doctor now."

They all sat on the benches hugging each other as they hoped and prayed that their girl Mercedes would be alright. They couldn't believe that she had been shot moments after she walked away from them. They were all in a state of shock.

The events happened so fast, and thankfully no one else got hurt. In a matter of seconds, they turned their backs and heard gun shots. They immediately knew that their friend was hit when they saw Mercedes sprawled out on the concrete. Her white track suit was drenched in blood.

The doctor emerged from the room with his pen and clipboard in his hand. His stethoscope comfortably rest around his neck. His blue scrubs were stained from the blood of Mercedes and others that he had cared for. Don, his wife, and the girls immediately jumped up. They all met face to face with the doctor.

"How are you doing Mr. and Mrs. Carter?" The doctor adjusted his glasses and wiped sweat off of his brow.

"I would be so much better if I find out that my daughter is fine?" Don anxiously anticipated the news. His heart was filled with anger and revenge for anyone that was associated with hurting his daughter. Maria couldn't even comfort him.

"Mercedes is doing well. She only has a flesh wound. The bullet grazed her arm and didn't puncture any main arteries. She lost some blood, but it's not a life threatening situation."

The doctor saw the fear in their eyes and made sure to comfort them. He was afraid if they heard the wrong thing they would take out their anger on him. He knew exactly who he was dealing with.

"So when can we go in to see her?" Maria asked.

"Well you can see her now, but only two or three at a time. That's the hospital regulations. Mr. and Mrs. Carter, come with me. I will show you where she is." The doctor advised.

The girls patiently sat outside while Don, Roy, and Maria entered the room.

Mercedes lie in her hospital bed and stared out of the window. She heard footsteps and turned to the door. She was so happy when she saw her family approaching her bedside.

"Hey Mami, hey Daddy," she smiled as her mother walked over to her and hugged her gingerly. "Hey, Uncle Roy." Mercedes greeted her uncle as he walked in behind her father.

"Oh Honey, thank God you're alright." Maria tried to hold back the tears, but they streamed down her cheeks.

"Just a little graze wound, I'll live." Mercedes assured them, "I'm a warrior just like Daddy." That comment brought a smile to Don's face. He knew his daughter was just as strong, if not stronger than he was.

"Baby, I'm so sorry-" Mercedes cut her father off.

"Daddy it's not your fault, you don't have to explain to me. Just tell me you love me and you will never leave me." Mercedes watched as her father swallowed hard. He absolutely adored and loved his daughter, but he couldn't promise her that he would never leave her. The only way he would leave his wife and Mercedes is if he got locked up or killed. Both of those were strong possibilities with the lifestyle he lived. Everyone eventually dies one day, some sooner than others.

"I love you." He kissed her on the cheek.

"When can I go home?" Mercedes asked.

"As soon as we get the discharge papers, we can head home." Don said.

"Your friends are outside waiting for you." Maria assured her.

"Bring them in." Mercedes happily said. She peered through the glass window and saw them all sitting on the bench. They were waiting to see when they would be able to visit with her.

"Alright Cedes, your mother and I will be back in a few while your friends come and visit. We need to talk to the doctor about your discharge papers." Don informed his daughter, as he kissed her on the forehead.

"Okay Daddy." Mercedes sat up in the bed and waited for her friends to come in. They entered through the doors and rushed over to her asking her a million questions about what happened.

"Damn, I only got one mouth." Mercedes chuckled. She told them what happened even though they were there. They wanted a first-hand account of what everything felt like. No one had ever been shot before and while it wasn't anything to be proud of; they felt honored to know someone whom it actually happened to.

"I'm just glad you're alright." Candy bent down and hugged her as tears welled up in her eyes.

"Why you crying girl?" Mercedes asked, as she got teary eyed too.

"You've been my best friend since kindergarten, we lost contact and we just got reunited. I can't see myself losing you already. I don't know what I would do." Candy cried as Mercedes pulled her in closer and hugged her again. Mercedes' arm was in a sling with bandages that would be off within a week. She would milk this for all its worth when she got back to school.

"I don't know what I would do if I ever lost you." Mercedes released a few tears of her own.

"Aww suck it up bitches." Shateeya joked. "Ya'll are about to make me cry up in this bitch." Shateeya said as she fanned her eyes, so she wouldn't cry.

Candy chuckled as she wiped her tears away.

"I love ya'll, my bad bitches." Mercedes giggled.

"I love you too Mercedes." Hazel added in. Her face showed the feelings of all the others. They couldn't believe this had happened to someone close to them.

"Well we were just stopping by to see how you are doing and shit, but we got to go. We don't want to hold you up on your next visit." Candy kissed Mercedes on the cheek and she wondered who she was talking about. Mercedes face lit up and replaced the confusion when she saw Chino standing in the door way.

"Bye girls," Mercedes smirked as they left the room.

Chino walked in with his arms behind his back and he removed a bouquet of pink tulips. He handed them to Mercedes.

"How did you know I was here?" Mercedes and Chino kissed softly. She was so happy to see him, but didn't want to show too much emotion.

"Your mother called me and told me you had been shot. I was heading into New Jersey, but came right back as soon as I got the news."

"Are you serious?" Mercedes asked. She didn't know Chino cared for her that much.

"Yes, anything for you." Chino smiled. "How are you doing?"

"Fine, its' just a flesh wound to the arm. I'm still around."

"Damn, shit's crazy." Chino shook his head. "Don't let me find out who did it. They will be buried six fucking feet under." Mercedes never heard him speak so protectively like that. She could tell he was into the streets; his swag told everything.

"Don't worry about it Baby." Mercedes tried to change the subject. "So why were you going to New Jersey?"

"Damn girl... nah I was heading over there to handle some business-me and my man Reem. He lives out there, but he be out here in New York kicking it. I just had to come and see how my Baby was doing."

"Oh I see, so when are you going back?"

"In a few minutes, he's outside waiting for me. I had to come and see you though to make sure you were okay. I was tripping the whole ride out here. I'm good now that I see you're okay. When I come back we'll chill." He kissed her on the lips and hugged her. He promised to call her later. At that moment, her mother and father appeared in the doorway. Mercedes' face froze knowing that her father would meet her boyfriend for the first time.

"Hi Chino, I see you made it." Maria smiled as she walked in. She gave him a kiss on the cheek and tightly held onto Don's hand. He eyed the young man suspiciously.

"Yes I did, I was just leaving. I have to head back to Jersey." Chino responded replacing his fitted on his head.

"Oh forgive me. Don, this is one of Mercedes' friends from school Chino. I let him know that she was here and he wanted to make sure she was well. Chino, this is my husband and Mercedes' father Don Carter." Both men extended handshakes and masculine hugs.

"Alright, have a safe drive and thank you Chino." Maria thanked him.

"No problem." Chino walked past her and Mercedes knew her father wanted to say something further, but he chose not to do so. The room was filled with silence but you could see the steam rising from her father's head.

Don showed him respect, for now. He was still not too happy that his daughter was already interested in boys. He was an overprotective father and didn't want anyone taking advantage of her. He decided to keep quiet about it, even though he wanted to be mad with Maria for keeping a secret.

Twenty minutes later Mercedes was ready to be discharged. On the drive home, Don and Roy wondered who would try to take him out-and why.

* * *

Back in Santiago de Cuba, Vicente sat at his desk with his hands folded and face filled with frustration. He was vexed. Sixteen years had gone by and Vicente had no idea where his daughter had run off too. He even put a gun up to Alana's head and asked her about Maria's whereabouts.

She cried and pleaded with him. She told him that she didn't know. He eventually let her go. Recently, Vicente received some valuable information from his former sister in law Maleese. He began to put the pieces together and he started to come up with a plan.

His thinking was if he couldn't kill him immediately, he would slowly plan it. His workers surrounded the table as he held the picture of his beautiful daughter. The man responsible for killing his daughter stood in front of him with his head held high, but inside he was shaking in his boots. The message was clear: anyone that crossed Vicente's path or hurt someone he loved had to pay.

"You killed my daughter." Vicente yelled. "I told you bastards to find him, kill him and bring my daughter back to me. And I said alive, it's that simple." He raised his voice, "I know that motherfucker is with my daughter!"

"We saw him with a young looking woman who resembled Maria, but I know for sure it wasn't her." The worker tried to explain himself, but Vicente held his hand up in the air for silence. He grabbed his gun jammed it against his forehead. The only sound in the room was the heavy breathing of the man looking down the barrel of Vicente's Glock 45. Sweat poured down his face in fear and his bowels released right there.

"You killed my daughter!" Vicente spat, "Now it is time for you to meet your fucking maker."

"Nooo... please, no I'm sorry Mr. Vicente." The worker begged him.

"Get on your knees you fucking coward." The man continued to beg and plead, yet Vicente didn't listen to or care about his cries of mercy.

"Please don't do this Vicente, I didn't kill-"

Vicente stood back and shot him in both thighs leaving him helpless and crying out for help.

"Ahhh." he cried out as he held his leg in agony. Blood poured from his injuries and onto the cream carpet, staining it permanently.

"Now that you're on your fucking knees like I kindly asked you, I have a question for you." He smiled, "You killed my daughter, my beautiful daughter. And you think that I should let you live?" Vicente's heavy Cuban accent came out mostly when he was very angry and vexed.

"Yes," he cried out. "I have a family, and I told you that I didn't kill your daughter."

"I don't give a fuck about your stupid bitch and kid. I will fuck her and then kill her like you did to Maria!" He barked. He shot him in the chest causing his shoulder blade to jump back.

"Ahhhh," he screamed again as his clothes were drenched in blood. To add insult to injury, Vicente used the butt of the gun and smacked the man directly in the jaw causing blood to ooze out from his mouth.

"See you in hell motherfucker."

"Fuck you!" The dude spat as he spit blood at Vicente and started laughing hysterically.

"You're jealous of Mr. Carter, you fucking spick!" Everyone in the room was shocked that he was speaking like this to Vicente. No one ever disrespected him, no matter what.

Vicente laughed as he raised his gun and shot him in the head. The room was filled with carnage from the torture that he inflicted.

"Clean this mess up." He demanded to one of his workers. Looking down at the mess he made, he spit on the carcass while saying "Fucking puta!"

As he was about to walk out, the phone rang. The voice on the other end began telling him that the body found wasn't his daughter. He was relieved. A wide smile appeared on his face as he hung up the phone. His plan continued. He knew he could rest easier since his offspring was alive and well. In his view, the murder wasn't in vain. He was always ready to get rid of those not useful to him. He had no regrets.

"So Plan B, Emilio you will go into work with Carter under an assumed purpose. You will be starting over. You will be working with him and I need you to gain his trust and be his right hand man eventually."

"You don't think he will suspect something?" Emilio asked.

"Listen, Mr. Carter is good for business. With what I've done for him, he will be fine returning any favors." He smiled and continued to give orders. "You're going to be an informant, letting me know his every move. Who he speaks to, where he goes, and when he breathes. Pack your bags, you're on your way to New York."

Emilio began to exit so he could get ready when a thought popped into his head.

"When I get all this information, what do I do about Mr. Carter?"

The answer was contained within a wide devilish smirk on Vicente's face. "Bring him to me alive so I can kill him!"

In Love With A Thug

Mercedes sat in the passenger seat of Chino's car as they drove down 125th Street in Harlem singing along to a song called "I'm In Love with a Thug." She nodded her head to the music as she discreetly gazed over at Chino. He was so sexy and perfect in her eyes. For about thirty minutes they drove around and Chino showed her where he grew up. He also took her shopping, although Mercedes wanted for nothing, he still wanted to be the man that provided for his girl.

When they were done shopping, Chino parked the car and took the keys out. Mercedes was puzzled as she looked around the area and Chino chuckled.

"Why you look all worried Ma?" Chino chuckled. "This is my crib." Chino got out of the car and walked over to the passenger door. He opened it to let Mercedes out. He led her with her hand in his toward the projects. As they passed by, he dapped up a few of his homeboys and kept it moving. She pulled her jacket closer to her cold body as she felt all their eyes gazing at her as they admired her body and beauty. They knew not to say a word out of respect for Chino.

Mercedes held her nose as she walked up the stairs following behind Chino. Making their way up to Chino's floor, they passed urine, graffiti and empty liquor bottles. Finally they reached his home and when he opened the door Mercedes was shocked. The outside damn sure didn't match the inside. As he opened the door and she stepped inside, she was greeted with a fresh aroma of warm vanilla scented candles. The house was flawlessly clean and well decorated with plush cream carpet, nice furniture and expensive electronics.

"You can sit down here, I'll be back." Chino informed her as he disappeared into the hall. Mercedes sat down and nervously looked around. Her nerves continued when she heard footsteps too light to be Chino's. They were the sound of heels worn by a woman.

As the woman appeared from the dimmed hallway, her appearance was the first thing that Mercedes noticed. She was short with a medium build. Her hair was styled in a blondish brown bob and she wore shorts that look like they were painted on. She rocked a wife beater that was so tiny her breasts poured out from the top and sides. She had a sexiness about her that couldn't be ignored.

She lit a cigarette and took a seat across from Mercedes and inhaled. She eyed her guest up and down and finally spoke.

"Who are you?" She inquired with a little attitude.

"My name is Mercedes...are you Chino's sister?"

The woman cackled and almost choked on her smoke. She reached over to grab an ashtray and answered the question that she found to be almost ridiculous.

"I'm Cassandra; Chino's mother. You're Mercedes right? Yeah I've heard about you." She smirked as she took a drag of her cigarette.

"You did?" Mercedes had no idea that she was a topic of conversation. Chino had not mentioned his mother to her at all.

"Yeah, my son talks about you all the time. I remember the first day I heard your name, Mercedes this...Mercedes that...he sounded like he was in love." She smiled as she waved her cigarette around in the air. "Don't tell him that I told you though." Mercedes smiled as she agreed not to tell Chino.

"You're a very beautiful girl." Cassandra smiled and said while admiring her.

"Thank you."

"You remind me of myself when I was your age."

"And how is that?" Mercedes eagerly wanted to know.

"You're beautiful and smart, everything a man could ever want. But you're in love with a thug, just like I was." She smirked as she blew the smoke into the air. "My mom kicked me out of the house at the age of seventeen over Chino's father." She pursed her lips together and bobbed her head up and down.

"Why did she kick you out?"

"She kicked me out because she didn't approve of my boyfriend and the type of lifestyle that he was living. I fell in love with him and not what he did. I loved him as a person and my mother couldn't accept it. I wasn't about to throw away my love for someone else's decision."

"Wow, that's crazy."

"Yeah, I loved that man to death. He asked me to be his wife and I married him. Shortly after that, I had Chino."

"Where's your husband now, if you don't mind me asking?" Mercedes inquired, she wanted to know more about Chino's past.

"He's dead," she took in a deep breath and finished the last of her cigarette. "He was into the streets hard and had a lot of enemies. One day it caught up to him and he got shot almost two dozen times.

Mercedes could tell she was trying to hold back the tears. Cassandra continued to tell the story and grew more emotional at the memory. "I just remember seeing him and him telling me that he loved me. Now I don't even get to hear him say that anymore."

"Oh, I'm so sorry to hear that." Mercedes sympathized for her.

"Yeah this world is cold as fuck, so make sure you snuggle up."

"Yeah, I know." Mercedes simply said not knowing how to comfort this woman. A few moments ago she was a stranger, now she seemed like an aunt.

"Baby Girl, don't let anyone make decisions for you or try to tell you who to date. Do what your heart tells you is right. Live your life and you will learn from your own mistakes. If you can learn from others mistakes, by all means do so. However, don't let their fear stop you from doing what you want." Cassandra informed her.

"Yeah it's best to learn from your own mistakes." Mercedes agreed.

"One thing I can tell you is that you are in love. It's in your eyes and on your face. I remember that look. It's the look of love."

"I'm really enjoying talking to you. It's nice to get to know my man through his family."

"Well you can call me Ma now." Cassandra smiled as she lit another cigarette. Chino appeared in the living room and leaned against the wall. He smiled from ear to ear.

"So are ya'll ladies in here talking about me?"

"Ain't nobody talking about you Chanito, so hush."

Mercedes laughed at his mother's comment. She tried to sound all young and hip.

"Whatever Ma, I know ya'll was in here talking 'bout me." He walked over, bent down and kissed her on the cheek.

"Ya'll aren't going to stay for dinner?" She asked as she put out the cigarette in the ashtray on the table.

"No Ma, I gotta go make moves. See you later, love you."

"Love you too Chino, be safe." She yelled out before he left out the door.

"It was nice meeting you Cassandra, I mean Ma." Mercedes said as she smiled. She loved having someone else to talk to openly about her love for Chino.

"Same here...remember, learn from your own mistakes and not anyone else's." She smiled as Mercedes nodded her head and left behind Chino.

"What was that all about?" Chino inquired.

"Oh nothing, me and your mother were just kicking it." Mercedes smiled.

"Uh huh." Chino smirked.

"Your mom is a nice woman." Mercedes said as they walked down the steps. Her quote was stuck in Mercedes' head. It was on repeat like a song on a CD. As Mercedes sat in the car, she looked out the window and replayed his mother's words, *"One thing I can tell you is that you are in love. It's in your eyes and on your face. I remember that look. It's the look of love."* Mercedes knew she was in love, but she didn't know the consequences that could go along with it.

* * *

Chino and Mercedes sat opposite each other as they ate dinner at a Spanish restaurant in Harlem. Mercedes felt Chino staring at her while she was eating. She swallowed her food and looked up to see him staring into her eyes. She smiled and with feigned attitude questioned him and his intentions. .

"May I help you?" Mercedes said sarcastically.

"What, I can't stare at you?" Chino chuckled.

"No you can, I was just kidding Babes." Mercedes smiled.

"I'm just mesmerized by how beautiful you are and how I've never met a girl like you." He admitted, "I'm lucky to have a girl like you."

"And I'm lucky to be with you too Chino." Mercedes reached across the table and kissed him slowly on the lips. She gazed at Chino's sexy features and finally took a good look at the long scar that ran down to his cheek from the corner of his right eye.

"What happened to your face Baby?" Mercedes inquired as she reached across the table and touched his face and caressed it.

"Oh this?" Chino chuckled as he pointed to his face. "It's a really long story Ma. I don't even want to talk about it." Chino took a sip of his drink and tried to change the subject, but Mercedes kept digging-not taking no for an answer.

"Come on Chino, I'm here for you talk to me." Mercedes placed her hand over his hand and stared him in his eyes with an eager look. The look melted his heart and he began to open up to her. Mercedes and his mother were the only women he trusted.

"Alright Ma, it happened a long time ago when I used to live in Harlem. When I was about twelve, my moms was in the kitchen preparing dinner and I was in my room playing with my toys. The door bell rings and I can hear my father saying 'I'll get it.' Then a few seconds later I heard a loud bang and my mother screaming. They were yelling where the money at, where the money at? That's when I came out my room to see what was going on and I dropped to my knees as I watched my father getting pistol whipped. The others tore up our house. I can never forget one of the dudes pulled my mom by her hair and smacked her in the face with the gun. I couldn't take it no more, so I ran downstairs thinking I was all tough and shit." Chino chuckled. "I tried to fight them, but one of them pushed me on the ground and told me if I didn't stop acting a fool he would shoot me right then and there. As the dudes came from the back rooms searching, they were upset because they couldn't find the money. They instantly shot my father twenty times in his chest. I felt like I was watching fireworks and shit, the bullets ripped through him from an AK-47. The only sounds were the shots and my mother screaming. One of them shot my mother in the leg to shut her up and tied her up in a chair while covering her mouth with duct tape. They snatched my little ass up and said, 'You lucky we might let your little spick ass live and your Madre. Your father deserved to die, and just so you remember your sorry ass father everyday-I'll leave you with his mark."

Mercedes noticed a tear forming in his eye, but he wouldn't let it shed.

"He sliced me in the face with a huge knife and stabbed me in the chest one good time, leaving me for dead. I pretended to die by staying still." Mercedes placed her hand over her mouth as she listened to the story. She couldn't believe what he was telling her and she wanted to cry, but held in the tears.

"Oh my God Baby, I'm so sorry." Mercedes walked over to him and she embraced him and whispered in his ear.

"It's not your fault Ma." He rubbed her back.

"It'll be okay Baby, I'm here now and I'll never hurt you." A tear slid down her cheek and she wiped it away before they parted from the embrace.

"Are you ready to go Ma?"

"Yeah I'm finished here, thank you." Mercedes smiled. Chino helped her put on her jacket and he threw a hundred dollar bill on the table and kept it pushing. As they drove Mercedes watched the sky out of the window and realized that they weren't going back to his house.

"Where are we going now?" Mercedes asked as they pulled up in front of a fancy hotel.

"We're staying here for the night Ma, if that's alright with you?" Chino asked. He wanted to make sure she was comfortable before getting out of the car.

"Yeah, I told my mom I was staying over at Candy's. So I'm good, I guess it was a good thing I packed some clothes." Mercedes said, as she looked down at her Louis Vuitton duffle bag that was filled with her clothes.

"Alright Ma, I just hope she don't find out and go ballistic on a nigga." They both chuckled as they exited the car and walked through the huge French doors. Chino checked them into their room and started walking down the hall. He took her bag as they hopped on the elevator and arrived on the 6th floor, which was the all suite floor. Chino slid the card in the door and the beeping noise went off. The door unlocked and they both entered the room.

Mercedes placed her bag on the floor and walked over to the bed and nervously sat down. Chino walked over to her and sat on the edge of the bed and began rubbing her leg.

"Yo, are you alright Ma?"

"Yeah, I'm good Babes." Mercedes smiled.

"Alright." Chino said and lifted her chin with his finger and started French kissing her passionately. Mercedes loved his tongue game. He was so rough but in a sweet and passionate way. She lay back on the bed as he continued kissing her and made his way down to her spot-her neck. She started chuckling as he kissed her neck.

"Baby that tickles." Mercedes said as he removed the straps from her Chanel dress and gripped her breasts. He started licking around her nipples as she moaned in pleasure. It was like he was making love to her breasts, he flicked his tongue across her them causing her juices to flow. He made his way down to her belly and planted kisses all over her body. He slid her dress off over her head and tossed it to the floor. Mercedes then kicked off her shoes.

Chino slowly slid her panties down her legs and placed his head between her thighs. Mercedes was so nervous that her legs began to shake. She was embarrassed by her inexperience. No one had ever eaten her pussy, or did anything sexual for that matter to her. Chino begin licking her clit slowly, he was taking his time as he tasted her sweet juices. Mercedes grabbed his head as she moved her hips in a circular motion. He began licking her up and down and sucking on her clit, she felt like she was going to explode.

"You like that Ma?" He asked as he got up.

"Mhmm hmm," she moaned feeling as if he was still eating her out. He grabbed a condom from his pocket and put it on his dick. He looked Mercedes in her eyes.

"Are you ready?"

"Ready for what?" Mercedes asked, knowing what he was talking about.

"For me to love and make love to you."

"Yes Chino, I'm ready." Chino lay down on top of her body and slowly inserted himself inside of her.

"Oww, that hurts Chino." Mercedes whined.

"Do you want me to stop?" He asked, as he stopped pushing himself further inside of her.

"No, don't stop." Mercedes softly spoke. She let out soft moans as he stuck his manhood deep inside of her tight vagina. She held onto his back, scratching him every time he hit the spot.

"Ahhhh Chinnnoooo." Mercedes cried out, with every stroke she called out his name.

"Does that feel good?" He asked as he thrust in and out of her softly.

"Mhmm hmm." Mercedes moaned as they made love for hours.

"I love you Ma." He whispered in her ear. Mercedes was shocked that she heard Chino saying this. She beamed proudly as she bit on her bottom lip and said it back.

"I love you too Chino."

They collapsed into each other's arms and slept. Chino wrapped his arms around her body and kissed her on the head. He smiled as he watched the woman he fell in love with fall asleep. He hoped and prayed that she would never leave him. Other than his mother, Mercedes was the only girl that he'd ever love. He held her tightly as they slept; he never wanted to let go.

A Gorilla in the Midst

Mercedes blinked her eyes up and down before opening them completely. Her naked body was wrapped tightly in the white linen sheets. Her jet black hair was a mess from their steamy lovemaking session.

A wide smirk appeared across her face. She was with the man she loved, and waking up in his presence made her feel grown. She turned over and noticed that Chino wasn't beside her. She heard water running in the bathroom and figured he was taking a shower. Her stomach growled when she smelled the aroma of breakfast lingering in the hotel room.

Chino emerged from the bathroom with a white towel wrapped around his waist line. Mercedes loved his six pack abs. His tattoos covered his arms and chest and stood out as the sun's rays peeked through the curtains. Mercedes bit her bottom lip as he walked towards her.

"Good morning Ma." Chino walked over to her and kissed her on the lips. He sat on the edge of the bed and gazed at her.

"Good morning Baby." Mercedes smiled.

"You're even more beautiful when you wake up." Chino shook his head.

"Oh shut up." she playfully hit him in the chest.

"Aarh" Chino barked as he held his chest.

"What Babe, what did I do?"

"Nah Ma you just hit me in my spot, where I got stabbed. Sometimes I still have chest pains." He informed her as he rubbed his chest.

"I'm sorry." Mercedes apologized as she covered her mouth.

"It's all good Ma." Chino graciously said while accepting her apology. Mercedes stared at his chest for several minutes. The long scar was thick and ran from his upper chest to his rib cage. "Can I kiss it for you?" Chino declined, but Mercedes reached over and planted a couple of kisses on his chest.

"You better stop; you know what went down last night." Chino warned her as he waved his finger side to side.

"And?" Mercedes inquired, with her eye brows arched.

"Nah, you ain't ready for all that Ma," Chino warned her. "You got a long way to go." He joked around. Mercedes burst into laughter.

"Whatever man."

"Are you hungry?"

"Yeah, I'm starving." As soon as Mercedes made that statement, her stomach started growling loud enough for Chino to hear.

"Yeah, I can tell." Chino chuckled as he made his way over to the table which contained a silver platter. He slowly removed the lid and the steam escaped the platter as he brought the food over to Mercedes.

"Mhmm breakfast in bed, I must be doing something good." She joked as she sat up in bed and placed her back against the head board. She wrapped the sheets around her chest.

"Yeah, you're special." He informed her, "I never did this for any other female." He assured her as he placed the tray on the bed. It had pancakes, scrambled eggs with cheese, sausage and a glass of cold pulp-free orange juice. Her eyes lit up and her mouth watered as the steam entered her nose. Mercedes dug into her food; within minutes she consumed it all.

"Damn Ma, you *were* hungry." Chino was amazed that she cleaned the entire plate as he placed it on the counter.

"Yeah Baby, thanks for the food." Mercedes licked her lips as she got up from the bed. The sheets dropped down to the ground and Chino gazed at her body. He shook his head.

"Damn Ma, you look better with no clothes on." Chino smirked as Mercedes looked back at him with a sexy grin.

"I gotta get home. Its 11:30 and my mom is expecting me back by noon." Mercedes rushed to put her clothes on, she wished that she could take a shower before she went home. However, she didn't want to be late getting home.

"Alright Ma," Chino sat on the bed still in his towel. As he dropped the towel to the ground, Mercedes paused and eyed his butt. It was so firm and perfect. She giggled as she continued getting dressed.

"What's so funny?" Chino asked, he turned around as he slid on his pants.

"Nada, hurry I have to go Babes." Mercedes whined.

"Alright Ma I'm coming, I just need to put on my kicks." He threw his shirt on his head and slipped into his Timbs. He grabbed his keys and they were on their way. As they sat in the car bumping to some Jim Jones, Mercedes replayed last night in her mind. The images of Chino making love to her sent chills down her spine.

"Last night was beautiful." Mercedes said as she relaxed in the car as Chino drove her home. She turned to look at him.

"Yes it was beautiful, like music to my soul." Chino smirked as he continued down 116h street. He was special to her, he was her first and she wanted him to be her last. She hoped that Chino felt the same way; she never wanted to leave him. More importantly, she didn't want him to ever leave her.

Mercedes looked around as she unlocked the door to her home. She noticed that no one was around. She could hear her father in his office talking on the phone. She crept down the hall and passed his office. She slowly walked up the spiral stairs and went into her room. She plopped her bag down on her queen size bed and quickly came out of her clothes and threw them in the hamper.

Mercedes entered her bathroom, turned on the water and hopped in. Flashbacks of her and Chino making love made her feel so special inside. She washed her hair and her body with one of her favorite scents from Victoria's Secret, Dream.

She hopped out of the shower, dried off her body and slipped on some blue jeans with a plain white shirt. She slid into a pair of white Nike flip flops. She stood in front of her mirror and removed the damp towel from her dripping hair. She dried her hair with the towel, and applied some mousse. She then headed downstairs. Just as she was doing so, she heard her father call out to her "Mercedes?" Don yelled.

"Yes Daddy."

"Come downstairs now." He demanded. Mercedes was scared shitless, her father sounded mad and she hoped he didn't find out about her and Chino. When she got down to the bottom of the stairs, she saw her father and a young man she had never seen before. He was about 5'8," he had a mocha skin color and his head was filled with curls. He had hazel eyes and his jaw structure was very masculine. He had a medium build, but his chest poked out of his shirt. He rocked a diamond earring in one of his ears. He was a plane Jane, but still cute though.

"I didn't even notice you walk by my office."

"That's because you were on the phone Daddy, and I didn't want to interrupt you." Mercedes smirked; she knew how to have her way with her father.

"Neither did I." Maria emerged from the kitchen and removed the apron from her waist. "When did you get in?" she asked.

"I got in about a half an hour ago; I was upstairs fixing my hair."

"How was your night at Candy's?"

"It was great; we watched movies and ate popcorn." Mercedes smiled as she lied through her teeth about where she was and what she had been up to. She hated lying to her parents, but she had no choice this time. She couldn't let them know she spent the night with Chino.

"Well, I cooked breakfast."

"I already ate."

"Oh okay." Maria smiled. "Well I'm going to go upstairs and take a little nap, I'm tired." Maria smiled as she kissed her husband on the cheek. "It was nice meeting you." She smiled as she shook the guy's hand.

"Mercedes I want to introduce you to one of my new worker's, Emilio. Emilio this is my daughter Mercedes Carter." He introduced them, "He's from Cuba and he'll be working for me."

"It's nice to meet you Emilio." Mercedes extended her hand, but he got on one knee and kissed her hand. Mercedes was impressed. He stood up and gazed into her eyes, he never looked away.

"It's a pleasure to meet you too Mercedes." He had a weird smile on his face and a devious look in his eyes. Mercedes had never seen a look like his before. He was sexy and mesmerizing, yet frightening at the same time.

"You've raised a very beautiful young lady." He looked at her father and smiled before licking his lips and staring at Mercedes.

"Isn't she the most gorgeous girl?" Don said while pinching her cheeks.

"Daddy!" Mercedes barked as she kept her eyes on Emilio. "So how long have you been staying in New York?" She asked him.

"I just moved up here not too long ago, I have a place not too far from here on Long Island.

"Oh really, what made you move up here?"

"Well my family lives up here, I was visiting and I liked it. I decided to stay. New York is very beautiful."

"So what do you do for a living?" Mercedes was getting extra personal.

"Alright, Mercedes," Don chuckled. "That's enough questions." He placed his hand on her shoulder and gave her the eye.

"I'm just making sure that he's on our Carter level." Mercedes smirked at him before turning and heading back up the stairs. She looked over her shoulder and he winked at her with a wide smile on his face. Mercedes knew there was something different about him, but she didn't know what it was. She was attracted to him a little bit, but her faithfulness to Chino wouldn't let her stray. She did want to know more about this Emilio. He was very different and they had a clear attraction.

Later on while upstairs, Mercedes called Candy to tell her about her evening with Chino.

"Girl you lying like a motherfucker." Candy couldn't believe the news she was telling her. She was also on three-way with Hazel and Chamari.

"I ain't lying." Mercedes said cheesing ear to ear. "Last night, he made sweet passionate love to me. That shit hurt like hell, but that nigga got me open."

"Damn girl, okay then you down with us now." Hazel chuckled.

"What you mean?" she eagerly asked. "Not a virgin click." They all burst into laughter. Their conversation was soon interrupted by a knock on Mercedes' bedroom door.

"Hold on you guys," she informed them as she placed the phone on her chest.

"Hello?" she sang.

"It's Daddy." He spoke loudly, "Can I have a few minutes?"

"Yes." Mercedes said as she placed the phone back up to her ear, "I'm going to talk to you girls later. My father wants to talk to me."

"Oooh you bouta get that ass beat." Chamari added in.

"Whatever ya'll, bye." Mercedes hung up and Don came in and took a seat next to her.

"So, what's new in your life?" he inquired. Mercedes knew her father was trying to get at something, specifically Chino.

"What do you mean?"

"Any new friends, new male friends, you know any boyfriends?" They both chuckled.

"Well yeah, this boy named Chino the one you saw at the hospital that day." Mercedes informed him.

"Oh really, where's he from?"

"He's from Harlem."

"Oh word," he nodded his head up and down.

"So when am I gonna meet him? Like really meet him, formally?"

"What?" Mercedes had a surprised look on her face.

"Well, I mean I want to know what type of dude I'm dealing with here. Especially when it comes down to my daughter, I need to see where his head is at. I'm not a perfect man Mercedes, but I want the best for you. I want more for you than *this* life."

"Daddy, I know that."

"I want you to finish school...go to college get a nice job and not have to depend on any nigga."

He smiled as he shook his head, "Mercedes what I'm trying to say is I want the best for you, that's all." He playfully slapped her on the knee. "I want to meet this dude."

"What about Friday night, that's when mom cooks dinner."

"Alright." he stood up and stretched. "I have to see if I approve of you talking to this dude or not." He seriously said.

"Come on Daddy."

Mercedes watched him as he disappeared in the hallway and wondered what would happen at dinner. She was in love with Chino, and she loved her father to death. To choose one over the other could cause dire consequences.

* * *

Friday night came sooner than Mercedes hoped. She helped her mother set up the kitchen table. Their maid Claudia was off, so her mom made dinner. Spanish yellow rice, baked seasoned chicken, vegetables and some plantains. Claudia was off, but insisted to stay and help set the table. Their thoughts were soon interrupted by the doorbell. Mercedes quickly stopped in her tracks and looked at her mother.

"He's here," she mumbled assuming it was Chino, "I'll be back Ma." "While I go to the bathroom and check how I look, can you open the door?" She quickly placed the napkins down on the table and rushed to the bathroom to check her make up.

"You look fine Honey." Maria yelled out as Mercedes made her way down the hall. She looked over at Claudia and they both chuckled. Mercedes stood in the mirror and made sure everything was straight from her head to her feet. When she was done, she found Chino sitting in the kitchen and greeted him with a kiss on the cheek.

"Hey Chino." She said as she blushed. The way he looked at her made her feel so special.

"Whassup?" he stared her down, "You look beautiful."

"Thank you." Mercedes saw that dinner was already served and quickly took her seat next to her man.

"I see ya'll already started eating dinner without me."

"No Mercedes, we were waiting for you to check yourself out in the mirror and all that good stuff." Her mother smirked.

"Whatever Ma, you know I just went to use the bathroom real quick."

"Where's Daddy?" Mercedes asked as she looked at her mother.

"He had to handle some business. He said he'll be here in a little while."

As soon as that was said, she could hear her father coming through the front door. Don walked in and took off his jacket and tossed it across the couch. He walked into the kitchen and rolled up his sleeves.

"Hey Baby," he walked over and bent down and kissed Maria on the cheek.

"Hey Honey." Maria returned the kiss, "How was your day?"

"It was alright." Don sighed.

"Hello sir, how are you doing?" Chino asked as he extended his hand, but Don completely ignored him.

"Daddy this is Chino, and Chino this is my father Don." Mercedes introduced them as her father pulled out his chair and took a seat.

"It's nice to meet you Don." Chino said.

"It's Mr. Carter to you." Don shot back with his nose flared up.

"Alright, it's nice to meet you Mr. Carter." Mercedes gulped hard as she looked over at Chino and noticed he was biting his tongue. He didn't let his pride take over him.

"This food is delicious Mrs. Carter." Chino nodded his head, savoring the taste.

"Thank you," Maria smiled, "I'm glad you like it."

"So, you like my daughter?" Don asked bluntly after clearing his throat. Chino looked up and was caught off guard by his question.

"Yes, I find your daughter to be a highly intelligent and a very beautiful girl."

"What do you want from her?"

"Excuse me?" Chino's cocked his head back as he looked at Don with a perplexed look on his face.

"What are you intentions with my daughter?" Don asked again more aggressively.

"I don't want anything from her sir. I like your daughter a lot. Matter of fact, I'm in love with her." Chino admitted.

Mercedes almost choked on her chicken as she heard him tell her father that he was in love with her. She quickly soothed her dry throat with a drink to calm her nerves. Don quietly eyed Chino to see how genuine he was with his response. He took another bite of food as Maria changed the subject and hopefully the vibe. Tension surrounded the table and it was thick.

"So Chino, what do you plan on doing after high school?" Maria inquired.

"Well I mean I want to go to college for business and open up a few businesses of my own you know." Chino smiled at the idea.

"What kind of business?" Mercedes chimed in, eager to know.

"Probably a nice clothing store, a book store, and maybe even own my own sneaker spot."

"That's really good, at least you're going somewhere with your life."

"Is it going to be a legitimate business or a drug front?" Don chimed in again, as he kept asking straight forward, blunt questions. Chino was really starting to get fed up with his smart ass questions.

"Legitimate." Chino bit into his chicken and softly chewed, trying to remain as humble as possible. His jaw clenched and you could see the anger swelling in his face.

"So what is it that you do for a living?" Don asked Chino staring icily into his face. He was playing judge, jury and executioner and depending what Chino answered would seal his fate.

"Seriously am I the target here?" Chino questioned as he looked around the table. He couldn't take it any more, he got up and said, "I'm sorry Mrs. Carter but I'm excusing myself from the table. Thanks for the dinner tonight." he walked over and kissed her and Mercedes on the cheek.

"So how do make your money?" Don asked his question in a different way, seeing he didn't answer his question. He stopped eating as he looked over at Chino and stared him in the eyes, waiting for a response. "I know your pretty ass don't work at Mc Donald's on 125th."

"Don Carter!" Maria raised her voice. She never raised her voice at her husband and was angry that he was showing a bad first impression.

"You don't have to answer that babe." Mercedes said to Chino. Her eyes began to water in embarrassment and shame at her father's behavior.

Chino squared his shoulders and took a deep breath knowing he wasn't going to win this fight.

"I get by, just like you do. I sell drugs like you and my father. I provide for my mother, just like you do your daughter." Chino's eyes burned and his nose flared up at the interrogation.

"We don't live in a fancy ass estate like this! We used to until my pops was murdered. The cops came in and took everything from us. They took everything we ever owned. They took my last pair of sneakers. I needed them because I didn't have any other shoes. I asked them why they were taking my sneakers." Chino laughed out of frustration. "They said they were brought with illegal money. So as a man, I have to do what I have to do to pay my mother's bills and for anything else she wants. I'm a drug dealer, a gangsta from the streets. I'm from Harlem, born and raised." Chino pounded on his chest as Mercedes watched her boyfriend carefully; she noticed the tears forming in his eyes. He wouldn't let them fall. He was too strong for that.

He stormed out of the door in anger and didn't look back. Mercedes quickly hopped up and tried to chase after him, but she couldn't catch him.

"Chino?" Mercedes yelled, but he was already gone and the tires of his car echoed. Mercedes displayed the anger on her face without saying a word.

"How could you?" Mercedes spat as she plopped down in her chair. Her mother held her close to comfort her as she glared at her father.

"He's a drug dealer Mercedes, you heard the boy." He continued eating his food.

"He's just like you Daddy." Mercedes cried. "Just like you, a regular person who has to do what he has to do to get by."

"I don't want you seeing him anymore." Don demanded.

"What? Why?" Mercedes questioned as tears streamed down her face.

"Because I'm your father and I said so."

Mercedes picked up a glass and threw it against a wall shattering it into pieces. She ran up the stairs to her room in a rage.

She put on some soft soothing music, but it only reminded her of Chino and how much she loved him. Listening to love songs from Keyshia Cole and other artists definitely didn't help. Mercedes sat up with her knees up to her chest and rocked back and forth. She heard loud footsteps walking up the stairs. Then she could hear her mother and father talking in front of her door.

"No Don, you aren't right." Maria sighed. "I mean she's young and she's in love with him don't you see that?"

"She's too young for love. She doesn't know what the hell love is. She's still fucking growing up, she's still a baby." Don barked.

"Wow, you're so naïve." Maria shook her head as she smirked.

"Naïve? I'm not naïve. I'm just looking out for my daughter. I don't want her fucking with no buster ass drug dealing niggas. What can he do for my daughter? Get her caught up in the trap life? Make her end up pregnant?"

"You should be the last one talking Don." Maria stated. She gave him the eye and he knew exactly what she was referring to. "I met you when I was eighteen and had my first child by you at a young age..." he cut her off.

"I don't know why you're siding with her. She's only sixteen Maria. This girl doesn't know what she wants in life yet." Maria didn't know what came over him, but she didn't like how he overreacted tonight.

"You definitely were excessive tonight." Maria said. "Asking that young man a whole bunch of inappropriate questions..." her voice was filled with rage. What's your problem?"

"What was inappropriate about them?" Don asked. "I asked him questions to see where his head is at. Now I know what he does for a living and I don't want my daughter around that. I absolutely will not allow it."

"Just know that you're being very selfish right now. I'll never say that you ruined my life by bringing Mercedes into this world; I love her with all my heart and support her through everything. Here you are being a hypocrite. You think this is the life I wanted? Yes a beautiful family, a nice house, expensive clothes and a nice car. I have all of that, but did I ask for a drug dealing boyfriend? No, I have to honestly say that I fell in love with who you are and not what you did. I didn't give up on you when I found out that you were a drug dealer. He's just like you Don. Don't you see that?" Maria sighed.

The conversation ended with Maria's last point. Mercedes heard her door open and she quickly tried to get under the covers and pretended she was sleeping.

"Mercedes?" Maria called out her name.

"Hmm?" Mercedes moaned as she turned around. Her mother wore a half smile on her face as she walked over and sat down on the edge of the bed.

"Are you okay?" Maria asked as she rubbed her hair.

"I'll be fine, I'm just thinking about Chino." Mercedes sighed. "He probably hates my guts and doesn't want anything to do with me now. I'm sure he thinks that Daddy's crazy. She cried as her mother extended her arms and held her.

"Don't say that baby, Chino loves you Baby Girl. No matter what, he stood up for himself tonight." Maria rubbed her daughter's back as she cried into her chest.

"I know your father is a tough guy and sometimes he's right. I do understand where he's coming from, but Honey he's a real nice guy. I don't understand why your father is acting like a complete fool tonight."

"So does that mean I can't see Chino anymore?" Mercedes asked. She removed her head from her mother's cheek with a hopeful smile.

"Sweetie, I don't know...honestly your father doesn't want you to see him and I'm supporting you all the way...but just don't disobey your father. He's still your father." Mercedes couldn't believe it, although her mother was on her side-it was still like she was siding with her father. She didn't have any words left for her mother, she was too upset. She rolled over turning her back toward her mother as the tears silently crept down her cheeks. She only wished that Chino was here to hold and console her. She never wanted to choose between the only two men that she sincerely loved.

Unfaithful

On Monday morning Mercedes' eyes were puffy and red from all the crying she did over the weekend. She refused to come out of her room. She had a full bathroom in there, so she had no need to venture downstairs. Claudia brought food to her daily, so she didn't have to face her parents.

Her father tried to talk to her several times, but she completely ignored him. She didn't have anything to say to him. Mercedes cried every time she dialed Chino's number. He ignored her calls each time. When she did finally reach him, he simply told her he needed time to think. As much as he loved her, he wasn't going to tolerate her father's disrespect. Mercedes was heartbroken and blamed her father for interfering with her happiness.

She hung up the phone and lay down, but was distracted by a sharp pain in her abdomen along with sudden nausea. She had the urge to vomit and placed her hand over her mouth. She quickly ran into the bathroom. As soon as she made it to the toilet, she vomited the remnants of last night's dinner. As she began to cry again, she brushed her teeth and got herself ready for the day. She prayed that it would be a better day, but somehow she knew she would have no such luck.

Walking over to her closet, she pulled out the first thing she could grab and put it on for school. She didn't care and her wardrobe choice showed it. She was very irritated and in a bitchy mood. She threw her hair in a messy ponytail and made her way downstairs.

As she made her way down, she crossed paths with her father. She avoided contact with him but he initiated a conversation with her.

"Have a nice day in school Baby Girl." Don said. Mercedes was already outside and slammed the door as she exited. She wasn't in the mood today; if anyone pissed her off it would be a day they regretted. As Mercedes walked outside, she stopped in her tracks. Mr. Gates wasn't there to take her to school. Instead it was Emilio.

He rolled down the window, "I'm taking you to school today." He smiled and rolled the window back up and replaced his sunglasses. Mercedes huffed as she walked over to the car. She opened the door and slammed it shut.

Emilio noticed that she was quiet throughout the ride. Mercedes felt the awkward silence; she always listened to music when Mr. Gates took her to school. She was about to reach her hand out to turn on the radio, but frowned up her face when she noticed Emilio didn't have a radio. He cleared his throat and decided to say something.

"Mercedes, are you alright?"

"Yeah I'm fine." Mercedes lied.

"Are you sure? Because your eyes are red and I know I don't know you like that, but I can tell something's wrong."

Mercedes tried to avoid eye contact so he wouldn't see the tears forming in her eyes. She rolled down the window to dry her tears with the morning breeze.

"If there's anything..." Emilio begin to speak, but Mercedes cut him off.

"I said I'm fine." Mercedes barked through clenched teeth. Finally, they arrived at school and she hopped out of the car. She didn't stop to acknowledge any of her friends.

After all of her classes, Mercedes bumped into her friends and they noticed something was wrong.

"Hey Missy, what's going on?" Candy asked.

"What up Cedes?" Hazel chimed in. As Mercedes got closer the girls noticed her eyes were red and puffy filled with tears.

"Aww, what's wrong Mercedes?" Candy began comforting her with a hug and Mercedes reciprocated.

"It's Chino." They all groaned at hearing his name.

"Who do I have to fuck up?" Shateeya asked.

"What he do to you Mercedes?" Candy asked. Mercedes wiped away the tears from her eyes and began to tell the story.

"Well, I invited him over for dinner Friday night to meet my father and it turned into a complete disaster. He told me that he didn't want me to see Chino again. Chino didn't want to agree, but he told me that he loves me but he couldn't disrespect my father. Basically he said he didn't want to see me anymore because he didn't want to cross my dad."

"I see where he's coming from Mercedes; Chino doesn't want to come between the bond you share with your dad." Candy informed her. "I know your father loves you and he knows what's best for you Cedes."

"She does have a point." Chamari added.

"But I love him and I can't stop my feelings because my dad doesn't like him." Mercedes yelled.

"Let's go in the cafeteria, you need to get some water to calm down." Candy insisted. She hugged her girl again before walking down the hall. Her legs turned into noodles when she saw something that caused her heart to drop to the pit of her stomach. Dejection was written all over face. Chino and India were back together and hugging.

"Mercedes don't." Candy tried to pull her back, but her feet moved too quickly. She was already exchanging words with them. "How could you?" Mercedes spat. India looked as if she'd been crying too, but as soon as she saw Mercedes' face everything changed. She had a devious smile on her face and began to clutch Chino.

"I got him." India mouthed. Chino turned around to face Mercedes. Before he could say anything, she ran down the hall as he yelled her name.

"Mercedes!" Chino yelled out. "Mercedes!" She ran until she reached the cafeteria. She wanted to hide from everyone and cried in anger at seeing her first love with someone else.

"I can't believe his ass was all hugged with that bitch like it was nothing." Mercedes spat as she sat at the round table with her girls. "It hasn't even been a fucking week!" She barked as she watched her fingers tremble.

"Fuck him!" Shateeya spat. "Mercedes he's like all these other nigga's out here, just want the pussy then bail out on your ass." Shateeya pursed her lips together as she filed her fingernails.

"Maybe we're blowing this shit out of proportion." Candy tried to assure them. "I mean, just because he was hugged up with her doesn't mean anything Mercedes. You have to talk to him." Candy insisted.

"The point is he was hugged up on that bitch. Especially that bitch India, he knows me and her have problems. I don't care if that is his ex, there are boundaries." Mercedes shook her head.

"Maybe something happened to her." Chamari added in. "Mercedes, I see how Chino looks at you and how he treats you. He loves you girl. Just because your father doesn't want you to see him and Chino agreed doesn't mean he doesn't still have love for you." Chamari rubbed her girls shoulder. Mercedes thought she did have a point. However, it still didn't change the fact that Chino was hugged up with India like it was nothing.

"Ain't nothing happen to that stupid bitch India." Shateeya laughed. She looked up and said, "And if she said something happened, she's a lying ass hoe-she's just jealous of you because you stole Chino. She'll do anything in her power to get him back." Shateeya severely pissed her off with her words. Mercedes excused herself as she got up from the table.

"I'm going to the bathroom."

"You want us to come?" Candy asked.

"Just in case a bitch try to get stupid, I got ya back sis." Hazel added.

"Nah, I'm good. Thanks anyway." Mercedes smiled and headed to the bathroom. She couldn't allow her girls and the entire cafeteria to see her upset and crying. She splashed water over her face in the sink. When she looked up, she saw India standing behind her with a smirk on her face.

"I guess you lost." India chuckled. She shrugged her shoulders and began applying clear lip gloss.

"Excuse me?" Mercedes turned to face her with her head cocked to the side and her eye brows arched. Her nose flared with anger.

"I said, I guess you lost." India turned and they were almost face to face. They had about one foot of space between them.

"Chino doesn't want you anymore. He's all mine bitch. Always has been and always will be. You came up in this bitch like you Miss Hot Shit and your pussy don't stink." India laughed. "You must have lost your fuckin mind. Every bitch in this school and in Harlem knows that he's my man always and forever."

Mercedes laughed, "Trick please, Chino despises your ass. So whatever little games you got up your dirty ass sleeves aren't going to work. So before you try to say someone's shit don't stink-check yourself out in the mirror. If you don't come correct then don't come at all." Mercedes smiled.

"You will never be me India, let alone walk in my Prada shoes. You will never have Chino again, he's mine bitch!" Mercedes assured her. "Believe that!" She added in with an evil grin. She turned to walk away, but India made a smart comment that caused her to quickly do an about-face.

"If he's your man, then why am I having his baby?" India blurted out and punctuated it with rolling her eyes. Mercedes quickly turned around and rushed straight at India. They both began to tussle as they fell to the ground. Mercedes had the upper hand; she was on top of India and punching her with both hands. She was throwing non-stop blows.

"You fucking stupid ass bitch!" Mercedes continuously punched her in the face. India extended her hands and tried to scratch Mercedes' face. Mercedes dodged her feeble attempt and grabbed a hold of India's face. She began banging it on the floor. India then tried to grab Mercedes' hair, but she didn't allow her. Mercedes backed all the way up and kept punching. Mercedes grabbed onto India's hair and wrapped it around her fist several times. She started pounding her face.

"Stop it Mercedes." India begged as she screamed. Mercedes knew she was trying to scream to get attention. She was looking for someone to come to her rescue.

Back in the cafeteria the girls knew something was up. Mercedes had been in the bathroom for a while and India went into the bathroom several seconds later. They rushed into the bathroom to see what was going on. They saw Mercedes on top of India punching her in the face. It was a bloody scene. Blood was all over India's face and on the tan marble floor.

"Don't you ever...in...your...mother fucking...life... try to come at me ...again!" Mercedes punched her one last time in her nose. "And keep Chino's name out your mouth bitch!" Mercedes banged her head onto the marble floor one more time. She got back up to her feet and looked behind her. The M.O.B.B. were staring at her in awe.

"What the fuck happened?" Candy asked.

"This bitch was talking crazy to me, she fucking asked for it." Mercedes looked down at India who was curled up on the floor. she was bleeding from her nose and mouth.

"Oh shit bitch! You got fucked up!" Shateeya chanted. India's clique came rushing into the bathroom and ran to her side. They were asking her what happened. Mercedes smiled and looked at her girls and said, "Let's go."

They walked from the bathroom and talked about how the fight started. Shateeya was real amped, saying she wished that she was in there when the fight broke out. She kept saying she would have jumped in and gave India a buck fifty to the face. They shook their heads and laughed.

"Oh yeah, there's going to be a nice ass party at this club down in Queens." Candy informed the girls.

"What, that 18 plus event?" Hazel asked.

"Yeah that one, I'm definitely going."

"But your only seventeen Candy, how you getting in there?" Mercedes inquisitively asked.

"Fake ID bitch!" She high-fived Shateeya. "We don't even need fake ID's because we some bad bitches." Candy chuckled. "You want to go?"

"I'm only sixteen, there's no way I'm getting up in there." Mercedes shook her head.

"Aww come on girl, it will be fun trust me." Candy smiled.

"Girl we'll get you in. Don't worry." Hazel smirked.

"It won't be any fun without our other bad bitch Mercedes." Chamari added. She looked at Mercedes with puppy dog eyes. "Pretty please," she batted her long thick extension eye lashes.

"Alright, I'm down. But I don't think my mom will approve. My dad won't for sure!"

"Just tell her you'll be staying at my crib again, or sneak out!" Candy insisted. "Chino's going to be there." Candy tauntingly added. She knew that's all Mercedes needed to hear.

"Alright, I'm down." Mercedes smiled. As they talked about the event, a security guard came walking down the hall and stood in front of them.

"Mercedes Carter, the principal wants you in the office now." The security guard informed her.

"Oh shit, you're in trouble." Shateeya cooed. Mercedes told her to shut up as she followed the guard down the hall and walked into the principal's office.

Mercedes walked into the principal's office and gulped when she saw India holding an ice pack on her face. She was sitting in the chair looking like she just went a few rounds with Floyd Mayweather. Mercedes struggled not to laugh at the sight. She sat across from India with a steely glare. India rolled her eyes and the principal came out of his office to address the two of them. He called them inside and they both sat down as he took his seat behind the desk.

"What happened?" He inquired. Mercedes and India sat silent.

"So no one is going to tell me what happened?"

Silence filled the room once again. Mercedes looked away and crossed her hands.

"Both of you ladies acted horribly today. Due to your refusal to talk about the incident, you both will be suspended for one week." The principal reclined back in his chair.

"What the fuck?" India yelled. "She started it."

"Watch your mouth young lady." He raised his voice. "So have a nice weekend; it's starting today."

Mercedes grabbed her bag and threw it over her shoulder and walked out of the office. She had never been suspended from school. She was a good girl, but she was tired of dealing with the drama. She already knew her parents would be notified, so she prepared to deal with their consequences when she got home. Mercedes hung around outside until school was dismissed. She refused to sit in anymore classes since she was already suspended. Also, she wanted to let the girls know what happened in the office.

"Alright, I'll see ya'll Friday." Mercedes waved.

Maria was waiting out front to pick her up. Mercedes got into the car and slid in the seat. She bit down on her bottom lip and looked out the window to avoid eye contact with her mother.

"What happened at school today?" Maria asked before she pulled off. She sat there with the car engine idling.

"This girl came out her mouth to me wrong and we ended up fighting."

"That's a good reason to fight Mercedes." Maria sarcastically responded.

"I mean she came at me Ma, she disrespected me."

"Mercedes, right now I'm so pissed at you I can't even put it into words. I will let your father deal with you." Maria waved her hand and dismissed her. Mercedes huffed and turned to stare from the window as her mother pulled off. The ride home was totally silent. When she walked into the house, Mercedes saw her father sitting on the couch. She said nothing and hoped that he wouldn't either, of course that was all a pipe dream. "Mercedes Carter." Don called out.

"Yes Daddy." Mercedes stood there in front of him.

"What's going on?"

"What do you mean?" Mercedes was acting stupid, as if she didn't know what he was referring to. Her father took a deep breath and let out a loud sigh.

"You know what I'm talking about Mercedes, the school called us and said that you had been in an altercation with a student and they suspended you for a week." He notified her as if she didn't know.

"Well, she came at me rude and was disrespectful. I had to stand up for myself."

"Mercedes you're only sixteen. You're very smart and that's why I didn't want you going to a public school! Because I knew this shit was going to happen."

"Well I'm a Carter, and I'm going to stand up for myself. I'm not going to take nobody's mess, ain't that what you taught me Daddy?" Mercedes asked him. She continued, "Don't let no one down talk you or disrespect you, you have to fight for what's rightfully yours." Don rubbed his temples as he shook his head side to side, he didn't even want his daughter in his presence right now.

"You know what Mercedes, you're right." he said. Mercedes was surprised and had a smile on her face. "Daddy did teach you well, but I'm going to have to put you on punishment until you go back to school." The smile quickly vanished, "WHAT?" Mercedes yelled, "I'm on punishment?"

"Yes, until you learn how to behave yourself."

"Wow, this is unbelievable!" Mercedes shouted as she stormed up the stairs and slammed the door behind her.

She was on punishment for a week at school and at home. That messed up her plans to go out with the girls. She had her outfit picked out and everything. She really hoped her mother would reconsider. She had to go out, especially since Chino would be there.

The Party to Remember

Mercedes rolled up to the club and Mr. Gates exited the car and opened her door. She didn't expect to be able to go. But since she was "Daddy's Girl" and never really got in trouble, her father was lenient with her. Her harshest punishment would be at school. She did have a set curfew that was strictly enforced; Mr. Gates was to pick up Mercedes at exactly 11 PM.

The line stretched all the way around the corner. The music was thumping so loud that you would have thought it was playing outside. As Mercedes made her way to the line, she noticed most of the girls were scantily clad. Mercedes and her friends were all dressed to the nines and all eyes were on them. They were focused on Mercedes especially; she always did a little extra to be noticed.

As soon as her heels clicked on the concrete, heads turned to see who she was. The boys wanted her and the girls hated her. She ignored them and made her way to the front of the line with her friends. Candy knew one of the guards and he let them jump the line.

Within minutes, they made their way through security and were in the club dancing to the music. The beat dropped so hard that they could feel the vibrations in their bones. They made their way over to the bar and were greeted with drinks, compliments of Candy and the bartender she flirted with.

"Girl you're crazy, we're underage." Mercedes said while shaking her head at her friend.

"Here Mercedes try it." Candy passed her a drink.

"Nah, I'm good." Mercedes replied.

"Come on girl, let's have some fun. Tonight is our night to have fun and show these niggas and bitches out here who we are M.O.B.B!" Candy yelled. Mercedes gave her an unsure look. Everyone wondered if she was actually going to drink it.

"Alright man, just this one drink." Mercedes took the drink and took a big gulp. The drink was Hennessy and Red Bull and it tasted funny. Once it entered her mouth, Mercedes made a weird face. The liquor slowly crept into her system and she got comfortable. She smiled while her girls took their drinks too. "Now let's toast." Candy smiled as they all put up their drinks. "It's M.O.B.B for life bitchessssss!"

As they scanned the club, they noticed the men staring hard at them and particularly Mercedes. The girls put her on notice.

"Damn Mercedes, this nigga is checking you out hard body." Candy said.

"Who?" Mercedes inquired as she looked around the club. She was trying to find out who her girl was talking about.

"That nigga right there with the Red Monkeys on and that long ass fucking chain. He is so fucking fine, Mhmm I love me some Dark chocolate."

"How you know he's looking at me?" Mercedes said. Her words were slurring already from the liquor.

"Here he come girl! You better holla at that nigga. Girl here he comes." Candy walked away and slipped into the crowd. Mercedes called out to her, she didn't want to be alone. Her friend was already gone. The dude walked over toward the bar and stood next to Mercedes and smiled, "Hey Ma, how you doing tonight?"

"I'm doing good and you?" Mercedes inquired.

"I'm just chilling, you know Ma. Seeing you definitely made my night though."

"Oh, really is that so?"

"Yeah, my name's Mike. What's yours?"

"Mercedes"

"What a beautiful name, it's nice to meet you Mercedes." Mike gently grabbed and kissed her hand. Christian Milian's "Dip it Low" came on.

"You wanna dance Ma?" Mike asked her. The liquor was already in her system and she was feeling nice.

"Sure," she responded as she made her way through the crowd and stood in the middle of the dance floor. The drink had Mercedes loose; she had never felt this feeling. Her dance partner held her hips and touched her sensually. They both were getting really turned on and it showed in their dance moves.

"Ma let's get up outta here and head to my crib." Mike whispered in her ear. It sounded good to Mercedes at that time. They were just about to exit the club when Mercedes looked up and noticed Chino walking towards her. The liquor caused her to forget that he was going to be there too.

"Mercedes, what the fuck are you doing?" Chino barked while giving her an evil glare. "You over here bumping and grinding on this nigga like you don't know what time it is." Chino yelled as he grabbed her arm and snatched her away from the guy. "Come on."

"Chino, let go you're hurting me." Mercedes whined as she tried to pull her arm away from his grip.

"Ayo man, let her go." Mike yelled.

"Nigga please, this is my shorty."

Chino laughed as he turned around. "Nigga, who the fuck you think you are?"

"I just met the bitch and you fucking up my groove." Mike said trying to defend his actions. His comment made the situation worse by calling Mercedes out of her name.

"Hold up, first of all she ain't no fucking bitch!" Chino assured him. "And nigga you just met my girl up in the club and think you gon' hit... nah nigga not my shorty."

"Nigga fuck you! What's popping den?" Mike was ready to fight, but Chino was from the streets. He didn't use his hands if he didn't have to. He quickly lifted his shirt to reveal the gun he held in his waist. Mike backed off immediately and went about his business. Chino covered his gun by pulling down his shirt. He took Mercedes to his car to talk. They had plenty to discuss.

Outside of the club, Chino stood in front of Mercedes staring at her in disbelief.

"What the fuck is wrong with you?"

"What are you talking about BayBay?" Mercedes speech was slurred.

"Don't act stupid Mercedes, you're drunk right now." Chino barked.

"How the fuck did they let you drink you're only sixteen?" He asked.

"Candy gave it to me, I mean it's nothing. Just a little Henny to set the mood." Mercedes chuckled and fell directly into him. Chino caught her and held onto her.

"Look at you Ma, you all stumbling and shit. You're coming home with me." Chino grabbed her wrist to guide her towards his car. Mercedes snatched her hand away and began yelling at him in the parking lot.

"No, no, no I'm not going with you because you're a liar and a cheater!" She waved her finger around in the air.

"How?" Chino inquired. "I wasn't the one in the club bumping and fucking grinding with another bitch!" Chino barked.

"Don't act like you wasn't hugged up on India the other day. I saw you." Mercedes yelled back with tears in her eyes. "And don't say nothing was going on between ya'll two." Mercedes tried to walk backwards and she fell.

"Are you okay?" Mercedes heard a familiar voice but couldn't place the face.

"Who are you?"

"Mercedes, it's me Emilio."

"Ohh shit, I hope I'm not in trouble." Mr. Gates sent Emilio to check on Mercedes and bring her home instead. He didn't want to draw attention to himself with the limousine.

"Nah, let's just get you home. It's not safe out here." Emilio picked up Mercedes and held her in his arms. Chino stood next to them and watched the exchange. He had no idea who this dude was and wanted to know why he had his hands on Mercedes.

"What the fuck are you doing with my shorty?" Chino jumped between them and prepared to grab his weapon.

"I suggest you back up, I'm taking shorty where she belongs."

"Nah nigga, she's coming with me son."

"It was my orders to take her home, Aight son. So I suggest you back the fuck up before shit gets crazy out here." Emilio demanded.

Chino and Emilio were arguing about who Mercedes was leaving with, neither of them noticed the black Cadillac speeding down the street. The tinted windows rolled down slowly to reveal a semi automatic weapon that began firing into the crowd. Everyone ran for cover or dropped to the ground to avoid being shot.

Mercedes was too drunk to know what was happening until it was too late. Emilio pushed her to the ground and lay on top of her for protection. The car sped away without anyone knowing who was inside, or who the intended target was.

"Are you okay?" Emilio looked over at her and admired her beauty. They both brushed themselves off and began to walk to the car to go home.

"Yeah, I'm fine." Mercedes wiped her forehead of sweat.

"Let's go. Your boyfriend will be fine. We need you to sober up." Emilio used that as an excuse; he spotted her and just wanted to take her away from Chino.

"So you're not going to tell on me?" Mercedes asked as she looked over at Emilio.

"Nah, whatever happens between us stays between us. As long as you sober up, there's nothing to be said right?" Emilio caressed under her chin with his fingers and winked at her. Chills went down Mercedes spine and butterflies took over her stomach.

She loved Chino with all her heart, yet the attraction between her and Emilio was undeniable. To avoid confronting her feelings, she looked out of her window until she arrived at home. When they arrived at the house, Mercedes simply thanked Emilio. She exited the car and they gazed at each other longer than normal. The butterflies came again and she swallowed hard. She prayed that they would go away. She slipped her keys quietly into the door and went upstairs to bed. She was still tipsy and now battling her feelings for two men. Only one of them would win.

* * *

There was no word from or about Chino as the following days passed. Mercedes even reached out to her friends to see if they had heard anything. No one had heard or seen him since the club shooting. Mercedes phone calls went unanswered. Mercedes texted him, but he still didn't respond.

Frustrated and feeling ignored, she decided to go find him herself. She hopped in the shower and threw on some clothes to make her way to see Chino. While in the bathroom, she felt queasy and began to throw up. It had been happening more frequently during the last couple of weeks and she didn't know why. One day after school she went to buy a pregnancy test. She decided to take it, just to be certain. She saw the results and wrapped it up in tissue and took it with her to toss. Now wasn't the time to deal with this issue, she wanted to see Chino.

Mercedes put on a pink velour Juicy Couture track suit. She wore a white wife beater underneath and her crisp white Air Force Ones. She threw on some big heart bamboo earrings and a gold chain that her father had given her for her 15th birthday. She threw her hair in a ponytail. She kept it simple, but she was still looking good. Nevertheless, she felt horrible on the inside.

She headed down the spiral staircase and saw her mother sitting at the kitchen table. She was reading the newspaper and sipping on her coffee.

"Good morning Ma."

"Where do you think you're going?" Maria inquired as she looked up at her daughter.

"I've been in the house all week Ma. I just wanted to get a little air." Mercedes explained.

"Yeah, you really haven't gone out since the club." Maria responded, "What's wrong, you look a little pale?" She walked over to Mercedes and caressed the side of her face.

"I'm fine Ma." Mercedes cracked a smile and moved her head slightly to the side reacting to her mother's touch.

"Are you sure? Because you know that you can tell Mami anything."

"Ma, I'm fine!" Mercedes barked. She then realized her tone and smiled, "I'm fine Ma." She spoke in a lowered tone this time.

Maria shot her daughter a stern look. She didn't like the tone that she took and said so without words. Mercedes got herself together and Maria moved on.

"So where are you headed?"

"Well, Candy and I are headed into the city to do a little shopping."

"You know how your father and I don't like you running around in the city without Mr. Gates or Emilio." She informed her, "Especially since you got shot."

"I know Ma, but we're just going to do a little shopping. Nothing serious, I'll be home before six." Mercedes gave her mother an innocent look. Maria shook her head and looked back into the paper.

"Alright, be safe. Make sure you're back before six or else," she warned her.

"Thank you mommy, I love you." Mercedes wrapped her arms around her mother's neck and kissed her on the cheek. "See ya later."

"Bye."

Mercedes was already out the door and was on her way to the subway. She clutched her purse as she endured the long train ride to Harlem. Although it felt good to be alone, she was always cautious of her surroundings. When she reached her stop, she hopped off the train and made her way down 125th Street.

As she neared her destination, she noticed a few guys standing in front of the project buildings near Chino's house. She took precautionary measures and hid her jewelry. She knew what type of environment that she was in. Avoiding them was no easy feat; she realized she failed when one of them grabbed her arm and pushed her up against a wall. He shoved a gun to her neck.

"Bitch, give me the chain or I'll kill you."

Her eyes widened with fear and she felt the barrel of the gun graze her cheek. He ripped the chain off of her neck and smirked.

"Snitches get stitches bitch!"

Just as the thief thought he won, he was met with a brick to his face. Chino arrived just in time and began beating him with the brick. He then started punching him the stomach.

"Ayo, let shorty go nigga!"

"Nigga...Argh...what the fuck Chino?" The thief yelled trying to protect his face and body from more injury.

"Nigga! What you mean what the fuck?" Chino pulled out his gun and pointed it directly at the dude's face.

"You fucking me up over some dumb bitch!" Red liquid left his mouth in clumps as he spit it onto the ground.

"First off nigga, this shorty right here is my girl." Chino's nose flared up.

"Come here Ma." Chino motioned for Mercedes to come over to him. She walked over and held him close.

"My bad Chino. Dawg, you know I'm sorry. Yo I didn't know. Shorty came through the block shining nigga, so you know how niggas get down out here in Harlem." The dude was trying to explain himself, his lips started trembling and his legs were shaky.

"Next time you fuck with anybody I fuck with...you going to end up in a body bag, real shit!" Chino cocked his gun to let him know what time it was.

"Now, give my shorty back her chain nigga." Chino placed his gun back in his waistband and watched as Mercedes got her necklace back. The dude also apologized for the disrespect.

"And I need whatever is in your pockets too son." Chino said trying to add insult to injury. He wanted to make sure this dude never fucked with anyone else.

"What, for what?" he raised his voice.

"A broken chain has to get fixed." The thief reached into his pocket and pulled off a few hundred dollar bills from the top of a thick pile.

"Nah nigga, I'll take the whole stack." Chino snatched the money from the dude's hand and walked away. He handed the money to Mercedes to put in her purse and they both walked away.

Everything seemed normal, but it soon changed. A few minutes later they heard tires screeching down the street. Mercedes and Chino looked back to see a black Cadillac; the same one from a few weeks prior. It was barreling down the street. Like the last time, the tinted windows rolled down and gunshots rang out of the driver's side window.

This time, Mercedes eyes connected with the driver's and the rest of their face was covered with a mask.

"Get Down Mercedes!" Chino yelled as he ran to her to provide cover. He covered her body and threw both of their bodies to the ground. Chino took out his gun and started shooting at the car as it sped off.

"Let's go Ma." Chino grabbed her hand and they rushed into his apartment building. The elevator ride upstairs was silent and seemed like it took forever. They arrived at his house to recover from the shooting incident. Mercedes walked into his bedroom and removed her jacket. She sat on his bed still and was obviously shook up.

"Why did you come here Mercedes?" Chino bluntly asked.

"Well...umm...Chino I just wanted to apologize for the other day at the club and..." Chino interrupted.

"Yeah, you should be-acting a damn fool up in there." Chino shook his head as he took off his Rolex and placed it on the dresser. Mercedes stood up and continued.

"I'm sorry Babe, but that day in school when I saw you and India-that really hurt me. What was that all about?" Mercedes crossed her arms across her breasts and awaited a response.

"Babe, do you want to know the truth?"

"Yes." Mercedes looked at him in his eyes. She hoped she didn't hear what she feared she would.

"Well, that day she came to me crying saying she wanted to talk to me. I told her that we were done and I was officially with you and shit. She said she didn't care about that; she just wanted to talk to me. While we were in the hallway, she told me that her grandmother passed away that morning and she didn't know what to do. Her grandmother was the only one who was always there for her. Her mother was a fiend. She left her when she was just a baby. I felt sorry for her, so I just hugged her and told her it would be alright. Mercedes, I would never cheat on you Ma so you don't got shit to worry about. I love you Ma."

Mercedes believed him, but she also remembered India said that she was having his baby. She knew India was jealous of her and wanted to walk in her shoes, so she just disregarded her statement.

"I'm sorry." Chino cut her off.

"Just tell me that you love me too." Chino lifted up her chin.

"I love you too Baby." Mercedes moved in and slowly and sensually kissed him.

"I want to apologize to you too Ma. Since that day your pops and I butted heads, I have been acting different. I didn't want to come between a father and his daughter. I feel that's something you just don't do. I understood where your pops came from, but he just doesn't know how much I love you Ma. He's just judging me by what I do, but that's why I fell back." Chino sighed.

"So are you still falling back?" Mercedes walked over to where he was standing and placed her arms around his neck. She cocked her head to one side and was searching his eyes for an answer. There was only one that she would be satisfied with.

"Nah Ma, I'm falling more in love with you. No one can ever keep us apart." Chino kissed her passionately as Mercedes pulled his shirt over his head. He began to undress her as well. Mercedes pulled her hair from the ponytail and it regally laid on her shoulders. Chino gently pulled her bra straps and unsnapped her bra. She giggled as she stepped out of her pants and he lustfully watched her hips and breasts.

Chino gently threw Mercedes on the bed and hopped on top. He palmed her breasts and put his tongue to work. Mercedes moaned as he skillfully licked and sucked on her breasts. Her hands wandered up and down his body. Mercedes bit the bottom of her lip as Chino found his way to her favorite spot, her pussy. Mercedes grabbed his head and grinded her hips as he gently and slowly sucked her fat pussy lips. Mercedes moaned like never before while Chino tasted her clit. He knew that she was in ecstasy and he was making her feel better than ever.

"You ready for me Ma?" Chino asked while winking at her.

"Oh I'm more than ready Baby." Mercedes propped herself up with a pillow while keeping her legs spread wide. Chino climbed on top of her and slowly entered her wetness. With every stroke she gripped his back harder. Her eyes began to roll upwards in pleasure. His name rolled off of her tongue in sheer bliss.

"Chino...Papi." Mercedes moaned. "That feels so good, don't stop." Chino made passionate love to her as they kissed exchanged freaky talk. They even cried together after the session was complete.

"Don't ever leave me Chino." Mercedes said as she stared into his eyes. He looked to her and placed his finger over her mouth, "I love you Ma, always and forever." He had never made a promise like that before. He was always afraid that he would not be able to keep it.

"Love you too Chino." A tear slipped down the side of her cheeks and she didn't bother wiping it away, "Forever."

Tomorrow Isn't Promised

Chino and Mercedes were spending every night together since they reconciled. Mercedes would sneak out of the house to be with him. She told her parents that she was staying with Candy on most occasions. Don Carter still didn't approve, but Mercedes believed in the old saying *'what you don't know won't hurt you.'*

One night, the loud ringing of the house phone startled Mercedes and awoke her from her sleep. She covered her head with the pillow and hoped the phone would stop. It continued ringing and she was extremely irritated. For some reason sleep had become her best friend lately; she couldn't get enough of it. She answered the phone to receive the worst news she could imagine.

"Hello," Mercedes mumbled into the phone.

"Mercedes," Candy sounded distraught.

"Hey, whassup Candy?" Mercedes yawned.

"Umm, I have some bad news to tell you."

"What is it?" Mercedes ears perked up and she listened closely. She pressed the phone firmly to her ears.

"Umm...it's Chino..." Her heart started racing at the mention of his name.

"What Candy? What happened to him?" Mercedes panicked as she sat up in the bed. She was wide awake now.

"Chino's...well...he's dead." Candy hesitated to say. "He was murdered last night."

Mercedes couldn't believe what Candy was saying. Tears exploded from her eyes and her heart fell to the floor at the news. "No...no...no!" Mercedes dropped the phone on her lap. "Why? Lord no...no...this can't be so!" Mercedes yelled.

"Mercedes! Mercedes!" she heard Candy yelling her name. She slowly picked the phone back up with trembling hands.

She cried uncontrollably and asked, "Candy, why did they have to take my Baby?"

"I don't know Cedes, I'm so sorry. I don't know how you feel, but damn I can only imagine." Candy shook her head.

Mercedes was inconsolable and didn't know what to do. Candy told her to meet her at the park in Manhattan on 116th St. Initially Mercedes didn't want to go, but she decided that she needed some fresh air and someone to talk to. Her mother was at the salon getting her hair done and her father was working as usual. Don was a busy man.

As soon as they hung up with each other, Mercedes ran to her closet. She grabbed the first thing she put her hands on. She put her hair up in a quick ponytail and grabbed her Sidekick. She rushed down the stairs and was on her way.

The park where she was to meet Candy was only a couple of blocks from Chino's house. She cried on the train ride for her lost love. When she got off the train, her eyes were red and people were staring at her. She didn't care, she kept it moving.

Mercedes sat on the bench waiting for Candy to arrive. While she waited, she looked around the park and watched a couple hold hands and kiss. It reminded her of the good times with Chino. She cried even harder and didn't bother to wipe away her tears.

Several minutes later, Mercedes noticed Candy walking towards her with her arms outstretched. She got up from the bench with her lips trembling and hugged Candy. They rocked side to side and held each other.

"It'll be okay Mercedes." Candy pulled back from the embrace and they sat on the bench together.

"I know...but damn Candy...that was my Baby...my man...my boo...my everything." Mercedes responded. She didn't know how to explain, "Candy, I fucking love him and didn't even get a chance to say goodbye." Mercedes cried.

"Damn, I know Mercedes. I didn't believe it when I found out."

"Who told you?" Mercedes eagerly asked.

"Well one of his boys that I use to mess with Keith called me. He said that some nigga was following him in a black Cadillac. Evidently it went down in a bloodbath. They were both shooting at each other and I guess the last shot hit Chino. His car flipped over and blew up...just some crazy shit."

"What, oh my God!" Mercedes covered her mouth as the tears flooded her eyes. She couldn't believe what she heard.

"Mercedes, you are a very beautiful person. You're smart and you're a great friend. You're a real ass bitch and I love you Mercedes. And I know Chino loves you too. I know he's looking down at you right now Ma. You had his heart." Candy nudged her shoulder. "Its life Mercedes, shit happens."

"Yeah, I know." Mercedes sighed. "Thank you Candy."

"No problem, just go home and try to get some sleep." Candy said.

"Aight, see ya later Candy." Mercedes responded as she and Candy parted ways.

When she got home, she immediately went to her room. She walked over to her closet and grabbed one of Chino's hoodies. He had given it to her one day when she was cold and didn't have a jacket. She smelled it and still had his favorite scent of Armani cologne. Tears formed in her eyes as she sat on the floor clutching his hoodie in her arms. Her cries were loud enough for anyone in the house to hear. She cried so hard that she had the sudden urge to vomit. She found herself rushing to the bathroom. She had been feeling funny for over a month, but kept ignoring it.

After vomiting her guts out, her face began to feel flushed and she was sweaty. She attributed it to the sadness that she felt inside about Chino. Somehow she knew it was more, but once again she ignored the signs.

Her thoughts were interrupted by a gentle knock on the door,

"Hey Baby, are you alright?" Maria asked from the opposite side of the door. Before Mercedes could respond, she was overcome with more nausea. Maria found her daughter with her head in the toilet releasing yellow stomach acid.

"Oh my God, what's wrong? Are you okay?" Maria panicked as she kneeled down to her daughter's side and rubbed her back. Mercedes wiped the side of her lip.

"Nothing," she mumbled as she got up and flushed the toilet.

"Baby come on, I know when something is wrong with you. I am your mother. It better not be that boy Chino because..."

"Chino's dead." Mercedes muttered through clenched jaws.

"Oh my God!" Maria covered her mouth in shock, "What happened?"

"Someone was following him and was shooting at him while he was driving. The car flipped over and now he's dead." Mercedes had no more tears left; she was all cried out. Her mother shed some tears for them both.

"I'm sorry to hear that." Maria said as she held her daughter close. Mercedes buried her face in her chest and Maria rubbed her silky hair. "It's okay to cry Baby."

"I love him Ma, and someone took him away from me." Mercedes pulled back from the embrace and stared into her mother's eyes.

"I know Baby, but sometimes life doesn't go how we planned or wanted it to go. Things happen for a reason.

Everything isn't always going to be good, we must also prepare for the bad." She kissed her daughter on the forehead.

"Baby you need some sleep. You've been crying and you're burning up. You might have a fever." She touched Mercedes forehead and it was scorching hot. "I'll bring you some tea okay?"

Mercedes slightly smiled and nodded her head in approval. Her mother left the bathroom and went downstairs to get the tea. Mercedes brushed her teeth and crawled back into her bed. Before she did, she grabbed Chino's hoodie and fell asleep with it in her arms.

Mercedes awoke hours later to the sound of knocking at her door. She didn't respond because she wanted to be left alone. However, she heard it open anyway. It was her father. He hated to see his daughter hurting. Don walked in and sat on her bed. He placed a cup of tea on the night stand and took a deep breath before speaking.

"Hey Baby Girl."

"Hey," Mercedes said solemnly as she tried to hold back the tears.

"What's wrong?" he asked. "Your mother told me that I should come upstairs and talk to you...is there something going on?" Don secretly panicked. His wife didn't tell him anything, she didn't feel as if it was her place to do so.

"Nothing," Mercedes lied as she sucked in her lips and tried to hold back the tears. She knew her father would get it out of her one way or another.

"Mercedes, I know you and I know we haven't been as close since Chino and I butted heads-but I want to apologize."

"It's a little too late for that." Mercedes sniffed as the tears streamed down the sides of her face and dropped onto her fluffy pillow.

"What do you mean by that?" Don asked; he was baffled by her comment.

"Chino's dead." Mercedes blurted out. More tears fell as the words came out of her mouth. Don quickly moved in closer and embraced Mercedes. He held her head tightly against his chest as she relentlessly sobbed. He laid his chin on her head and rubbed her back.

"Shh Baby, I didn't know that." Don said. Mercedes pulled back from his embrace with her eyes as red as blood. She stared her father in the eyes.

"Did you kill him Daddy?" Mercedes asked bluntly.

"Of course not Baby Girl, why would I kill him?"

"I don't know." Mercedes shrugged her shoulders. "Maybe because you hated him and didn't want me to ever talk to him again, I just figured I'd ask."

"Baby Girl, listen to me. I would never hurt anyone that you love unless they put their hands on you. I love you Mercedes, and I could tell you loved him with all your heart...but" Mercedes cut him off.

"But what Daddy?"

"But I want you to be happy and I want you to finish school and go to college."

Mercedes knew he was leaving out something, so she pushed for more answers.

"Daddy, what was it about him that you didn't like? She asked while wiping her eyes.

He knew that his daughter loved Chino sincerely. He could see it in her eyes and in her face. She was always glowing when she spoke of him. He wanted her to be happy, but just not with Chino. When he saw Chino, he saw himself. Don and Mercedes stared at each other. They were searching for the truth and concealing it simultaneously.

"To be honest Mercedes, you know what I do for a living. I live that life, that fast life. Your mother is a beautiful woman and I love her. I didn't want this lifestyle for her. I wanted to provide a good life for you and her. The price that comes along with it is usually too high. I don't want you to have to worry about whether or not your husband is coming home at night because he's a hustler. Either the streets will get him or jail will. Either way, that's no way to live life."

Don was finally real with her about his feelings. That still wouldn't stop her from living her life.

"I hear you Daddy, but he's gone now. You don't have to worry about that." Mercedes wanted him to understand how hurt she was that her dad was cruel to the man she loved.

"I'm just so sorry to hear that Mercedes, you just have to remain strong. You're a Carter." Don winked at her.

"Yes I am...Mercedes Carter" Mercedes smiled.

"I love you Baby Girl." Don reached for a hug and Mercedes smiled as she hugged her father tightly. He got up to leave and turned to his daughter.

"Remember, no matter what The Carter family will never die!"

Mercedes processed the information that her father had given her. Although her man just died, the conversation with her father was long overdue. It helped her to put a few things into perspective. Mercedes pulled the covers back and lay her head on the pillow. She fell asleep remembering the words her father said before leaving her bedroom, '*The Carter family will never die.*'

* * *

Chino's funeral was held in his home town of Harlem. Mercedes wore all black and her hair was simply parted down the middle. The funeral home was packed with people who came to pay their respects. The funeral was closed casket, with a picture of him on top. The parlor was filled with flowers from many who showed their love. Mercedes was accompanied by her mother and father. They wanted to come as a show of support for their daughter. When Mercedes entered, she was greeted by Chino's mother Cassandra. Cassandra looked over with tears in her eyes and Mercedes grabbed and held onto her hand. Tears streamed down her face as the pastor begin to speak. She never would have thought this would happen to him so soon. She had lost her husband and her son to the streets of Harlem.

After the eulogy and remarks given by family and friends, Mercedes looked at Cassandra for approval. It was her time to speak. Cassandra nodded and Mercedes rose from her seat to approach the podium.

"Good morning everyone. My name is Mercedes and I'm Chino's girlfriend. I can't say I was his girlfriend, I still am. I still carry him in my heart and I will never forget him. The first day I laid eyes on Chino it was love at first sight. His eyes, his long hair and his beautiful personality instantly won me over. Everything about him was pure and so beautiful. I don't understand why someone would want to take his life. He's a good person and I love him and I just want to say this to Chino."

Mercedes looked up to the ceiling and placed her hand over her heart. She stood there with tears filling her eyes and blurring her vision.

"Chino I know you're up there staring down on me, your mother, your family and everyone else. I love you Chino and no one will ever take your place. Your place is locked in my heart." A tear crept down the side of her face and she wiped it away with her glove and laughed.

"I'm sorry ya'll, I'm breaking down- but its tears of joy and pain. I'm just so blessed to be alive today; tomorrow isn't promised for anyone. In closing, my message to you all is to stay strong and live your life as if it is your last day."

Mercedes smiled as she walked back to her seat. Cassandra greeted her with a hug and kiss and thanked her for her kind words.

After the ceremony, Mercedes was walking down the corridor of the funeral home with her head down. She accidently bumped into India.

"I'm sorry," Mercedes apologized. She didn't know who she bumped into.

"You better watch where you going next time bitch." India barked.

"Or else what?" Mercedes nose flared up as India tried to get in her face. She tried to keep her cool, but with India it was impossible.

"India, this is not the place or time for this-definitely not at my son's funeral." Cassandra stood in between them as they exchanged cold glares of anger.

"I'll see you around puta." India looked Mercedes up and down and walked away with her group of friends. Mercedes turned to Chino's mother and apologized, "I'm sorry..." Cassandra cut her off.

"No, it isn't your fault. India just doesn't know how to act, bringing that damn nonsense up in here." She shook her head from side to side.

"Alright Mercedes, take care."

They hugged each other and Cassandra stared Mercedes in her eyes. Mercedes felt like she wanted to say something, but the words never left her mouth. Cassandra wanted to tell Mercedes the truth badly, but she couldn't.

"Goodbye Mercedes."

Cassandra turned on her heels and rushed out of the funeral home. Mercedes didn't know Cassandra that well, but she knew something was up. Mercedes walked back inside for one last talk with her love. She approached the casket and wished she could see him one last time. She figured his casket was closed because his body was charred in the explosion. She hovered over the casket. She placed both hands on the edge and started crying.

"I love you Chino and so does your baby that I'm carrying. Mercedes rubbed her belly as she cried. She had not told anyone yet that she was pregnant with Chino's child. She wished that Chino would be able to see his daughter or son grow up. Mercedes didn't want to bring her child into this world without a father, but she was happy she had a life to remind her of

Chino. Mercedes said one last thing before turning and walking away.

"Love you forever Chino."

Moving Forward

Weeks after laying Chino to rest, Mercedes walked down the cold Harlem streets. Her parents gave her time alone since she was so distraught. The cold whipped through her body, but she pulled her jacket closer to her trying to keep warm. She spent an hour at Chino's gravesite and placed flowers on his tombstone. A tear crept down her cheek and onto her jacket. She was tired of wiping her tears away. The tears were a mixture of sadness for losing him and excitement for the new life growing inside of her.

The cold air coupled with the grief caused her stomach to ache. She dipped into a store to get some water and an Advil. She rubbed her belly as the water coated her throat. She remembered how she felt when she went to the doctor and found out that she was nine weeks pregnant. So much had happened in a short period of time.

The one thing that she pondered was how she would tell her parents. She knew this was exactly what they didn't want for their daughter. Nevertheless, it was happening and she knew they would be very upset. She was keeping her baby, but no one-not even her friends would know.

As she walked and thought about her life without Chino, she looked up and noticed a group of girls approaching her. She rolled her eyes as she recognized them to be India and her clique, the Queen Bee's. Mercedes knew for a fact that they were going to fuck with her just because she was alone and without her friends. Mercedes stopped in her tracks when she saw India with a mischievous smirk on her face.

"Excuse me?" Mercedes said with an attitude.

"Where do you think you're going?"

"You're in my way, so I advise that you move." Mercedes retorted.

"No I'm not going nowhere!" India yelled. "If it wasn't for you, Chino would still be alive." Mercedes looked at India and didn't know what the hell she was talking about. She waved her hand in her face and said,

"Bitch please you're just jealous because he didn't want to be with your no class having ass any way." Mercedes rolled her eyes.

"India, don't let that bitch talk to you like that." One of girls from India's crew said as she sucked on a lollipop.

India pushed Mercedes. It was enough to move her off of her feet, but not enough to do any harm. She wanted Mercedes to make the first move.

Mercedes looked back and laughed, "Don't fucking do it to yourself bitch, I'm preg..." India pushed her again, it was harder this time. Pregnant or not, Mercedes knew if she walked away or decided to hit India back they were going to jump her.

Mercedes put her guard up her and started throwing blows at India. India began slapping Mercedes and Mercedes grabbed her by her hair as they fell to the ground. She hopped on top of her and started punching her in the face. India was desperately trying to block the blows. Despite the size difference, Mercedes still had the upper hand.

Mercedes was putting in work and inflicting serious damage. One of the girls had to pull Mercedes by the hair to get her off India. That act allowed India to gain an advantage and like wolves, they all surrounded Mercedes. They were kicking her in her face and stomach. Mercedes was only concerned about her baby and was trying to block the stomach blows.

"My baby...my baby..." She screamed to anyone that could help her from the painful torture they were inflicting.

"Hey! Stop that!" An older woman yelled; she had become a witness to the drama.

India and her girls scattered down the street and disappeared around the block. The damage had already been done. The woman helped Mercedes to her feet. She doubled over in pain and began to cry. Her cries increased when she looked down and saw a trail of crimson dripping down her legs onto the concrete. She was bleeding and possibly losing her only memento of Chino. She began to get dizzy and immediately fainted.

"Somebody please call an ambulance!" The lady shouted as she held Mercedes in her arms.

XXXXXXXXXX

Mercedes sat on the hospital bed waiting for Emilio to pick her up. She felt that he was the only one she could trust at this time. Her parents could never know what was going on. She would have to tell them eventually, but not now.

Mercedes hopped down from the hospital bed and limped into the bathroom. She stood in front of the mirror and slowly brought her hands up to her face and touched it. She was still gorgeous, but the bruises made her look like she was a hood rat. She lifted her dress and observed the bruises from her waist down. India and her girls would pay for the pain they caused, inside and out.

Several minutes later she heard a knock at the door. Mercedes was already back in bed and watching TV. She looked up and saw Emilio at the door holding a bouquet of red roses and a get well card. A smile crept across her face and she motioned for him to come in. Emilio slowly walked in and handed her the flowers and the card.

Mercedes smelled the roses and placed them on the bed. She opened the card and it read 'I hope you feel better'-*Love Emilio.*

"Thank you Emilio."

She got down from the bed and stood in front of him. Emilio caressed her face and smiled. Mercedes felt chills from his fingertips and blushed.

"You're welcome, anything for you princess." He kissed her on the forehead. "Despite some bruises, you still look gorgeous."

Mercedes pulled back and smiled. She was happy that he asked no questions. She was anxious to leave the hospital and they walked out to the car. Emilio opened her door like a gentleman should. *'He is such a nice gentleman.'* Mercedes thought to herself as she got into the car. She clutched her red roses and card. They rode in silence until Emilio turned up the radio. A smile appeared across her face as she thought about Chino.

"I see you invested in a radio." Mercedes let out a light chuckle.

"Yeah," Emilio smiled. "The other one was broken, so I just bought a new one." Mercedes nodded and turned her head to look out the window.

As she sat in the car, the song "In Love with a Thug" by Jim Jones came on. Tears fell silently from her eyes. It brought back the painful memories of when they she used to be in Chino's car listening to this song with him. They pulled up in front of her house and she took a deep breath. She noticed her father wasn't home, but her mother's car was parked in their garage.

"Thanks for the ride Emilio, I really appreciate it."

"No problem," he said. Mercedes opened the car door and got out. She slid her key into the door and her mother was sitting on the couch. She tried to avoid her mother and prevent her from seeing her face, but it was too late.

"Oh my God Mercedes!" Maria screamed. She jumped up and rushed over to her. "What happened to your face?" Her mother caressed her face, noticing the bruising and scratches that were present. Mercedes burst into tears. She had lost Chino and the baby in a matter of weeks and had no one to talk about it with. Her emotions were overwhelming and she finally had a release. Maria wrapped her arms around her daughter as she cried into her arms.

"My baby...they killed my baby..." That's all that Mercedes could say as she cried in her mother's arms. *'Baby?...Your baby?'* Maria said to herself with a perplexed expression on her face.

"You were pregnant, Mercedes?" Maria astonishingly asked. She had no idea and felt that she should have paid more attention to her daughter.

"Yes Ma...I'm so sorry." Mercedes pulled her mother closer to her and hugged her. She buried her face in her chest. "I'm so sorry Ma...I know...I'm sorry...I should..."

"Mercedes, what happened?" Maria whispered in her ear and pulled back from the embrace. She grabbed both of her shoulders and stared into her eyes.

"Chino's ex-girlfriend India...Her and her girls jumped me when they saw me. I was a little over two months pregnant. I'm sorry, Ma ..."

"Damn, Mercedes." Maria shook her head. "That's exactly why your father didn't want you to go to a public school." She continued shaking her head as she spoke.

"Are you okay Honey?" Maria asked in a worried tone. "How do you feel?"   Mercedes shrugged her shoulders, "I'm hurt...I mean I know I'm only sixteen but, after Chino died Ma I was excited at the opportunity to have his baby. I would have had a piece of him with me; it would still feel as if he's alive you know?" Mercedes looked up at her mother and stared her in the eyes.

"Are you mad Ma?"

"I can't judge you. What mother wants a pregnant sixteen year-old? It's definitely not ideal, but it happened and we just need to get through it together. I had you at eighteen and that's still young, you know. I don't want you to make the same mistakes that I did. I just want you to be happy. As you get older, you'll find the man to make you happy. You will fall in love with him. You will know him when you see him. "

Mercedes was happy that she was able to share this with her mother. She felt like a weight had been lifted from her shoulders.

"Your secret is safe with me." Maria reached over to embrace her closely.

"You promise you won't tell Daddy?" Mercedes asked. Don walked through the door at that moment.

"Tell me what?" He asked.

He surprised them by interrupting their bonding session. They pulled back from their embrace as if they had seen a ghost.

"What the hell happened to your face?" Maria forgot about her daughter's face, she ran over to Don to explain.

"Some girls jumped her. She's fine though." Don rushed over to Mercedes and caressed her face. He began examining her bruises.

"What girls jumped you?" Don asked. He clutched his gun that he wore in his waistband.

"Some girls from school, they're jealous of me."

"See, that's why I didn't want you going to a public school."

His teeth gritted, he spoke in an angry and regretful tone. "You're gorgeous and bitches are always gon' hate."

"I know Daddy, but I didn't know it would happen." Mercedes began to regret convincing her father to allow her to attend a public school.

"You don't need to apologize. If they were niggas, they would be six feet deep before you blinked. Nobody fucks around with the Carters, NOBODY!" Don barked.

Maria flinched at his angry and vengeful tone.

"You're going to a private school, no questions asked. Your cousin Sean goes there and my sister Brenda said that school is good and there's no drama there. So that's where you're going on Monday."

Mercedes looked at her mother with pleading eyes. Her mother's eyes responded with an 'it's out of my hands look.' Mercedes got the message and simply said,
"Okay Daddy."

"Give your Daddy a hug." Don smiled and pulled his daughter into his warm embrace. "You're still gorgeous Mercedes."

"Thanks Daddy." Mercedes smiled.

"Alright ladies, let's go." Don said retrieving his car keys from his pocket.

"Where are we going?" They both said in unison.

"It's a surprise for your mother; a present for my appreciation to the most beautiful wife in the world, for our sixteenth anniversary." '*He never forgets.*' Maria said to herself, she smiled while looking at Don behind her oversized Chanel shades. Mercedes and Maria were still anxious to know what it was.

"Close your eyes." Don said before arriving at the destination. He parked the car and walked over to the passenger side. He opened the door for his wife and helped her get to her feet.

Don slipped a key into his wife's hand and whispered in her ear, "Open your eyes." When she did, she screamed "Oh my God! Oh my God!" Maria jumped up and down in elation; her eyes were watering with tears of joy. They were standing in front of a pink building that read Carter's Beauty Salon. Although Maria was a little skeptical about the name of the salon, she was ecstatic. She could always change the name if she wanted. She turned around and kissed her husband passionately. Mercedes playfully rolled her eyes at her parents as they kissed.

"Thank you Baby, I love you." Maria cooed.

"You deserve the world, and I know you always wanted your own salon. Go ahead and open it." With her hands quivering, she finally got the key into the hole and turned the knob. Once they were inside, Maria and Mercedes both wore wide grins. It was decorated lavishly just like their home. She knew that no other shop would have shit on her salon, for the taste was exquisite and so upscale. The Carters were expanding their empire and they felt invincible. The only question was how long would it last.

2 Years Later...

18th Birthday

Mercedes never felt more alive than on the morning of her 18th birthday. She woke up with a smile on her face and thanked God that she made it this far. She thought of Chino and her unborn child that were taken from her. During the last two years, Mercedes coped with their deaths and became a responsible young woman. After changing schools and graduating, most of her time was spent working at her mother's salon. She worked as the receptionist. The relationship between her and her father strengthened over time. Reminiscing about the past few years, Mercedes got up and walked over to her bureau and pulled out the dresser drawer. She grabbed the sonogram picture of her unborn baby. Tears fell onto her hands as she fingered her only photo of the baby. She regretted not telling Chino about her pregnancy, but she wanted it to be a surprise.

Every night they would enter her dreams and she would dream about life with them as a family. Soon she would be awakened and reliving the moment she found out Chino was dead. Her dreams would turn into a nightmare and she would break into sweats in the middle of the night. Sometimes she would start yelling out his name and it only brought tears to her eyes.

Her thoughts were soon disrupted by a knock at the door. She tossed the picture back into her drawer and saw her mother entering the door with a birthday cake.

"Happy Birthday Mercedes." Maria sang.

"Thanks, Ma." Mercedes smiled as her mother held the cake in front of her singing the birthday song.

"Make a wish." Maria said. Mercedes closed her eyes to make her wish.

"Are you excited? It's your eighteenth birthday!"

"Yeah, I know." Mercedes smiled. "It feels good knowing that I'm alive and so is the rest of the Carter family."

"You got that right."

Don walked in just in time to greet his daughter. He grinned with pride.

"Happy Birthday, Baby Girl."

"Thank you Daddy." Mercedes kissed him on the cheek.

"You're welcome. Make sure you're ready for later. I'll be home to give you your gift. It's a surprise.

"Aight, I got some business to handle so I'll see you ladies later."

Don kissed his wife on the cheek and Mercedes on the forehead. He then disappeared down the hall to begin his day.

"Alright Mercedes, let's get ready to go to the mall. Daddy left me the Black Card." She winked at Mercedes as she waved the card around in the air.

Later that night, Mercedes was looking as beautiful as ever. She was getting dressed for her night out with her parents to celebrate her birthday. As she entered the white limo which her father left, she pondered where she was going. Her mother was running late and her father was still handling business. She noticed a dock as she looked out of the window with boats floating on water. Her father stood dressed in a suit with a huge smile on his face. She had no clue what was going on.

"What the fuck is this?" She mumbled. The driver exited the car and walked around to the passenger side door. He graciously opened the door for her.

"Hey, Daddy." Mercedes smiled, as she greeted her father with a hug.

"Happy Birthday, Baby Girl."

Don hugged his daughter and gave a signal to one of the men at the dock. As soon as he did, they removed a cloth revealing a huge yacht. "And it's all yours." "What?" Mercedes blurted out with a baffled look on her face. "What do you mean it's all mine?" She was a little puzzled.

"That's your own private yacht." Don assured her. "It's yours; I brought it just for you."

"Oh my God! Thank you Daddy."

Don took his daughter by the hand and walked her up the dock to her boat. They stepped into the darkness; just then, the lights came on and Mercedes mouth dropped again in shock.

"SURPRISE!" The first people she noticed were her mother, Emilio and her high school best friends. Everyone else in attendance was family and friends.

"Happy birthday cuzzo." Mercedes' cousin Sean walked up and hugged her tightly.

"Hey Sean!" Mercedes said as she hugged him back, "I haven't seen you in awhile boy." Mercedes pulled back from the embrace as she stared at her cousin. She was grateful for the love from her family and friends. They were all she had.

The night was more beautiful than ever, the skies were dark and the stars glistened-illuminating the sky. Mercedes wanted to get some fresh air and went out onto the deck to get a view the city. The tall beautiful buildings lit up and reflected off the waters. It was the perfect skyline.

Mercedes stood on the deck of the yacht with her elbow rested on the bar. She held a glass of Moet in her hand. She looked up at the stars. They reminded her of Chino and the day that they were at the beach and he talked about his father. A tear crept out of her left eye and streamed down the side of her cheek as it tickled her face.

"Beautiful stars aren't they?" Emilio walked up from behind her and stood next to her.

"Yeah, they are." Mercedes replied as she wiped away the tear. "I was once told there are plenty of stars in the sky, but there's always one that catches your eye. When it does you will never forget it, and always see that star. It will be in your heart....scars are like..."

"Stars..." Emilio replied finishing her thought. His comment brought a chill down her spine and she looked at him in amazement. Only Chino knew those words and Mercedes found it really odd that Emilio did too. She shook the thoughts out of her head as she continued looking up into the sky.

"Ohh, it's getting really chilly out here." Her teeth began chattering.

"That's because I came out here." Emilio smirked at her, causing Mercedes to crack a smile.

"Oh boy please, you so silly." Emilio took off his blazer and placed it around her shoulders and slowly rubbed her arms.

"Why thank you, that's really nice of you." Mercedes said.

Emilio looked deeply into her eyes and placed his hand on her chin. He then leaned in and kissed her lips slowly and sensually. Mercedes didn't fight and she kissed him back. She felt something between them that was unexplainable.

They both pulled away unaware of how to continue. He cleared his throat as he leaned over the railing and looked out into the sky.

"So what made you come to New York? Did you want to start a new life here or what?" Mercedes curiously asked.

"Well like I said before, I have family out here, but I also needed a new start. I am here in New York for business."

"Really and what kind of business is that?" Mercedes looked over at him with prying eyes.

Emilio laughed, "Damn you ask a lot of questions." Her eyes waited for an answer and he sighed knowing that she wouldn't let up.

"No, I came here because I have to handle some business with your father. I'm here basically doing us all a favor." Emilio responded and turned to Mercedes.

"Yeah, well my father doesn't need any help. He is one of the top drug dealers in New York City, he's well respected. His mentality is so strong that it will never die. It will always pass on and stay in the Carter family."

"And what do you mean by that?" Emilio tilted his head to the side.

"The Carter family will never die." Mercedes spoke with pride.

"It's already dead." Emilio winked at her as he walked away and disappeared into the dining room. Inside, everyone was laughing, chatting and enjoying themselves. Mercedes stood there frozen; her eyes were focused as she stared through the glass watching Emilio talk to her father. She was thrown off by his comment and didn't want to jump to any conclusions.

"Mercedes?" Maria called out.

"Yes Ma?" She responded as her mother invaded her thoughts.

"Are you alright?"

"Yeah, I'm fine." She lied, as nervousness swept over her. Emilio's words deeply troubled her.

"There's another surprise for you."

"Close your eyes." Maria said guiding Mercedes to her next birthday surprise.

"Alright open your eyes." Mercedes removed her hands from her eyes. She stood in front of a big white truck that opened as her mother counted to three. Don came driving a car off of the truck. Mercedes began jumping up and down in glee.

It was a black and pink 2010 Mercedes Benz E350 coupe, with Lamborghini doors. Mercedes sprinted over to her father and hugged him to death. If her hugs could kill, her father would have been strangled to death. He handed her keys to the Benz and she screamed in excitement. She quickly hopped into the car. The fresh aroma of the leather seats made her smile. She loved the view that the sunroof gave of the city. Mercedes sunk in the leather seats as she held her heart and smiled. She couldn't ask for anything more.

"Mercedes, you need a place to park your new car." Don handed her keys and she looked puzzled.

"Daddy what's this?"

"Those are the keys to your new fully furnished penthouse apartment. Enjoy Baby Girl." Mercedes couldn't ask for a better birthday. If only she had Chino to share it with.

xxxxxxxxxx

Mercedes awoke to her father calling her name. She adjusted her eyes and saw him waving his Black Card. It was time to go shopping. She quickly got dressed and grabbed the keys to her car. She had to make a stop before she went shopping.

She decided to visit Chino's grave and she placed a few flowers at the tombstone. She thought about his mother and felt bad because she hadn't visited her since Chino's funeral. A visit to her was long overdue, so she bought some roses to give to her.

Driving her new Benz through the streets of Harlem felt so good. She finally arrived, parked and walked up the breezeway. The smell of urine attacked her nose as she walked up the staircase. She took a deep breath and began to knock on the door. She stopped when she felt someone watching her. She shrugged her shoulders and started to knock again. As she raised her hand the door flung open. Mercedes gulped hard when a black woman answered the door. She was smoking a blunt and blew the smoke in her face.

Mercedes coughed and waved the smoke from her face.

"Who the hell are you?" The woman rudely asked.

"Um...I'm looking for Cassandra...this is where she lives."

"No, nobody by the name of Cassandra lives here."

"That's impossible she lives…"

"Listen honey, I've been living here in these Harlem projects for two years." The lady informed her, "Nobody by the name Cassandra lives here." The woman slammed the door in her face before she got a chance to say anything else. Mercedes turned to walk away; she looked over and noticed a Spanish woman standing in the doorway of her apartment. Just then her white fluffy cat ran outside startling Mercedes. It rubbed its' white fur on her pants.

"I'm so sorry…so… so sorry." The Spanish woman apologized repeatedly as she picked up her cat and held it in her arms. "You need to stop running from me Kitty." The woman patted her cat, rubbing its soft white fur.

"It's okay." Mercedes smirked while rubbing the fur of her skinny jeans.

"Are you lost?" The woman questioned.

"No." Mercedes chuckled as she removed a piece of her hair from her face and placed it behind her ear. "I was just looking for a woman named Cassandra who lives right here across the hall from you."

"Yeah, well she doesn't stay here anymore." The woman said.

"Do you know where she moved to?"

"No…" the woman shook her head, "The last time I saw Cassandra was two years ago. She was leaving one night in the middle of the night. She had her suit case and her son with her."

"Her son?" Mercedes questioned. She cocked her head back with a mystified expression across her face. "No…no that's impossible." Mercedes shook her head side to side. "He passed away two years ago."

"Well, I don't know." The woman shrugged her shoulders. "All I know is that she left and said that she had to leave town and she left here with some guy. It was too dark in the hall to see anything, these lights are always broken." The woman stated angrily.

"Is there anything that she said to you that could help me find her?"

"No I'm so sorry Honey, I don't know anything." The woman walked back in with her cat and locked the door. Mercedes knew that the woman knew more than what she was telling her, but she couldn't do anything about it. She exited the projects and got into her car. She sat there thinking before she turned the car on. *'There's no way that that guy was Chino. There's no way he's still alive. He had a funeral and he was in the casket. There's no way, he's dead.'*

Mercedes thought to herself and wiped away the tears that formed in her eyes. She wondered where Cassandra might have gone-maybe she just needed to get away after Chino died. Mercedes shrugged her shoulders, started up the car and pulled off. She headed to the mall to do a little shopping.

xxxxxxxxxx

Maria rolled over in their king-sized bed and Don was absent. She pulled back the covers and slid her feet into her slippers. She left her bedroom and walked down the hall to talk to Mercedes.

"Mercedes wake up Babe; we have to go to work." Maria removed the blanket and Mercedes wasn't there. She walked over to the window and noticed her Benz wasn't parked out front. *'Where did she go this early in the morning?'* Maria said to herself and exited the room and entered hers. As she walked back into her room, she heard the bathroom water running. Don was washing his face. She wrapped her arms around him and kissed him softly on the neck.

"Good morning Baby." Maria smiled as she stared in the mirror looking at Don.

"Good morning Gorgeous." Don said as he finished wiping off his face.

"Where's Mercedes?"

"She went out shopping; I gave her a Black Card."

"Aww isn't that sweet." Maria cooed, "I know she's happy to get out of this house."

"Yeah, well she's still is my Baby Girl." Don smiled as he turned around. He wrapped his hands around her waist and kissed her on the lips. "What time are you heading to the shop?"

"Well I'm about to hop in the shower now, I told the girls today I would be opening up the shop at ten. I needed to get my beauty sleep." Maria smirked.

"Aww please, with all that beauty sleep shit." Don shook his head, "You don't even need beauty sleep Baby because you are beyond beautiful." He caressed the tip of her chin with his index finger and caused her to blush like the first time she met him.

"Aww, thank you Honey," Maria cooed. She pinched his cheeks. "Well let me get ready. My first client is coming exactly at ten o'clock." Maria playfully shoved her husband out of the bathroom and got ready for her day at the salon.

"Damn you look good." Don blurted out as she exited the bedroom ready to leave. Maria was putting on her lip stick and stopped in her tracks and turned around. She wore a smile on her face and shook her head.

"Thank you Babe," Maria turned around and looked in the mirror again before turning away. She grabbed her bag and keys and was off to make her own money.

"I'll see you later."

"Yeah, you just might. I'll probably be stopping by the shop for a line up." Don said as he brushed his waves on top of his head.

"Boy please, what happened to the barber you always go to?" She asked while watching her husband walk over to her. He wrapped his arms around her waist and pulled her closer.

"Well, I heard my Baby is the best in town." He winked, "I heard you gave my brother Roy a fresh clean cut the other day."

"Yeah, I did. I guess I'm aight." Maria scrunched up her nose and smirked.

"You ain't aight, you got skills." Don said, "Well I won't keep you any more, you got to get to work." Don kissed her on the forehead not wanting to mess up the peach MAC lip stick she applied to her thick succulent lips, "Love you."

"I love you too Mr. Carter." Maria smiled. She turned and walked down the spiral staircase and headed straight out the front door. Getting into her car, she dialed Mercedes on the car phone and began chatting with her before work.

"Hey Baby." Maria said enthusiastically when Mercedes answered her cell phone.

"Hey Ma, what's up?"

"I'm heading to the shop now, where are you?" Maria wondered.

"Oh, I was out shopping buying stuff for my new condo." Maria could tell there was something wrong with Mercedes, she could hear it in her voice. She decided to leave it alone until it was time "I was just wondering if you were coming to work today." Maria asked, "Because if you're busy today you don't have to come in."

"No Ma, its fine. I'm on my way." Mercedes said, "I'm only ten minutes away."

"Alright see you there."

"Alright Ma." They both hung up in unison. Since she had some extra time, she stopped at Dunkin Donuts to get coffee and donuts for breakfast. She then made her way to the salon. As soon as she pulled up in front of her hair salon, she noticed Mercedes pulling right in right beside her. She put the car in park and hopped out the car. She waited for Mercedes to get out of her Benz. "Hey Ma." Mercedes and Maria both exchanged kisses on the cheek.

"Hey." Maria smiled, "Hold this for a second while I get the keys out of my bag." Maria handed Mercedes her stuff so she could get her keys. With her head buried in her bag she didn't notice the damage, but as soon as she did, she shrieked in horror. "What the fuck?" Maria said surveying the damage. Mercedes never heard her mother curse like that, so she knew she was pissed.

"What happened?" Mercedes asked. She was in awe as she stepped into the salon behind her mother. Tears began to fall from Maria's eyes and her jaw dropped when she looked around. Her perfect salon was trashed. She put all of her hard work into it after Don purchased it for her. Everything in sight was ruined. Her walls were spray painted and everything was knocked over. The windows were smudged with red lipstick.

Maria walked in and carefully stepped over broken glass. All of the pink chairs were knocked over. She glanced up and noticed something spray painted in big bold letters on the wall. It read 1.15; Maria had no idea what it meant. She was thinking that the kids were pretty cruel to do this to her store. She only cared about how she was going to repair her shop. She and Mercedes put in considerable effort in decorating her salon.

"Oh my God!" Maria panicked and the tears poured down her face. She thought about calling Don, but he never answered when he was working. She threw her phone against the wall in anger, causing it to shatter. Mercedes jumped as the shards flew all over the room.

"Call your father." Maria demanded.

She exhaled deeply. She didn't know what to do next, but whatever she was going to do needed to be done quickly. The Carters were all about action.

Mercedes dialed her father and he answered on the first ring. Maria rolled her eyes. She hated that he rarely picked up for her.

"Hey Daddy...can you come to the shop...no now... someone broke into the shop and trashed everything...ok...bye." Mercedes hung up the phone and walked over to her mother and rubbed her back, "It's going to be alright Ma."

"Who would do such a thing?" Maria asked while looking around at her destroyed shop.

"I don't know; you don't have any enemies Ma." Mercedes shrugged her shoulders.

"A bitch did this. Someone your father has beef with." Maria eyed the damage, specifically the lipstick and the spray paint.

"Wait, what are you trying to say Ma?"

"This is the work of a woman scorned. Your father has another woman, I'm sure." Maria barked as tears engulfed her eyes again. She couldn't believe what she was seeing. She wished that she was in a dream and could wake up any second now. Don walked into the salon minutes later and stopped in his tracks.

"What the fuck happened in here?"

"You tell me." Maria stated nonchalantly. She stared her husband in the eye.

"Shit I don't know, I just came here and walked into a mess like you!"

"Stop fucking lying to me!" Maria got up to walk away and Don grabbed her arm. She snatched her arm back and rushed out of the door. She slammed the door causing the remaining glass to fall to the ground.

"Daddy, who did this?" Mercedes asked. Don stood frozen staring at the wall. The numbers told him exactly what he needed to know. He knew who did this, but kept it to himself.

"I got to go handle something, tell your mother I'll be home later." Mercedes and Don exited the salon. He hopped into his car and Mercedes decided to follow her father. She followed him to Harlem. She watched him. He was like a man on a mission. Mercedes saw him take his gun and cock it back. He was obviously plotting revenge on someone, but Mercedes didn't know who it was.

She sat patiently in the car watching, as her father entered a building. She was curious because her friend Hazel lived in the same building. Just as she was about to get out and go see where he went, Don came running out. He was angry, and whatever it was that made him that way was inside this building.

Mercedes drove around and tried to figure out who was exacting revenge on her family. She finally went to her mother's house to check on her. She decided to help her prepare dinner and calm her down from the day's events. Dinner was complete in no time and they both sat to eat. Maria was clearly disturbed, but Mercedes was more concerned that her mother and father were at odds.

"Aren't you going to wait for Daddy?" Mercedes carefully asked. She picked up her fork and was eager to eat as well.

"No, he knows what time dinner is every night." Maria said as she calmly ate her food. A few minutes later, they heard the front door unlock and Don walked in. He entered the kitchen and kissed Mercedes on the forehead. He walked over to Maria to do the same. He attempted to kiss her on the neck, but she quickly moved away. In frustration, he took off his jacket and flung it onto the chair. He angrily sat down to eat.

"Where's Claudia?" Don asked.

"She's in Puerto Rico for a family emergency." Maria calmly stated.

"Oh, well Honey, I apologize for the hair salon..."

"What are you apologizing for? You didn't do it." Maria barked.

"I know how much work you both put into it. When I find out who ruined your dream...."

"Who is she?" Maria said without looking up from her plate. Mercedes looked up and watched as the room grew silent. She took that as her cue to exit the room before things got messy. As if reading her mind, her mother asked her for privacy. "Mercedes, can you excuse us please?"

"Sure Ma, I have to go wait for my furniture to be delivered anyway."

"At this hour?" Maria questioned with an arched brow.

"Yes, it's a rush delivery so it can arrive anytime." Mercedes said goodbye to her parents and headed home.

"Again Don, who is she?" Maria grabbed her cup of red wine and took slow sips. There was silence in the kitchen. Don stopped eating his food to assess the situation. His lack of response was pissing her off. Maria slammed her wine glass on the table shattering it and creating a stain on the crisp white tablecloth.

"I know it's one of your little hoes!" Maria yelled as she ran upstairs and slammed the door behind her. Don followed and found Maria standing in the mirror with her back to him. She was staring at her wedding ring and removed it when she saw his face. To ease the mood, Don walked over and placed his arms around her. He kissed her gently on the neck, but she refused to succumb to his charm.

"Get off of me." Maria barked. She tried to wiggle out of his arms. She threw her wedding ring at him and it bounced off of his chest and onto the floor.

"You can take this fucking ring back because it doesn't mean shit...after eighteen years..." Maria cried.

"Maria, please calm down." Don whispered in her ear. "I swear to you, I never cheated on you a day in my fucking life. I may have fucked with them before, but not since you told me you were pregnant with our child. I love you and only you. I will never risk fucking with another female. I can't lose the most important two ladies in my life Ma, come on now." Don sincerely said. Maria looked up in the mirror and saw Don staring at her.

"You really mean that?" Maria asked.

"Yes Babe, I love you with all my heart. I never cheated on you and I never will. The hair salon will be up and running in a couple of days, I called up my people and they are on it. Don't worry about who did it. Just know that I set them straight and it won't happen again." Maria turned around, wrapped her arms around his neck and cried.

"I love you Mr. Carter...always and forever." Maria hugged him tightly, as if it were her last time that she would see him.

"I love you too Mrs. Carter and when I'm gone I won't ever stop loving you."

Cuban Links

Within the next few days, the damage done to Maria's salon was repaired. Mercedes finally got her condo furnished and decorated to her liking. She had an exhausting day and lay in her bedroom after moving around in the condo. Her friends had left an hour ago and Mercedes just wanted to relax. She wanted to talk to her father about what Emilio said to her at her party, but she couldn't even get in contact with him lately.

Several hours later, she was asleep and interrupted by the loud ringing of her doorbell. She checked the clock and it was almost eleven o'clock.

"Who the hell is this at my door this time of night?" Mercedes ran downstairs while putting on her robe and looked through the peephole. It was her father. She opened the door and felt the artic breeze rush into her home.

"It's cold as fuck out there." Don walked in still rubbing his hands together. "Got your pops out there freezing and shit." They both chuckled.

"Sorry Daddy, I was upstairs sleeping." Mercedes smirked as she closed the front door behind them and locked it.

"The place looks nice." He looked around and nodded his head in approval. "I see you have exquisite taste, just like your mother. You two and pink-boy I tell you." Don laughed.

"I know; it's the Carter taste." Mercedes smiled from ear to ear.

"Yeah, it's in our blood." Don smirked as he scratched his chin.

"You've been busy all week Daddy; I've wanted to talk to you."

"I know Baby Girl, I apologize. I had a lot of shit on my plate. I was out of town and just came back. Daddy's a busy man."

"Yeah, I know." Mercedes nonchalantly stated.

"So what you wanna talk about?"

"Well...lately...I don't know Daddy, I've noticed Emilio's been changing and I..." Mercedes was cut off by the ringing of her father's cell phone.

"Hold on Baby, one second." Don quickly answered his phone and walked into the kitchen. Mercedes rolled her eyes at the rude interruption.

"What up Bro? Nah I'm talking with Cedes right now...What? What the fuck you mean? Nah, he can't be dead...well we gotta handle this business first bro. Business first no matter what, Vicente is waiting on us. I'll see you in a few."

Don ended the call and slid his phone into his pocket. He had to leave immediately and found Mercedes in the foyer.

"I'm sorry Baby Girl, but something popped up and I gotta go." Don walked over to her and kissed her on the forehead. "We can talk in the morning." He assured her.

"It's really importa..." Mercedes words stopped as her father turned to walk away from her. "Love you Baby." Don Carter jumped in his Range Rover to fix the problem he encountered on the phone.

"I love you too Daddy." She was overcome with anxiety as she watched him drive off. She had a feeling that something was about to go down, but was unsure of what it was.

* * *

Don drove to his brother's house and thought about Mercedes. He hated leaving her like he did, but he needed to handle business. He would make it up to her later. Within a few minutes, he arrived and blew the horn for his brother to come out of the house.

"Whaddup, Bro?" Roy said as he got in the car.

"Just left Cedes crib, but y'all interrupted us. "So what happened?" He nervously asked. He wanted to know what the urgency was about.

"Man, I don't know how this shit happened. Niggas is saying Frank was at one of the spots and some nigga just ran up in there and shot him up. They took everything-the drugs, the money and the guns." Roy shook his head.

"Was he alone?"

"Yeah, I don't know how this shit happened. It's gotta be someone from the inside-a set up. They told him to meet him at the spot and offed him. That shit's fucked up, he didn't deserve to die." Roy inhaled deeply. "Our team has been tight for a long time bro; I know something just ain't right."

"Yeah you're right." Don responded. "Where's Vicente?"

"He said meet him at the warehouse, the one in China Town. The same one we went to for the last meeting." Roy told him. "So what did Mercedes have to talk to you about?" Roy asked.

"I'm not sure; I told her we could talk in the morning."

"You sure it isn't anything serious?" Roy looked at his brother and stared him in the eyes.

"Yeah, it can wait until the morning." Don said. He was really hoping that it could. Don and Roy drove in silence towards China Town. They pulled up in front of the warehouse spotted Vicente and his workers. Don parked his car diagonally across from them and put the car in park.

When he got out of the car, he knew something wasn't right. Emilio was there standing right next to Vicente with a devilish smirk across his face. Roy and Don already knew they were looking at the problem—a dirty rat.

"Mr. Carter," Vicente smiled.

"Mr. Vicente," Don looked at him dead in the eye.

"Do you know why this meeting was called?" Vicente asked.

"Yeah, it's to discuss business so let's do this." Don looked at his brother and gave him a nod to get the money out the car. Roy went to get the money and handed it to Don. He threw it to Vicente. Emilio glared at Don with hate in his eyes.

"It was nice doing business with you." Vicente smirked. Don extended his hand to Vicente. He grabbed his hand and held it tightly. He pulled Don in close and spoke directly in his ear.

"You think I had visions of you fucking my daughter and stealing her away from me?" Don pulled back and quickly let go off Vicente's hand. His heart quickly dropped, he had no clue Vicente would have ever found out about Maria and him.

At that moment, he knew Emilio was the snake creeping around and playing both sides.

"You betray me!" Don barked at Emilio. He knew Emilio had been sent by Vicente to work for him. Don couldn't believe that he slipped up; he fucked up, big time.

"Life is a big gamble isn't it?" Emilio sarcastically said.

Everyone laughed, except for Don and Roy.

"I let you in my home and I introduced you to my family!" Don gritted.

"It's all a game Don, and you should know that. I apologize for any misunderstandings, but I had to do my job and I did it well." Emilio retorted.

"Fuck you, you will pay!" Don spat at him. Emilio walked up to him and punched him in the face. Don pulled out his gun, but Vicente's security guards surrounded him with their heavy artillery pointed directly at Don and Roy.

"Your daughter is a very beautiful girl." Emilio whispered in his ear. He didn't want Vicente finding out about Mercedes because he would kill her.

"Fuck you, stay away from her!" Don spat as blood dripped down the side of his mouth. "I swear to God if you lay your hands on either one of them, your dead son!" Don said in a low tone. He didn't want Vicente to hear. Emilio started laughing hysterically and walked away. Vicente slowly walked over.

"You didn't think I would find out huh?" Vicente laughed.

"You don't understand; I love your daughter." Don sincerely spoke.

"Maria doesn't love you, she loves me! She wasn't supposed to run off with a nigger like you. She will never have love in her heart for you." Vicente insisted.

"She's the love of my life and no one will ever come in between that." Don courageously stated.

"You stole my daughter from me. All these years you have been fucking her and buying from me. You can't have both even if you think you can."

"So what do you want, money? I can give you that? What do you want from me?" Don yelled.

"I don't want your money, Mr. Carter. I have plenty. I want you dead."

"Let's do this then." Don put his hands up. He knew his time had finally come.

"What the fuck you doin' Bro?" Roy asked.

"It's my time to go Bro." Don simply replied.

"No, it's not your time to go. Not yet at least." Roy shook his head knowing whatever he said or tried to say wasn't going to help. Vicente was a very serious and powerful man. Whatever he said went and when he wanted something done-it got done.

"If you're alive, tell Maria I love her Bro with all my heart, and tell Mercedes I love her too. The Carter family never dies." Don said before he turned away from Roy.

"Get down on your knees." Vicente ordered with the gun pointed to his head.

"If you're going to kill me, kill me standing because I'm a strong man. I'd rather go out on my feet like a man than on my knees like a punk." Don spoke with pride. He stared Vicente in his eyes to let him know that he was not scared. Vicente laughed at his act of valor. He was actually kind of impressed.

"I always liked that about you, you're a very wise man Carter. But when you chose the wrong man to fuck with, you have to pay. My daughter is my heart, she's everything to me. You just took her from me like it was nothing." Vicente yelled as tears came to his eyes.

He slowly backed up to put some distance between himself and Don. Don's only thoughts were of leaving his wife and daughter. He loved them with his entire being. He didn't know that they had just spent their final moments together. The guards stood around Vicente. They had their guns pointed at Don and Roy, ready to fire. Don knew that it was two against a group of them, but he decided to put in work before he died. He lifted his gun and started shooting, with Roy following suit. Bullets riddled him and ripped through his skin. He was fighting for his life. He fell to his knees as he succumbed to his injuries. The gun smoke cleared and Don's body slowly dropped to the ground. He was filled with multiple bullet wounds. Roy was on the ground as well, shot several times.

"Let's go." Vicente said in his Cuban accent. He walked over to Don's body. Don's eyes struggled to stay open as he noticed the dark figures standing above him. It was Vicente and Emilio coming to finish him off. Vicente held a 9 millimeter and pointed it in his face. He released one more shot to the head. It dropped Don's head against the concrete. Vicente kneeled down and started laughing hysterically.

"I won motherfucker." Vicente spit on him and got up and walked away. Emilio stood there and raised his gun. He shot Don a couple more times in the chest. He turned around and dashed to the car. He got in and left the scene with the others. Roy crawled over to his brother as blood oozed from his mouth. He grabbed his phone and called for help before it was too late.

"Yes! My brother has been shot...I need help, Downtown in China Town at a warehouse." Roy hung up the phone.

"It's over now Roy." Don said as he gasped between breaths. His body was riddled with bullets and it was becoming increasingly difficult to breathe.

"Nah Bro, hold on. The ambulance is coming for us Don, you can't die." Roy said as he held the back of his brother's head and stared him in his bloody eyes. He thought that Don would have already been dead with all of the bullets he had been hit with.

"The Carters...don't die..." Don uttered. He forced a smile on his face. With that being said, his eyes closed for good. Don Carter was gone. Roy let his brother go as he heard a car's tires screeching behind him. It was the same car that had just left.

"Shit!" Roy mumbled as he tried to crawl away. Emilio had come back to finish the job. He pulled out his gun and aimed it at Roy.

"No witnesses," he said as he shot Roy at point blank range.

I'll Be Missing You

Mercedes lay sound asleep in her bed. Her sleep was disturbed by her ringing phone.

"Ugh!" Mercedes begrudgingly grabbed her phone to answer it.

"Hello?" Mercedes whispered into the phone.

"Mercedes?"

"Mom?"

"Yes Baby it's me." She could tell from the sound of her mother's voice that she had been crying.

"What's wrong Ma?" Mercedes fretfully asked.

"It's your father..." The words exploded out of her mouth like fireworks.

"What? Is he okay? Is he home? What happened?" Mercedes began to panic and paced back and forth trying to figure out what was wrong with her father.

"He's been shot!" She screamed. "He's in the hospital!"

"Calm down Ma." Mercedes heart was beating faster than a cheetah could run. Her head started to spin.

"I'm on my way over there now." Mercedes hung up the phone and quickly got dressed to go to her mother's house. Tears filled her eyes and blurred her vision as she sped to her parent's home. She wiped them away with the back of her hand and arrived at her mother's house within minutes. She saw her mother sitting on the steps sobbing uncontrollably. Mercedes quickly got out of the car and raced over to her. They both embraced as Maria released her bottled up feelings into her daughter's arms.

"Ma, he'll be okay." Mercedes assured her as she rubbed her mother's back. "Let's go." Mercedes pulled back from the embrace and rushed to the car.

"What hospital is he in?"

"He's in the New York Downtown Hospital." Maria sniffled as she wiped away her tears with the Kleenex tissues.

As soon as they arrived at the hospital, they parked and rushed from the car. They set their sights on the receptionist's desk. They needed answers about Don Carter.

"I...I'm looking for my husband D-Don Carter." Maria stuttered. She had tears streaming down her face. Her demeanor, much like her clothing, was disheveled. "He's in surgery right now Ma'am. You can't go back there right now." The receptionist advised, "You can take a seat in the waiting room."

"FUCK THAT!" Maria barked, "I need to see my husband." She startled everyone in the waiting room and they suspiciously eyed her. Mercedes tried to calm her mother down and spoke to the receptionist on her behalf.

"I'm sorry ma'am, but my father has been shot and we need to see him."

They eyed the double doors for patients and doctors only and took off to sneak in.

"I'm sorry, but you can't go back there." The receptionist said as they dodged doctors and searched the rooms for Don.

"DON CARTER!" Maria cried out as she rushed down the hall looking in every room. A doctor rushed over to them and told them that they needed to leave.

"Doctor please, my father has been shot and we need to know if he's okay." Mercedes' voice cracked as the tears began to fall.

"Are you Mrs. Carter, the woman I called just a little while ago?"

"Yes, I'm Mrs. Carter. Is my husband okay?" Maria searched the doctor's face for a glimmer of hope.

"Well, he's in critical condition and he has almost a dozen gunshot wounds. It's a miracle he's still alive, but he's a fighter." Mercedes and Maria both covered their mouths in horror. He was just fine the last time they saw him.

"Oh my God!" Maria cried. "How could someone do such a thing?"

"I know Mrs. Carter, I'm terribly sorry." The doctor sincerely replied. "He's undergoing surgery as of right now."

"Thank you Doc." Maria said. The doctor smiled and turned to walk away. He stopped in his tracks and said, "Is Roy Carter related to you in any way?"

"Yes he is." Maria said, "That's my brother-in-law."

"He was also shot several times including the head. He's currently in a coma."

"Oh Lord!" Mercedes cried out. She couldn't believe it. It seemed as if everyone in her family was going through something and she had no way to help.

Mercedes saw her mother slowly losing control. Her leg trembled as she cried and rocked back and forth. She intently prayed for Don and Roy. Forty-five minutes passed and the doctor came back with an update.

"Is my husband going to be alright?" Maria asked, while still hoping for the best.

"I'm sorry; Mr. Carter didn't make it." The doctor's eyes said it all. Maria wailed and collapsed to the ground in sorrow. She had just lost the love of her life.

"Mercedes stood still in utter disbelief. It felt as if someone just sucked all of air out of her. She cried and fell to her knees. She looked at the ceiling and asked God why. She cried until her tears abandoned her. Maria tried to comfort her daughter, even in her own time of sorrow. She knew Mercedes loved her father dearly. After several minutes passed, they finally calmed down and dried their eyes enough for them to see where they were walking. They noticed the doctor approaching them to talk.

"You know, we usually don't do this...but do you want to see him?" He asked.

"Yes please." Maria said in a hushed tone. They followed the doctor and entered the room where Don's body lie. She stopped in her tracks and began sobbing once more. Seeing her husband in that condition was surreal. Mercedes tightly grabbed her mother's hand. They both stared as they touched his lifeless body, praying that it was all a dream.

"I love you Daddy." Mercedes turned and ran from the room. She couldn't believe her father was gone. She kept wishing it was a dream and when she woke up things would be normal. Unfortunately, it wasn't a dream-it was reality.

"Don, Babe I will always love you. Why did you have to leave me so soon? I promise to look after our daughter and keep her safe. We'll find out who did this and they will pay. Goodbye my love, see you on the other side."

Maria slowly walked out of the room while wiping her tears away. They checked on Roy once again and he was still in a coma. They decided to go home and check on him tomorrow.

They drove in silence back to the home that Maria and Don once shared. When they arrived, they noticed the lights were on. Mercedes thought she switched them off before they left. Maria wondered the same and she grew tense. She knew Claudia wasn't back from Puerto Rico yet. She went to care for her sick mother.

"Keep driving Mercedes." Maria told her while looking out the window.

"Why Ma?" She was puzzled by her mother's request.

"Just drive Mercedes! Please!" Maria raised her voice and turned toward her.

Mercedes did as she was told and kept going. She was concerned to see her mother scared. She didn't know what to make of Maria's actions.

"I didn't mean to yell Sweetie, but please just let me spend the night with you." Mercedes kept driving and without asking any further questions. She noticed her mother turned and suspiciously looked as she passed their house. She wondered what could be happening.

Mercedes pulled up in front of her condo and parked. They held hands and entered the house together. They went directly upstairs into Mercedes' bedroom. She grabbed a set of pajamas for her mother to sleep in and got some night clothes for herself. They turned off the light and climbed into bed lying next to each other.

"I love you Mercedes."

"I love you too Ma."

"Mercedes?" Maria called out her name barely above a whisper causing her voice to crack.

"Yes Ma?"

"Can you hold me?" Maria sniffled.

Mercedes moved in closer to her mother and held her as they cried themselves to sleep in each other's arms.

xxxxxxxxxx

Claudia sat in the yellow taxi clutching her purse. She pressed it against her abdomen. She was due back from Puerto Rico early this morning and already had confirmed with Maria that she would be home. She stared from the window as the taxi drove up the path to the Carter's mansion. Claudia opened her purse and pulled out a fifty dollar bill and handed it to the driver to pay the fare. The trunk was popped and Claudia got out and grabbed her Louis Vuitton luggage from the trunk. She closed it and walked up to the door. She looked at her watch and noticed the time was eleven-thirty. She saw that the lights were on, so someone was awake. She didn't like having to disturb them. Claudia proceeded up the stairs with her bags and rang the doorbell. The door opened and she picked up her bag to carry it inside when she was grabbed at the neck and pulled in. She didn't know who it was but they were strong and her breath was slowly leaving her body.

"Let her go." Vicente said as he calmly sat.

Emilio released his hand from around her neck. Claudia dropped to the ground. She coughed loudly and put her hand over her chest. She was desperately trying to catch her breath.

"Who is she?" Vicente asked. He was eager to know who this woman was.

"Claudia." Emilio said, as if Vicente knew who she was supposed to be. "She's the maid."

"They have a fucking maid?" Vicente's eyebrows arched as he looked around, "You got to be fucking kidding me!" Vicente slapped his knee as he laughed and everyone in the room laughed as well. They laughed at whatever Vicente laughed at. If they didn't, he would take offense. He had that much power over his cronies.

"Really, he has a fucking maid? This man sure was living it up-but not anymore." A devilish smirk appeared across his face. One of his workers came down the stairs and Vicente looked over his shoulder.

"Did you find anything?" He asked.

"No, no money or drugs sir." The worker informed him, "He must have it somewhere else."

Vicente knew Don was a smart man and wouldn't keep any of his drugs and money in the house. The burning question was-where did he hide everything? Vicente walked over to Claudia who had a look of sheer terror. "Where's my daughter?" Vicente bluntly asked.

"Who's your daughter?" Claudia pretended to be unaware of the situation; she was trying to save her life. She knew that Vicente was Maria's father, but didn't want to be involved. She already knew too much. Maria and Claudia grew close over the years. They were friends, even though Claudia worked for Don and Maria. Vicente didn't like the answer and backhanded her. Blood began to trickle from the side of her mouth.

"You think I'm fucking stupid?" Vicente asked, "Huh?" Claudia still held onto her face as she looked up and stared into Vicente's eyes.

"I don't know," Claudia sarcastically said while shrugging her shoulders. When she spoke, her thick Spanish accent came out. Vicente thought she felt like she had the upper hand.

"I'm going to ask you one more time." Vicente growled. He was getting mad. "Where is Maria?"

"I don't know where she is."

Vicente grabbed her hair with a firm grip and balled it up in his fist. He yanked her head back. He stared into her eyes and didn't blink.

"I know you know where the fuck my daughter is!" He let go of her hair and backed up like he was going to leave her alone. He then balled up his fist and rocked her jaw several times. Claudia's head moved back and forth, not once falling to the ground. She may have seemed like a sweet woman, but she came from a poor family. Her father always told her to never bow down to no one and to never let anyone disrespect her. Claudia remembered those words; she kept them in mind as Vicente kept punching her in the face.

"Where is she?" Vicente's voice cracked. "I just want her back." He softly said.

He stopped hitting her long enough to get those words out. Finally, he sounded like a father instead of a gangster. Claudia grabbed her sore jaw and moved it side to side. She was trying to regain feeling in it. Thick gobs of blood poured from her mouth and oozed down the side of her lip.

"Why would I tell you, even if I knew?" Claudia barked. "You're going to kill me anyway!"

"Emilio, kill that bitch!"

"Your daughter hates you! She hates your fucking guts and she will never be with you!" Claudia barked. These statements made Vicente enraged.

"Oh yeah, we'll see about that." Vicente bent down and sat eye level with Claudia. "No one takes my daughter and gets away with it. As for you...you were just at the wrong place at the wrong time."

Vicente spit on Claudia and got up, "Puta!"

He turned to Emilio and gave the signal as he walked towards the front door with his crew.

"Kill this bitch."

"You will pay!" Claudia said as she starred at the barrel of Emilio's gun. "You're fucking with the Carters! You will pay!" Claudia closed her eyes and said a quick prayer. They were her last words as Emilio cocked back the gun and smiled.

"It's too late to pray to God."

He pulled the trigger and put a bullet in the middle of her forehead. He watched as she slumped over. He stepped over her lifeless body to join the others.

Just to Get By

Mercedes hated that she had to wake up so early. Her eyes were red from crying through the night. She looked at her mother's eyes and they were identically swollen and bloodshot.

After getting dressed for her father's funeral, she slipped on her oversized Chanel shades to hide her face. She felt and looked like a hot mess. Mercedes checked herself out in the mirror and her mother watched her.

"Girl, no one is going to see you." Maria let out a chuckle, "You look fine."

"Please Ma, you woke me up at seven." Mercedes rolled her eyes, "I look like shit and feel like shit."

"I know Baby, we just have to remain strong." Maria cracked a smile and rubbed Mercedes shoulder. Mercedes drove up the path to the place that she once called home. She parked in front of the house. They both exited the car and walked to the front door. It was suspiciously ajar. Maria looked back at Mercedes, "Someone was here."

Their suspicions were confirmed when they walked in and saw Claudia dead on the floor. She was surrounded by blood and remnants of her brain.

"Oh my God! What's going on Ma?" Mercedes screamed and fought the urge to release the contents of her stomach. She was losing everyone close to her and it was heartbreaking. She had never seen anything like this before and it made her stomach turn. Mercedes turned around and she was standing next to Claudia. She looked down at her with tears in her eyes.

"She was such a nice woman." Maria recalled. "She didn't deserve to die like this. Call the ambulance please."

"She's like family Ma."

"No, she was family." First Chino, then her dad, and now Claudia. For some odd reason, she felt like she was going to be next.

The ambulance arrived within minutes, with the police shortly thereafter. Maria watched as they brought Claudia out on a stretcher. Her body was covered in a plastic bag. She was soon approached by detectives. They wanted to know more about Claudia's death.

"Hi, I'm Detective Morris and this is my partner Detective Hanks..."

"I know who you are." Maria shot back, cutting him off. Detective Hanks blew cigarette the smoke in the air.

"Are you Mrs. Carter?"

"You know damn well who I am." Maria cynically said. She rolled her eyes at the detectives. She knew the two of them very well. They were often arresting Don, but couldn't keep him because the charges never stuck. They had to release him every time. Maria was sure they were like giddy bitches when they found out he was dead. They were also probably elated when they got the call for a murder at his mansion.

"Can we come in Mrs. Carter?" Detective Hanks politely asked. Although Maria hated the cops, she knew Hanks was a nicer detective than Morris.

"Come on in, but you can't smoke that cigarette in my house." Maria said with a demanding tone. Detective Morris smiled and took a long last drag on his cigarette before tossing it to the ground. They sat down and waited for someone to speak.

"So, do you know who may have killed your maid?" He flipped his note pad and glanced at the paper, "Claudia Hernandez."

"No, I don't know." Maria said nonchalantly, "I have no clue."

"So you're telling me you have no clue who killed your maid?" Detective Morris asked with a questionable brow. Maria shook her head from side to side.

"You're full of shit." Detective Morris chuckled and placed the tiny notepad in his shirt pocket. "Your husband was killed and his brother Roy is in critical condition. Now your maid ends up dead and you have no clue who's behind this?"

"It's not like you give a fuck about my husband!" Maria barked. Mercedes walked in and sat beside her mother; she was furious.

"You're right! I don't give two shits about your fucking drug dealer husband! You got that right!" But something isn't clicking; you probably know who it is. Maybe someone is after you and you don't want to admit it. You put your family in jeopardy; I'm willing to bet this isn't the last time I'll see a body in a bag in your presence." The detective said before getting up and walking out of the house.

Maria began to cry. She wondered if her father killed her husband and maid. He was the only one who had a vendetta. He couldn't be so heartless and ruthless, could he?

"Here's my card, if you have any questions or concerns." Detective Hanks said while handing Maria a card. She gently took it from his hand. "I'm so sorry for your loss." He walked toward the door. Maria looked down at his card and crumbled it into her hand.

"Ma, what was that all about?" Mercedes inquired.

"Nothing Baby," Maria lied as she got up. "I'll be back, I'm going upstairs real quick to get some clothes. I'll be staying at your house for a couple of days. After that, I'm going to contact your father's sister Brenda to see if I can stay there."

"You can stay with me Ma."

"No, I refuse to put you in jeopardy. No one must know you exist." Mercedes was astonished by her mother's last comment. "What do you mean? People know who I am."

"No new people Mercedes," Maria said. "Trust me, we'll talk later."

Mercedes took her mother's word for it and decided to let the conversation end there.

"Mami, does this mean whoever killed Daddy and Claudia will come after us too?" Mercedes was suddenly putting the pieces together and facing her fears head on.

"I don't know Baby." Maria said with a shrug of her shoulders. "We'll be fine though."

Mercedes sat on the couch with her hand to her chin and pondered their next move. She knew her mother knew something, but obviously she didn't want her to know. She could only trust her mother's word that all would be well.

* * *

Later that afternoon, the funeral home was filled with dozens of roses and other flowers, as well as hundreds of people. Maria made sure that they prepared the best service for her husband. They had an exquisite, one of a kind, marble casket. It had diamonds embedded on the sides of it. Maria knew her husband wanted to go out in style; he left orders for burial in case of his demise. Don was dressed in a black Giorgio Armani suit. His make-up was done, so it looked more like him. He was almost unrecognizable when they saw him last.

Mercedes sat in the front row. She was decked out in her best gear-just as her father would have wanted her to be. He only wanted the best for his Baby Girl. She represented the Carter name well. Her hands were clasped with her mother's for support and encouragement as they walked up to the casket. Seeing her father in such a catatonic state caused her to break down and weep.

Maria stood next to her. She had to be helped up as she fell to her knees, overcome with grief.

"Why did they have to take my husband? Why Lord, why?" Maria cried out. She placed her hands on the side of the casket. Mercedes continued to cry and saw Emilio through her tears. He was walking down the aisle toward her. She shot him an icy glare and he stopped in his tracks. He walked up to Maria and rubbed her back as he whispered something in her ear.

"Thank you Emilio." Maria turned around and hugged him. She cried into his arms as he rubbed her back. He stared into Mercedes' eyes. Emilio escorted her mother back to the seat and sat down next to Mercedes.

"If I find out that you had anything to do with my father's death, you will pay." Mercedes whispered in his ear with a soft voice.

Emilio swallowed hard. Mercedes knew something was wrong. *Where was he when her father was murdered? Why didn't he contact us to let us know that her father was killed?* Those questions floated around in her mind and she gave him one last look before she got up and walked over to her father's casket. At that moment a flood of emotion overtook her and she couldn't take it anymore. She sobbed for Chino, for Claudia, and most of all for her father. She bent over the casket and kissed Don gently on the forehead. She said goodbye for the final time.

"I love you Daddy, and the Carters will never die." Mercedes cried. "I will make sure of that. The Carter family soul will always live on." Mercedes gave her father one last look before she walked away and said, "See you later."

After the funeral service, Mercedes noticed her girlfriends sitting in the back of the funeral home. They were always there for her when she needed them.

"We're so sorry about your father Cedes." Candy said as she hugged her.

"Thank you girls," Mercedes cracked a smile. She sensed that her friend Hazel was as overcome with grief as she was.

"Hey Mercedes." Hazel nervously said. She could feel Mercedes staring at her.

"What's up Hazel?" Mercedes asked.

"I'm sorry about your father's death." Hazel hesitated to get the words out of her mouth and her voice seemed cracked. "I have to go." Hazel left in a hurry, causing everyone to wonder about the awkwardness of her presence.

"What's wrong with her?" Mercedes wondered as she watched Hazel disappear from the funeral home.

"I don't know; she's been like this since she got here. We asked her, but she said she didn't want to talk about it." Candy told her.

"Damn, well I hope she's alright." Mercedes worried about her girl. Besides Candy, she loved Hazel more than any of her girls. She loved her like she was a part of her family.

"She'll be good." Candy smiled. "What about you? How are you holding up?"

"I'm good for now, we'll have to manage. I never imagined losing my dad." A tear crept down the side of her face.

"Thank you girls for stopping by and showing my family some support, I really appreciate it." They all embraced and promised to keep in touch.

As Mercedes was about to leave, she noticed Emilio outside smoking a cigarette. She brushed past him and he tossed his cigarette and followed her.

"Mercedes!" He called out, but she ignored him. She was headed to the limousine that sat waiting for her in front of the funeral home.

"Please Mercedes, can I talk to you for a minute."

"What the hell can you possibly say to me?" Mercedes asked. "That you had something to do with my father's death?" She was extremely suspicious of Emilio.

"Are you going to hear me out?" Emilio asked as he genuinely looked into her greenish puppy dog eyes. Mercedes titled her head to the side and folded her arms across her breasts.

"You have one minute."

"Alright, thank you."

"You don't have time to thank me. Just talk." Mercedes advised him.

"Well, the other night at your birthday party, I wanted to apologize for saying what I did." Mercedes turned away; she didn't want to hear his bullshit. He grabbed her arm and made her look at him so she could see the sincerity.

"Mercedes, please listen to me. I didn't mean what I said. I was drinking and everything was so overwhelming for me. My family has lost people too. My parents died and my aunt is in the hospital. Having so many people close to me that are gone or hurt had me feeling like fuck the world. I'm sorry. I truthfully apologize and if you don't accept, that's fine." Emilio was laying on the charm thick and even threw in a few tears to make it authentic.

"Just because you lost your mother doesn't mean you should wish death upon my family!" Mercedes retorted with tears in her eyes, "You got what you wished for."

She walked away and climbed into the limousine slamming the door. Maria saw her daughter was upset after talking to Emilio and wondered what happened. However, she kept her concern to herself. The family had endured enough and she just wanted some peace for once.

The time had come for them to bury Don and they arrived at the cemetery. Mercedes and Maria held each other as they cried together. It was hard to believe the man they loved was being put to rest. They knew it could happen with the life he led, but didn't know it would be so soon. Mercedes walked over and kneeled down near the burial site as tears fell down her cheeks. She kissed her teddy bear that he bought her as a child and placed it on the casket. She wiped away her tears and embraced her mother.

"It's okay Ma, he's in a better place now." Mercedes whispered. All they could do was believe that to be true and focus on carrying on the Carter name.

New Beginnnings

It had been a week since Maria moved out and was staying with Don's sister Brenda in Queens. Mercedes got a call from her mother asking her to meet her at the diner down on 125th. This morning she was feeling refreshed. It was the first time in weeks that she was able to sleep after losing her father. Maria told her it was urgent, so she had no choice. She threw on something casual and drove to the diner.

"Hey Ma." Mercedes greeted her mother with a kiss on the cheek.

"Hey Baby." Maria smiled as she continued to sip on her coffee.

"So, what's up Ma? How have you been holding up?"

"Alright I guess; I still miss your father you know." Maria turned and looked away as her eyes began to water.

"I never would've thought that he would die so soon. Mercedes your father was a very powerful and well-respected man." Maria sniffled and grabbed the napkin off the table to wipe away her tears. "How are you taking it?"

"I mean...I think about him every morning and when I go to sleep. I can never forget about Daddy. I cherish the times that we had and the memories we made. I still love him as if he was still here, but what can we do Ma? Just live for him, that's what he wants us to do; the Carter family will never die. Daddy always told me that. Yeah we will die one day-but he meant that our family is so strong, our morals, beliefs, the love is so strong. No one can ever break it or take that away from us, and I'm here to stay and keep the Carter family moving."

"I understand completely." Maria smiled. "You're just like your father; I can see it in your eyes Mercedes. I've decided that I'm going to put the house up for sale and I wanted to talk to you about it."

"What?" Mercedes yelled. She forgot they were in a diner with other people. Some of the other patrons looked their way. She lowered her voice and looked around. She noticed people were staring at her, so she changed her tone of voice

"You're selling the house?" "Mercedes, I understand why you're upset. You have your place and I'm going to be all alone. Besides they will be back to finish what they began."

"Who are they?" Mercedes asked. She really wanted to know who or what her mother was afraid of.

"Don't worry Mercedes; I'll be fine as long as I don't go back to that house."

"Where are you going to stay Ma?" Mercedes worried.

"Well I've been searching for a small apartment, but for right now Aunt Brenda said I could stay with her."

"No Ma, that's absurd you can stay with me." Mercedes insisted. "I don't see why not."

"Baby, that's fine. I'll be okay. Don't worry about me." Maria smiled. She loved the fact that her daughter was very caring and generous.

"Alright Ma, if that's your decision I'll have to respect it." Mercedes sighed. "What about your clothes, cars and jewels?"

"Yeah, well I might have one of your daddy's workers go back to get my things. I checked the safes and they didn't get into them."

"Oh yeah, that's good. Ma how is Uncle Roy doing?"

"Well he's in ICU and they said that he's going to make it. He's out of his coma and responsive, but he's still critical. He'll need lots of physical therapy."

"Wow, that's crazy. At least he's going to make it. I'm going to visit him one day this week." Mercedes said.

"Yeah, that would be nice. I'm going to get going and head on out to Queens. Brenda wants me to watch the kids tonight." Maria got up and embraced Mercedes.

"I love you Ma." Mercedes smiled at her mother.

"Love you too Baby." Maria walked out of the diner and Mercedes watched as she hoped into her BMW and drove off. She jumped into her car, since she was already in the city she decided to trek to the mall and do some shopping. Mercedes shopped until her arms were tired. Shopping took her mind off of recent events; she needed it after the stress she had been going through. Retail therapy always did her good. She took her bags home to get ready for the next day, no matter what it entailed.

* * *

Mercedes woke up the next morning to her mother calling her on her cell phone.

"Good morning Ma." Mercedes answered the phone.

"Hey... Mercedes" She could tell her mother had been crying. It was obvious that she was still mourning for the loss of her husband. Mercedes totally understood; she missed her father too.

"What's wrong Ma?" Mercedes sat up and wiped the sleep out of her eyes. She had been mourning Don's loss especially hard and it broke Mercedes' heart.

"I'm not going to be able to work this morning." Maria sniffled, "Can you open up the shop for me and make sure everyone is at work on time."

"I got you Ma; I'll make sure everything is handled. Take it easy. I love you."

"Alright thanks Mercedes, I know I can count on you." Maria smiled a little. She was happy she had her daughter to depend on.

"I'm going to get some rest. I really miss your father."

"I know Ma." Mercedes inhaled deeply, trying to hold back the tears. She was unsuccessful and shed a few tears of her own.

"We just have to remain strong for him Ma, he's in a better place and he still loves us. Be strong."

"Alright I'll try. Thanks Cedes, love you."

"Love you too Ma." Mercedes hung up the phone and got dressed. She was prepared to go open the shop and take charge as her mother asked.

Everyone arrived on time as Mercedes sat in the shop and waited. She told the workers that her mother wouldn't be in today. Condolences poured in and they all understood what she was dealing with. As Mercedes answered calls, a delivery man entered with a package. Mercedes had been receiving things for her mother all day, but this time it was for her. She ended the phone call to accept the gifts.

"Are you Mercedes Carter?" The delivery man asked as he looked down at the white note attached to a bouquet of roses.

"Yes, I am?"

"These are for you." He handed Mercedes a vase of long stemmed roses and a gift from Edible Arrangements. She had no idea who it was from. These gifts were a bit more personal than one expressing condolences. Everyone wanted to know who it was from. Mercedes told them to get to work and mind their business. She was blushing profusely and they were happy this put a genuine smile on her face. She finally opened the card and read to herself. *I'm sorry for the loss of your father, he was a good man. I want you to know that I didn't have anything to do with your father's death. I'm not going to keep apologizing, but my heart goes out to you and your mother. I know you've been working at the salon, but I set up a day for you and your mother at the spa and a weekend at the most expensive hotel in Manhattan. Enjoy- Emilio*

Mercedes smiled and put the card away. She spotted his number on the card and was thinking about calling him. She opened the fruit basket and began munching. She pondered if Emilio was indeed innocent and had nothing to do with her father's murder. She wanted answers and decided to close the salon in time to relax for the rest of the day. Everyone understood and bid her farewell. It was seven-thirty and Mercedes decided to take her mother some dinner. She picked up some Chinese food and made her way to Queens. What she felt would be a pleasant visit, turned sour quickly. When Maria opened the door her eyes were red and puffy and her hair was disheveled. Mercedes was greeted by a strong hug from her mother and she could only accept the love and reciprocate. She knew her father was on Maria's mind and she was having difficulty dealing with his death. They entered the apartment and tried to eat something to take their mind off of things.

"Thanks Mercedes." Brenda smiled while eating a piece of chicken. "I was going to cook some spaghetti and meatballs, but the damn kids were running around and spilled it everywhere."

"No problem Auntie." Mercedes smiled, grabbed her plate and motioned for her mother to walk with her. They grabbed their dinner and headed in the den to talk privately.

"Mercedes...I- I don't know what to do." Maria held back the tears.

"What do you mean Ma?"

"I mean, I'm strong, I'm not this person. It's gone from bad to worse. I never use to be like this. I'm drinking; I'm too emotional and vulnerable. This isn't me."

Mercedes didn't know what to say, but she did know her mother was a wreck. She never saw her mother take a drink outside of a special occasion.

"Ma, don't say that. You're a strong person and you have to remain strong for Daddy and for me. You are all that I have left and I'm all you have left."

"Yeah, that's true." She managed to say between sniffles and drying her tears with a napkin.

"You and I are going to spend the weekend in a hotel and indulge in their spa. It would help us get our mind off of things. We haven't had a day for us in a while." Mercedes smiled.

"Sounds like a plan." Maria finished drying her eyes and smiled.

* * *

The next day Mercedes and Maria went to the salon to get their hair done. They decided to also get manicures. After that, they went to the spa that Emilio helped reserve. They felt extremely relaxed as two men massaged their shoulders with scented oil. Mercedes pleasantly smiled at this experience. After they were done, they headed to the hotel room. It was filled with desserts and shopping bags. Mercedes found a designer dress on her bed.

"Wow, who did all this?" Maria asked looking at Mercedes' gifts.

"Emilio." Mercedes smiled and exposed her dimples.

"Why are you smiling so much?" Maria asked with a smirk. Mercedes opened her eyes to find her mother staring at her.

"I don't know Ma." Mercedes shrugged her shoulders.

"I was just asking. It's just...I haven't seen you smile like that since Chino died." Maria shrugged her shoulders. "You're glowing. Do you like Emilio?" Mercedes plopped down on the bed and sighed. She shrugged her shoulders; she didn't know how to feel.

"Honestly Ma, I don't know." Mercedes admitted. "I want to dislike him, but then he does things like this."

"Emilio's a nice guy, why would you not like him. You don't even know him."

"I have no idea. He gives me a strange vibe. I'm not sure if I can trust him. Maybe I'm just paranoid..."

"Honey, I know it's because of Chino. I know you're still in love with him, but he's gone now...you have to move on." Mercedes was a little upset by her mother's comment.

"Yeah, I know Ma. I don't know, I'll see."

"I've seen the way he looks at you. I think he's in love with you. He just doesn't know how to tell you."

"Yeah, I guess he is. He lost his mother and his aunt is in the hospital. He's probably scared of getting close for fear of losing."

Maria covered her mouth with her hand. "Wow, that's crazy. Mercedes maybe you should be a little nicer to him, since he lost a loved one too. Give him a chance."

"Maybe, I'll think about it." Mercedes said. She remembered she had his number in her purse and retrieved it. She decided to give him a call.

"Hey Emilio."

"Hey gorgeous, I thought you would never call." Mercedes smiled and shook her head.

"Yeah, well my mother said I should give you a chance."

"You should always listen to your mother." He joked.

"Well, thank you for the spa, the hotel, and everything." Mercedes said. She was forgetting some of the stuff that he brought her. "You have nice taste in designer bags too."

"Thanks. I know that if I want to be around you, I have to keep up with the latest fashion."

They both laughed and Mercedes felt comfortable talking to him.

"Well anyway, how is your aunt doing? Is she okay?"

"What are you talking about?" Emilio had already forgotten the lie he told her.

"Didn't you say that your aunt was in the hospital?"

"Oh yeah...she's still in critical condition and when I'm not busy I'll go see her."

"Oh okay, well I hope she feels better. Sorry for the loss of your mother."

"It's cool." Emilio was eager to change the subject. "So can I take you out tomorrow night?"

"I called you to thank you for the gifts. Who said I wanted us to go out?" Mercedes rudely said. She was joking and still playing hard to get.

Emilio nervously chuckled. "Ok, I understand that Mercedes."

"I'm just kidding." Mercedes laughed at him. "You can take me out tomorrow."

"Are you serious?" Emilio enthusiastically asked.

"Yes you can. Just know that I have my eye on you Emilio."

xxxxxxxxxx

The next evening, Mercedes stood in front of her mirror checking out her outfit for the night out with Emilio. She smoothed down her jet black hair and it cascaded down to her shoulders. She wore a fitted strapless black dress from Nicole Miller that accentuated her curves. She wore black Christian Louboutin red-bottom stilettos. As usual, she had the finest jewelry on from head to toe. She looked and felt amazing for the first time in a long time. Mercedes took one last look in the mirror before exiting the bathroom. She heard the doorbell ring and went to go answer it. She grabbed her clutch off her dresser and headed down her steps as her heels clicked on the steps.

She slowly opened the door to a waiting Emilio. Neither of them said anything. They both stared at each other in amazement as the other was dressed eloquently.

"Damn Mercedes, you look very beautiful." Emilio was amazed.

"Thank you." Mercedes blushed as he complimented her beauty and attire.

"Why thank you. You're looking quite handsome yourself."

"Thanks," Emilio smirked. Mercedes smiled and eyed him up and down. She never really noticed how handsome he was. Mercedes saw a very different side of Emilio. She smiled at the fact that he opened the door for her. She felt that it showed he knew how to treat a woman. Emilio entered the driver's side and they both drove to their destination.

They arrived at the restaurant and Emilio took her hand. He opened the door for her to enter. The restaurant was crowded and Mercedes was worried that they wouldn't be able to get in.

"Emilio Pouche." Emilio stated his name to the waitress as she quickly acknowledged him and grabbed a menu. She simply said, "Right this way sir." They both followed behind the woman as she guided them upstairs to a private area.

As they sat at the round glass table, the restaurants lights were low. It provided a nice ambiance and a very classy look. She noticed Emilio staring at her as her eyes scanned the menu. She glanced up still with the menu in reading position and asked,

"Is there something wrong?"

"You have really beautiful eyes Mercedes." Emilio complimented her.

"Why thank you." Mercedes blushed. She briefly looked away but glanced up and caught Emilio staring yet again.

"I never noticed the color of your eyes, I thought they were hazel."

"Well, you have never actually been this close to me to notice."

"That's true, well I'm getting close enough to you now." Emilio placed his hand on top of Mercedes' and a quick shiver went down her spine. Before either of them could say anything else, the waitress came over and asked them if they were ready to order.

"I'm ready, are you?" Emilio asked Mercedes as she still perused the menu.

"Yes, I'll have a Pina Colada."

"I'll take a Long Island Ice Tea." He told the waiter.

"I would love to try the Serrated Shrimp and Chicken with the lemon cheese and mashed potatoes please, thank you." Mercedes ordered and closed her menu.

"And how about you sir, what would you like?"

"I'll take what my lady is having." Emilio smiled at Mercedes and handed the waitress the menu. Mercedes looked at him and smiled.

"I thought you would go for the steak or something." Mercedes chuckled.

"Nah, I mean I love steak. But I'd rather have what my lady is having."

"Oh, is that so?" Mercedes mischievously smiled. He called her his lady twice already.

"Very much so."

"Question, how come you asked me to go out on a date with you? What do you want from me?" She asked frankly.

"I mean, isn't it obvious Mercedes? Ever since the first day I saw you, I've been amazed by your beauty and wanted to whisk you away. You have such swagger for a young woman your age. It's attractive to me and I like it a lot." Emilio winked at her.

"That's interesting." The waitress came back and placed her food and drink down.

"Mhmmm, this looks delicious." Mercedes licked her lips as she eyed the steamy plate.

"Yeah, so do you." Emilio was clearly enchanted by her and was making it known.

"I'm not the dessert menu." Mercedes teased while batting her eyes at him. He loved the flirting and she had a habit of biting her lip. Emilio found that sexy.

"Girl, if you keep biting your sexy lips like that you will be my dessert. They continued to laugh and drink. They were getting tipsy throughout the evening. Mercedes began to feel closer to Emilio and he knew he had her in the palm of his hands. They decided to leave the restaurant get to know each other a little more.

Mercedes invited Emilio up for a nightcap and he graciously accepted. During their conversation, Mercedes kept bringing up Chino and how much she missed him. Emilio didn't like that at all, but Mercedes was so intoxicated that she didn't notice his displeasure.

"Thank you Emilio for taking me out tonight." Mercedes words were slurred as she talked.

"No problem Ma." Emilio smiled, "I think I need to help you get out because you aren't okay to walk."

"Shut up." Mercedes giggled at him and playfully nudged his shoulder. Emilio hopped out the car and quickly walked around the passenger side. He opened the door for Mercedes. She handed him the key and he opened her door. He took her the bedroom as she directed. He plopped her down onto the bed. She grabbed her pillow and began to cry.

"Good night Baby Girl, Emilio stopped in his tracks when he noticed she was crying. She began to sob harder and he walked over to the bed.

"What's wrong Mercedes?" Emilio asked.

"Just everything," she said between tears.

"Aww Ma, please don't cry on me now." Mercedes wrapped her arms around his neck and cried in his arms. He felt sorry for her; he never had a woman cry in his arms. He felt awkward watching her cry, but she eventually cried herself to sleep. He held her tightly as his shoulder became her pillow.

The next morning, she awoke to his hands tightly gripping her waist. She looked over to see Emilio staring at her. She didn't remember much due to her drunken state. She wondered if they had sex.

"Good morning beautiful lady." Emilio smiled.

"Did we have sex?" Mercedes wanted to get right to the point. She didn't want to assume and go about her day like nothing happened. Emilio loudly laughed at her question.

"Nah Ma, we didn't have sex. You're still fully dressed. If we had sex, your clothes would be on the floor."

"Whatever." Mercedes smiled as he grabbed her hand and began caressing it. "So you don't remember us going out to eat. We laughed, talked and drank."

"Of course I do, but after a few drinks I was done. What happened later in the evening?" Mercedes seductively asked. Emilio pulled in closer and whispered in her ear.

"You were looking so fucking gorgeous I wanted to eat you up. You told me you weren't on the dessert menu, so I guess you got a free pass."

Mercedes listened to him speak and began to get aroused, but Emilio's phone began to ring and interrupted the moment. He removed himself from her grasp and went to speak privately in the bathroom. Mercedes wanted him now more than ever. She would have to wait for another time. He returned from the bathroom with bad news.

"Sorry Baby Girl. I wish I could stay longer, but I got some business to handle." Emilio slid his phone back into his pocket.

"I understand." Mercedes sadly replied. She watched Emilio put on his jacket, then walked him to the door and opened it.

"Thank you for letting me take you out last night." Emilio said with a wink.

"No! Thank you, and thanks for staying with me last night. I really appreciate it."

"Anytime," their eyes connected and Emilio leaned in for a kiss. She turned her head and his kiss landed on her cheek.

"I guess I'll see you later."

"Alright Ma, until then."

"Bye." Mercedes smiled and waved as she closed the door behind him. She pressed her back against the door and sank down to the floor. She knew she was falling for him, and it scared her.

Slip & Fall

It had been several weeks since Mercedes last saw her friends. In fact, she hadn't seen them since her father's funeral. They spoke on the phone collectively, but hadn't had a chance to get together.

One day they all decided to meet and chat at a diner on 125th Street in Harlem. They sipped on Mimosa's as Mercedes gazed from the window. She was oblivious to the conversation going on.

"Mercedes," Candy called out.

"Huh?" Mercedes was interrupted from her thoughts when Candy called her.

"What the hell are you thinking about?"

Mercedes quickly begin to blush, as the girls looked at each other and smiled.

"Ohh, is that a blush I see?" Hazel snickered.

"I haven't seen her blush like that since Chino." Shateeya joked.

"It sure is girl. Spill the beans! Who is this new guy that makes you blush so much?" Chamari asked.

"Oh shut up." Mercedes smiled and nodded her head.

"It's nothing, no one." Mercedes lied and sipped on her drink. She hoped they would change the conversation.

"Aww, come on Mercedes. We are girls, sisters you know. We don't keep secrets." Candy opened her mouth and Mercedes wanted to stick her foot in it. She knew Candy was hiding a secret of her own.

"Yeah we ALL have secrets, ALL of us that no one knows about." Mercedes replied while looking at Candy.

She directed her attention to the rest of the girls and decided to tell them about Emilio.

"It's actually a guy I've known since I was sixteen."

"Well, who is he?" Candy inquisitively asked.

"His name is Emilio, he worked for my father."

"Oh *his* sexy ass, he is a fine motherfucker." Chamari smiled as her and Candy high fived each other. "I remember him from your party."

"Ya'll are so silly." Mercedes said as they all laughed.

She began to tell them about the events surrounding her date. "The other night he took me out to dinner and we were eating, drinking, and laughing-all that good shit. He took me home and I ended up breaking down and crying about Chino and my dad. He just held me all night until the morning." Mercedes beamed, showing off her dimples.

"Get the fuck outta here." Shateeya smartly said.

"Aww that's sweet, he's a real nice gentleman for that." Candy implied.

"So ya'll didn't fuck?" Shateeya jumped in.

"Damn Miss Nosey Bitch." Mercedes joked, "Nah we didn't have sex yet."

"Please! So that entire night ya'll was drinking and you woke up with your clothes on?" Shateeya laughed. "Yeah aight bitch, now we all know that she's lying. My panties would've dropped to the floor OKAY! That nigga was definitely up in the panties. Real recognize real." She started hysterically laughing while everyone looked at her in shock.

"Well, a wise woman knows not to fuck on the first night. And real recognize real, but I keep it classy." Mercedes rolled her eyes and her phone rang before Shateeya could respond. "Excuse me ladies." Mercedes left the table.

"Hello?"

"Hey, beautiful, how are you?"

"What's going on stranger? Long time no see or hear."

"Yeah, I'm sorry Mercedes. I was in Cu-I mean I was out of state taking care of some business. I just came back this morning." Emilio lied.

"Yeah, okay. Whatever." Mercedes pursed her lips together.

"Aww Ma, come on now. What you mad? I apologize, I'll make it up to you." Emilio didn't want her to be mad. She was actually warming up to him. Mercedes' teeth were chattering due to the wind outside.

"Yeah okay Emilio, I gotta go."

"Where are you now?"

"I'm out for lunch with my girlfriends."

"Well when you leave there, get ready and I can pick you up from home."

"Alright, see you later." She smiled at his effort to make her feel better. Maybe he wasn't so bad after all.

Mercedes hung up her phone and slid it into her Coach purse. She walked back into the diner.

"Well I have to get going ladies. It was good seeing y'all." Mercedes didn't even bother to sit down.

"Where are you headed?" Candy eagerly asked.

"Home, Emilio just called me and we're going out tonight."

"Aww shit, go on girl." Candy gave her a pound.

"Alright you ladies be safe, love ya'll." Mercedes gave each of them kisses on their cheek before exiting the diner and hopping into her car.

When she got home, she called Emilio to let him know that he could come get her soon. She fixed herself up shortly after heard the doorbell ring. She walked to the door and found Emilio with flowers behind his back.

"You look gorgeous, Mercedes."

"Thank you Emilio." Mercedes kissed him on the cheek and Emilio pulled out the flowers and handed them to her.

"Aww, you're so sweet."

"I try, are you ready to go?" He asked as he took her hand.

"Let's go." Mercedes and Emilio walked down the path to his car. He helped her get in and closed the door.

They spent a wonderful day together. They shopped on Fifth Avenue, went to a movie and had dinner. Mercedes noticed after the movie that he stopped in front of a hotel. As they entered the hotel, Mercedes loved the ambiance and décor.

"This is a beautiful hotel." She remarked as she looked at the 16 story hotel in amazement.

"Yes it is beautiful, one of the most expensive hotels in the city." Emilio grabbed her hand as they proceeded into the hotel. He checked them in and they rode upstairs on the elevator.

As they entered the hotel room, Emilio helped her take off her coat. He put on some Jazz to set the mood and she noticed the bed was covered in rose petals.

"I know you had a long night, so I prepared a bath for you." Emilio smiled as he led Mercedes into the bathroom.

"This is very nice Emilio." Mercedes smiled. He handed her a bag from one of her favorite stores, Victoria's Secret.

"No problem. I'll be waiting for you when you get out. I'm gonna go watch TV. " Emilio smiled as he closed the door behind him.

As he left, she got undressed and stepped into the bath. It felt magnificent. After thirty minutes she decided it was time to come out and see what else was in store. She put on the lingerie from the bag and came out of the bathroom. She found Emilio on the bed flipping channels.

"Damn Ma, you look great." Emilio lustfully said.

"You're so silly." Mercedes blushed as she sat on the edge of the bed.

"Yeah, I can be sometimes. I made a little dessert for you."

Emilio reached over and retrieved some chocolate covered strawberries that were waiting for her.

"Mhmmm, this is delicious." she licked her lips and still had a piece of chocolate hanging on the side.

"Well, except for this chocolate sticking to the side of my lip." She giggled and tried to remove it.

"Let me get that for you." Emilio moved in closer to Mercedes and he licked the chocolate off and started sucking on her full lips. He massaged her tongue with his and placed his hand behind the back of her neck as they kissed passionately. Butterflies flew around in her stomach sending chills down her spine. Emilio helped remove her bra exposing her C cup breasts. He kissed her over her neck and leaned her back onto the bed. He slowly sprayed whip cream all over her nipples. After making love to her breasts, he put whip cream all over her stomach and started licking her belly button. Mercedes loved the way he was taking his time exploring her body. As Emilio went below her panty line, she began to moan loudly.

He slowly removed her thong and slid it down her legs. He dropped it to the floor. His tongue made his way down to her sweet, tight pussy. He began licking around her fat lips. He took his time licking and sucking her pussy nice and slow. Mercedes' eyes rolled in back of her head as she grabbed the back of his head. Emilio tasted and swallowed all of her juices. He picked his head up and was licking his lips.

"You finally let me get the dessert." he smirked.

"That was just a little sample." Mercedes badly wanted him inside of her.

"Oh yeah, well can I get the whole meal?" Emilio removed a condom from the package and placed it on his stiff dick. He slid it inside of her and she began moaning and bucking in discomfort.

"Are you alright Ma?"

"Yeah, I'm fine," she moaned. "It just hurts a little. It's been a while you know?"

"Do you want me to stop?" He stopped and looked her in her eyes. She shook her head 'no' and they continued making love. She bit the bottom of her lip and decided she was going to take the dick. He continued to slide in her and finally made it all the way inside. He hit her with the slow strokes, making her a fiend for his dick. She tried to hold back her moans, but it was futile. She moaned loudly and scratched his back with each deep stroke.

"Chino!" Mercedes accidently called out her ex's name. Emilio didn't even stop; he kept going. With each and every stroke he thrust a little harder. Emilio knew he didn't have to worry about anything. Chino was long gone and out of the picture. He had Mercedes all to himself. As they reached their climax together, they fell asleep in each other's arms until the dawn.

Mercedes woke up with the sheets wrapped around her body. She smiled thinking about the events from the previous night. She couldn't believe that she and Emilio had sex. She never thought it would be possible. She reached over the bed to retrieve her cell phone and noticed that she missed several calls from her mother.

"Oh shit!" Mercedes scurried about grabbing her clothes and getting dressed. Emilio heard her and asked what was going on.

"What's wrong Ma?" Emilio asked, with a concerned look on his face.

"I was supposed to meet my mother at the hospital." Mercedes put on her coat and slipped on her stilettos. "Can you take me there please?"

"Sure, let me get dressed." He threw on some clothes and drove to the hospital.

"Thank you so much Emilio."

"No problem Ma, is your mom okay?" Emilio curiously asked.

"It's my Uncle Roy."

"This shit is crazy, I thought he was dead." Emilio couldn't believe that Roy Carter was still alive.

"What?" Mercedes asked him, she did not hear what he said.

"Oh nothing, I didn't know he was still in the hospital." Emilio responded.

"Yeah, why don't you come up and see him?" Mercedes insisted.

"No," he yelled. "I mean, I can't today Mercedes. I know he's messed up and everything from what happened. I'll let him rest and come see him another time." Emilio smiled as he rubbed his hands over hers.

"Alright," Mercedes shrugged.

Emilio reached over and moved in for a kiss. This time, she kissed him back.

"See you later." She smiled and made her way to go see her Uncle Roy. Mercedes talked to the nurse at the desk and she told her where to go. She made it to the room and looked in to see her mother holding his hand and talking to him.

"I'm sorry I was late Ma I........" Maria cut her off.

"It's okay Mercedes." Maria was dry and didn't want to hear any excuses from her. Mercedes walked over and saw her uncle lying in bed. He was filled with tubes. The monitors recorded his every move and the beeping sounds were continuous.

"How's he doing?" Mercedes asked as she walked over and touched his hand. Tears began to drip from her eyes as she watched his eyes flutter. At this point, that was the only motion he could make.

"The doctors said he's still in critical condition, but he'll make it. He can barely talk and the doctor said he can't really remember much either. Your uncle was shot several times. If he didn't call the ambulance, he would have been right there with your father." Maria began to cry again, even though she tried to hold back the tears. "Aww Mama please, please don't cry." Mercedes rubbed her back. "Everything's going to be just fine."

"Yeah, I hope so. I just hope your uncle makes it." Maria said. "The bastards who killed your father and shot your uncle need to pay." Maria had an idea that Vicente Santiago was behind the death of Don Carter and the near death of Roy. She just didn't want to say anything to Mercedes.

"He will, I know he will." Mercedes hoped and prayed as she smiled at her Uncle and rubbed his hand. "Hey Uncle Roy, I know you can hear me. You can't talk back to me, but just know that I love you and everything's going to be alright."

He simply looked at her and blinked. That was the only way he could let her know he heard her. The nurse came in to tell them they needed to leave.

"So he doesn't remember anything that happened?" Mercedes asked.

"Not yet. The police asked him questions, but their efforts were in vain. He can't speak to answer their questions. All he can do is open his eyes. He's lucky to be alive." The nurse smiled and adjusted his pillow.

"Yes he is; he's a Carter." Mercedes smiled thinking about her father.

Maria watched how Mercedes stared at her uncle Roy. She hated that he was an example of the life they led. She wanted her daughter to lead a healthy, normal life. Sadly, she was in way too deep and there was no turning back. The Carter blood ran through her.

xxxxxxxxxx

Flash Back

The night was silent and Mercedes was sound asleep in her bed.

POP! POP! POP!

Gunshots rang out jerking Mercedes out of her sleep. She jumped out of her bed with her heart almost beating out of her chest.

She tip-toed from her bedroom and slowly walked over to the spiral stairs. She peeked through the wooden bars and noticed four men rummaging through their things downstairs. Suddenly, someone grabbed Mercedes from behind and she wanted to scream. It was her mother and she placed her hand over her mouth. In her other hand she held a gun, ready to protect her home and family. She placed one finger over her lips and told her to be quiet.

"Shh, don't say a word." Maria said as she picked up her daughter. She took her up the hall to be protected from harm. From her peripheral, Maria saw a shadow. It was soon revealed to be one of the intruders. He began shooting and she quickly hit the floor. She opened one of the bedroom doors and locked it. She panicked, with her hands trembling with fear.

"Mercedes go and hide under the table." Maria told her. Mercedes stood there with her teddy bear in her hand and watched her mother in fright.

"I said GO!" Maria yelled. Mercedes ran and hid under the table as she was told. Maria pushed a chair against the door as a barrier. The intruder began banging on the door, but the chair prevented his entry. He then decided to shoot at it to get in. Maria ducked as the bullets pierced the door.

She ran to the table where Mercedes was and held her close. Her eyes were locked on the door as the shooter made his way in.

"*Where are you? Come out and play.*" *He laughed. Maria noticed him walking over to the table. She saw his feet get closer and they both remained quiet. He knew they were there, however, and flipped over the table. Maria quickly got up and kicked him in his nuts before he could even cock back his gun. He had his nuts in one hand and the gun in the other. They both began shooting at each other and Maria was caught in the arm with a bullet. "Argh!" Maria screamed. She still held onto her daughter tight, with all of her strength. They ran down the long corridor and dashed down the steps. They reached the garage, where their truck was parked. She quickly ran around to the driver's side of the truck. She fumbled with the keys as she tried to unlock the door. Tears came to her eyes out of fear for her daughter's life. She was not so much concerned with her life. As she unlocked the door, she quickly placed Mercedes on the seat. Shots echoed within the garage as the shooter entered behind them, still threatening their lives.*

"*Mami!*" *Mercedes cried out loud.*

"*It's okay Baby, lie down.*" *Maria shot back but soon ran out of bullets. Reaching over to the glove compartment, she found another gun and cocked it back. After exchanging several shots, she hit the shooter and his lifeless body fell to the ground. Blood and brains covered the concrete floor. "Mami watch out!" Mercedes screamed as a man approached her mother from behind. He grabbed her neck and they struggled. He was too strong for her. There was another struggle and guns erupted. Maria's heart pounded rapidly and she gasped. She looked over to see the attacker with a fatal bullet wound in his head. She looked over and saw her husband Don with his gun in a shooting position.*

"*You alright Babe?*" *He asked.*

"*Yeah, I'm fine.*" *Maria took a deep breath, "I'm just hit in the arm.*"

"*Alright, let's hurry up and get the fuck up outta here.*" *Don hopped in the driver seat and Maria scampered to the back* seat with Mercedes. Don pulled out of the garage and fled the scene.

"Yo, I swear them nigga's in Harlem got something coming for them!" Don barked.

"How do you know it was them for sure?" Maria said, she was referring to the Spanish dudes in Harlem who Don had beef with.

"I just know! It's a war going on between me and them right now." Maria sighed in relief, she thought her father had found her and sent people to kill them.

"Mami, what's going on?" Mercedes cried.

"Nothing, Baby." Maria held her arm as she groaned in pain from the bullet wound. Mercedes turned around to look out of the window and spotted a man shooting at them from the middle of the street. Glass shattered and Maria hovered over Mercedes to protect her from harm. Mercedes was too young to know what was going on, but her young mind wanted to find out.

An Awakening

Mercedes sat and watched her Uncle Roy sleep for four hours. Chills crept down her spine when she looked around the room. She cried when she looked around and saw the IV attached to his arm and the machines that were keeping him alive. She now had a glimpse into what her life would be like as a hustler's wife.

She smiled slightly when she saw her uncle's face. His features closely resembled his brother, Don Carter. Uncle Roy was a very handsome man, just like her father. Roy wore cornrows that reached a little past his neck. His complexion was lighter than her father's. He had full lips, a little mustache and big brown eyes.

Mercedes' eyes lit up with joy when she noticed her Uncle's eyes slowly fluttering up and down. His lips parted slowly as he tried to speak. Mercedes moved closer to her Uncle.

"Shh, Uncle Roy. I know it's painful to talk, take it easy."

Mercedes smiled as she held onto his hand and felt him squeeze her hand tighter. She knew he was making progress; just a couple of weeks ago he couldn't move any parts of his body except his eyes.

"I see you're doing a little better. You're a very strong man, a very strong man. There aren't too many guys who could make it through something like this."

Mercedes wiped away her tears and said, "Uncle Roy, you're like my second father. You were always there for me when my father wasn't. I mean, my father was always there, but when he was out of town you were there. I remember that day when I was having trouble at school with one of the boys and you came up to the school to check him for me. You snatched him up by his collar and let him know that the Carter family doesn't mess around." Mercedes giggled. She knew he remembered that story too. She wished she could hear him laugh.

She continued to reminisce and began to cry. She wanted her old life back, when she didn't have to live in fear and her family was intact.

"The Carter family never dies Uncle Roy, no matter what. Our souls will always live on and our hearts will always remain strong." Mercedes placed her hand over his chest. Roy slowly placed his hand on top of hers and forced a smile on his face.

"It's really been different without my father being around. It's been very hard on me and Ma." Mercedes couldn't hold back her tears. "I've just been trying to move on and live with it, but deep down inside I'm truly hurting Uncle and I just wish I could bring him back."

Mercedes inhaled deeply. "I never use to like Emilio for some reason, but now he's all that I have besides Mama. Emilio..." The mere sound of Emilio's name sent Roy into a fury. His blood pressure rose and he struggled to speak. He wanted to tell Mercedes to stay away from him, but the words wouldn't escape his lips.

"What Uncle? What are you trying to say?" Mercedes' eyebrows arched as she stared at her uncle wondering what he was trying to tell her.

"Who did this to you? Who killed my father? Please tell me...please I need to know...?" Mercedes begin to break down. Roy looked at her and shook his head; he really wished he could talk. Mercedes knew he had the answers she sought.

"Whoever did this to you will pay!" Mercedes promised to herself and to Roy. She wiped the tears from her eyes and stood up.
"I'm gonna head home now Uncle Roy, I'll call and check up on you here and there to see how you are doing. For now, try to get some rest okay Unc, love you."

Mercedes reached over and kissed him on the forehead. On the ride home, Mercedes was thinking about what her uncle was trying to say. She knew he wanted to tell her something, but he just couldn't. She hoped he would get better really soon; there were questions that still needed to be answered. She was unaware that her answer was closer than she imagined.

* * *

Mercedes sat at the kitchen table reading the newspaper. She was sipping on her fifth cup of coffee. Emilio walked up behind her and wrapped his hands around her. He kissed her gently on the neck.

"Hey, Babe," he smiled.

"Hey," Mercedes smiled as she rubbed the back of her neck.

"What's wrong Babe?" Emilio sensed something was wrong with her because she never drank much coffee.

"Oh nothing, I'm just thinking about my Uncle Roy." Mercedes sighed.

"Baby don't stress it, he'll be fine." Emilio took a deep breath.

"I know Babe. I was talking to him and he was trying to tell me something, but I don't know what he was saying." Mercedes looked at him.

Emilio got up from the table and paced back and forth in the kitchen. He turned his back to her so she couldn't see his guilt.

"I know you already told me no, but I mean you can tell me the truth. Did you have anything to do with my father's death Emilio?" Mercedes looked at him and wondered what he was thinking.

"Are you alright?" Mercedes asked. "Is there something on your mind?" Mercedes asked in a concerned tone. Emilio looked at Mercedes and sat back down in the chair.

"No, I didn't have anything to do with your father's death." Emilio lied again, "I told you before Ma. I would never have wanted your father to die; I know how much he meant to you and to your mother. I'm just thinking about your father and how good of a man he was to me. He took me under his wing, showed me the ropes and everything. He introduced me to his beautiful loving family, I felt as if I was a part of the Carter family. I mean, I wish I was there that day to be there for him. Instead I was out of state taking care of business." Emilio inhaled deeply and placed his hands in front of his face.

"It's not your fault." Mercedes began to cry. "I miss him so much. I mean, I wish I had the chance to tell him how much I love him and to say goodbye. I mean life is so short and it can be gone in the blink of an eye."

"I know how you feel Baby, trust me, I know." Emilio embraced her and rubbed her back. "Just take it easy Ma. I'm here for you Baby Girl and I'm not going anywhere." He lifted her chin and smiled, "You're so beautiful."

"I want you to be my girl, my world, my everything. I've never met a woman as beautiful or as smart as you. Mercedes Carter, I think I'm falling in love with you." Those words shocked Mercedes and made her heart flutter.

"Really," she asked.

"Yes, I want to make love to you." Emilio said placing his hand around her waist. She wrapped her arms around his neck and they begin kissing passionately. Emilio picked her up and carried her up the stairs. He placed her gently on the bed. Emilio made sensual love to Mercedes. They both explored each other's bodies and took their sweet passionate time.

As they made love, Mercedes cried and he kissed each and every single tear drop away. She was torn; lost in the love of two men. She liked that her love was growing for Emilio, but her heart would always belong to Chino. Even though he was dead, she still felt like she was cheating on him.

Silent Death

Emilio hopped into his Benz and rushed to the hospital that housed Roy Carter. He had the chance to do what he had to do while Mercedes was out running errands. The hospital told Mercedes that he was progressing well and could now speak. That meant he would be able to tell her who tried to kill him and who succeeded in killing Don Carter. Emilio couldn't risk being exposed. He was falling deeply in love with Mercedes and wasn't ready to lose her. Emilio wanted to be with her since Don first introduced them.

He desperately wanted to reach the hospital before Mercedes did. He accelerated well beyond the speed limit and finally reached the hospital. He exited the car and put his hoodie over his head in an attempt to conceal his identity. He approached the receptionist who sat casually filing her nails.

"Hello, how are you doing?" Emilio smiled while making eye contact with the lady.

"I'm fine and you, how may I help you?" The receptionist seductively said.

"Well, I'm looking for Roy Carter."

"What's your name?" She asked him. Emilio stumbled for a second, but remembered his alias that he always used.

"Francisco Sanchez." He used Francisco Sanchez as an alias and had that name on his fake ID. She typed his name into the computer and shook her head, denying his request for admittance.

"I'm sorry, but your name isn't on the visitation list. Only his family members are allowed to see him." She sternly spoke, obeying the strict orders that were given.

"He's like my father, I just moved up here and he was taking care of me. I just found out he was in the hospital, I was just trying to check up on him. Thanks anyway." Emilio sighed as he turned around and begin to walk away.

"Sir?" The lady called out. Emilio deviously smiled as he turned around.

"He's in room 313." She gave him the information and smiled at him. His plan actually worked. He smiled back and thanked her as he made his way to the elevator. Upon reaching the third floor, he searched for the room number. Once he spotted it, he glanced around to check his surroundings and walked inside. He couldn't afford to have any witnesses.

Roy was watching TV as Emilio entered the room. He watched him shut the door behind him. He had no idea who was here to see him. Once Emilio came in and removed his hood, Roy's eyes widened in fear. He tried to reach the button for assistance, but Emilio snatched the plug from of the wall.

"I see that you're still alive." Emilio coyly said.

"Yeah, I'm still alive motherfucker!" Roy spat. "What the fuck are you doing here?"

"You know why I'm here Roy, don't play with me." Emilio let out a sinister laugh. "Don is dead, Frank is dead, and all the others are dead. You have no reason to be alive."

"I have a family to live for!" Roy defiantly stated. "What the hell do you want?"

"You know what I want Roy. Since Don is dead, I know he left you with all of the goods. Where's the safe?" Emilio demanded.

"What safe?" Roy knew exactly what he was talking about. All of the Carter money, drugs and weapons were stashed there. No outsiders had ever been to the safe house, but they knew it existed.

"Don't fucking play dumb with me!" Emilio snatched one of the tubes out of his nose and Roy grunted in pain. "The safe with all of the money...the drugs where is it Roy?" Emilio asked as he continued to torture him.

"I don't know what you talking about."

"If you won't tell me where the safe is, I'll find it through Maria."

"You stay away from her and stay away from Mercedes. Don will kill you!" Roy threatened Emilio, not remembering that Don was dead.

"The Carter family is already dead." Emilio informed him. "Mercedes is all mine, and she is so beautiful when she's lying beside me." Emilio hysterically laughed.

"If Don ever found out you were fucking with his daughter, he would kill you." Roy gritted his teeth. "And when Mercedes finds out you were the one that helped kill her father, she will kill you."

"Yeah right, she doesn't have the heart to kill." Emilio couldn't imagine his sweetheart killing someone. "We're in love and I'm going to propose to her one day. I won't have you or Maria standing in the way of the love of my life." Emilio stated. "With Don being dead and Maria and you gone, no one will be able to stop me." He smirked, "Don't you agree."

"You're a sick motherfucker!" Roy yelled.

"Say your prayers real quick before you meet your maker." He walked towards Roy fully prepared to end his life, this time he would be sure of it.

"Fuck you Emilio!" Roy spat at him. "You won't be able to live to see that Carter money motherfucker." Emilio pulled all of Roy's tubes from his body and snatched the IV bag and unplugged it. Roy struggled to breathe, so he grabbed the pillow from behind him and placed it over his face. He suffocated him. Roy struggled because his legs were still not fully functioning; his mobility was limited. Emilio watched as he stopped moving.

"Sleep tight," Emilio smirked. He replaced the pillow to make it appear that Roy was sleeping. He threw his hoodie over his head again and exited the room. He walked down the corridors of the hospital and thought to himself 'mission accomplished.'

Just when he thought he was in the clear, he was frozen in his steps. Standing before him was Roy's niece and his girlfriend...Mercedes.

xxxxxxxxxx

"What are you doing here?" Mercedes asked him.

"Oh, I just stopped by to see my ummm...Aunt." Emilio lied. "I have to go now Mercedes, I'll see you later." Emilio kissed her on the cheek and quickly rushed down the hallway. Mercedes knew something was wrong with him. The way he was sweating profusely and seemed to be in a rush-it just didn't sit right with her.

"Okay," she whispered. She turned around and continued walking to her uncle's room. When she walked into the room, she noticed her uncle's face was facing her. He was blue and looking at her with bulging eyes.

"Oh my God!" She screamed as she realized he wasn't awake-nor was he asleep. He was dead. "Somebody help please! HELP!" Mercedes screamed out for the nurse's assistant. Immediately nurses came rushing into the room and one of them tried to push Mercedes out of the room.

"Nooo, Uncle Roy! Please don't leave me." Mercedes barged past the nurses and cried over her uncle's dead body. "Why? Why?" Mercedes shrieked as she hovered over her uncle's body. The nurses and doctor tried to pull her away, but they were unsuccessful. After several minutes of trying to get Mercedes out of the room, she fainted.

When she came to, she noticed she was in a hospital bed. She quickly patted her body down to make sure she was okay.

"Help!" Mercedes screamed as she saw an IV in her arm. The nurse came rushing in to Mercedes' side and calmed her down.

"What am I doing here?" Mercedes asked with a perplexed look on her face. A nurse came in to tend to her. She was a hefty dark skinned woman with fiery red dreadlocks and a mole on her lip. The mole was quite distracting, but Mercedes tried not to focus on it.

"Mercedes, sweetie, you're fine." The nurse checked her vitals and looked at the chart.

"You were just taking it hard, your blood pressure rose and you fainted." Mercedes remembered going to see her uncle, and she could barely breathe.

"Where's my uncle? Is he okay?" Mercedes panicked. The woman looked at her sadly. She didn't want to tell her the bad news, but it was written all over her face.

"He died at twelve forty-five this afternoon. They tried to save him, but he removed all of the tubes that were helping him stay alive." Mercedes broke down again and the nurse tried to keep her calm as she embraced her.

"No, No, No!" Mercedes knew deep down inside that the picture wasn't right and her uncle would never commit suicide.

"I'm so sorry Mercedes."

"Why? Why?" Mercedes yelled out in anger. "You don't understand, first they killed my boyfriend Chino, then my father and his people. Now it's my uncle. Who's going to be next, me?" Mercedes cries were mixed with laughter. "This shit is unbelievable!"

"Oh sweetheart, don't ever say that." The nurse hushed her. "Everyone has to go someday, but I know for a fact it isn't your time to go yet. You're still a little baby." The nurse touched her face and wiped away her tears. "You're a beautiful young lady with a bright future in front of you." The nurse smiled.

"Thank you." Mercedes forced a smile. "I just wish that I could have talked to my uncle. He was like a second father to me. I was here for him to get better. He wanted to tell me something, but he didn't live to tell me." Mercedes said. She tried to hold in her tears, but they eventually exploded.

"Mercedes, your Uncle Roy and I talked the other day. He seemed like he was worried about something. He kept saying he wanted to talk to you. That's when I called you so you could come down here. He told me he had something to give you...one second." The nurse disappeared into the hall and came back with a box in her hand.

"Your uncle to said cherish this box and make your father proud."

"What? I don't understand..." The nurse handed Mercedes the box. Mercedes looked at it and had no idea what to do.

"Honey I don't know, he just gave me the message. He said it holds the Carter future." The nurse smiled. "Now get some rest." She insisted as she disappeared from the room again.

Mercedes waited until the nurse exited the room and she ran her French manicured nails over the white box that had the initials MC written in black cursive letters. She carefully opened the box and it revealed two sets of keys, a small key and a shiny long key.

"Keys?" Mercedes had a bewildered look on her face as she held the key in her hand and examined it. Under the keys, she found a piece of paper with writing on it. She picked up the paper and it was a New Jersey address. She pressed the key up against her chest and thought of what the nurse said. "It holds The Carter future." Those words ran through her mind. It made her wonder what the key was for and why her father gave it to her and not her uncle. She would soon find out everything.

Mercedes returned the keys and paper to the box and closed it. Just as she did, there was a knock on the door. It was Emilio. She hid the box under the covers and smiled.

"Hey Baby." Emilio walked over and gave her a hug and a kiss on the lips. "How are you feeling?"

"I'm alright, how did you know I was here?"

"Well, I did see you earlier. But I kept calling your phone and one of the nurses must have gotten aggravated and answered the phone." They both laughed.

"They told me you fainted." Emilio sighed. "I also heard about your uncle; I'm sorry to hear that. I wonder why he would commit suicide, I mean I don't understand." Emilio placed his hands on his temples and shook his head.

"No, my Uncle Roy didn't try to kill himself." Mercedes nodded her head, "He would never do such a thing. He was getting better. He was going to live, I know he wouldn't take his life. Someone murdered him." Mercedes yelled.

"Honey, you never know what people are thinking. Cedes, Babe, you have to wake up and smell the coffee." Emilio caressed her face. "Your uncle was in critical condition and maybe he wouldn't want to live like that and have the guilt of your father's death on him."

"Excuse me?" Mercedes eyebrows arched as he tried to explain.

"I know he must've felt guilty that he couldn't save his brother when he was murdered. I mean it hurts to see someone you love get murdered and sometimes people blame themselves." Emilio assured her.

"I know what you're saying, but Babe I know Uncle Roy didn't..." Emilio cut her off placing his fingers over her lips.

"Babe just relax, you've been through a lot you need a lot of closure. I'm here for you Mercedes; you don't have anything to worry about." Emilio hugged her and kissed her on her forehead.

Tears streamed down her face and he wrapped his arms around her. Something in her heart didn't feel right. There was something going on, and she soon would find out what it was.

Safe House

One Saturday morning, Mercedes decided to get up and drive to the New Jersey address that was in the white box. She threw her legs over the side of her bed and quickly looked over at Emilio. He was sound asleep. She snuck out of the bed, hoping he didn't wake up. She showered, dressed, and tried to leave before he woke up. As she was about to leave out the front door, Emilio woke up yawning. He looked over and caught Mercedes exiting the room.

"Where you going Babe?" Emilio asked.

"Oh," Mercedes stopped in her tracks and looked at Emilio. "I'm going to hang out with Candy and the girls today for brunch." She lied.

"Have fun Babe and call me later." Mercedes waved to him and walked down the steps and hopped in her Mercedes-Benz coupe. She didn't know that Emilio was standing on the balcony watching as she pulled off. It felt good driving the Benz, with her seat reclined. The fresh smell of leather hit her nose as she drove. She had just copped the new Nicki Minaj mixtape and it bumped from the speakers as she drove to New Jersey. On her way there, she noticed her gas was getting low. She pulled over at a local gas station near the Manhattan Bridge. She walked into the gas station and handed the clerk fifty dollars to fill the tank. She went back outside and pumped the gas.

Mercedes hopped back into her car and pulled off. While on the highway, she noticed a black Cadillac behind her. Mercedes didn't pay it any attention until she realized it stopped at the same gas station as her and followed her back onto the highway. It would switch lanes as she switched. It was obviously following her, but Mercedes wanted to be sure. She pressed her foot down on the gas and accelerated and so did the black Cadillac. Mercedes suddenly slammed on her brakes in the middle of the street causing the black Cadillac to swerve from behind her and it kept driving. She took the next exit and drove into New Jersey. She kept staring into the rear view and side mirrors, but she didn't see anyone following her.

As she arrived in New Jersey, Mercedes followed the directions of the navigation system and it guided her to her destination. Mercedes noticed that the neighborhood was nice and only had a few houses on the block. She pulled up to a small white condominium. She decided to pull around the back of the condo. She got outside and looked around. Mercedes quickly walked around the condo to the front door and walked up the steps. She took out both keys and used each one of them to try to open the door. The small key worked and the front door easily opened.

She walked around the condo and saw furniture and doors. She saw a wooden door, but when she tried to open it-it was locked. She decided to try one of the keys and chose the long one. The door quickly turned to reveal an entrance to a basement. The basement was made out of steel and it was freezing. Mercedes looked around and her eyes lit up. There were several weapons hanging up on the walls, including AK's and various handguns. She walked around the basement, not knowing what to expect. Her jaw dropped when she saw tons of kilos of cocaine. She knew her father dealt in drugs, but had never seen it up close. She spotted several duffle bags sitting on the ground in the corner of the basement. Mercedes walked over and knelt down to unzip the duffle bags. Inside of them, she saw stacks of money held together with rubber bands.

She got up and stood scanning the room. She noticed a safe embedded in the wall. Mercedes walked over to the safe and wondered what was inside. She tried a couple of numbers, none of them worked. Then she tried her birthday, the combination of 10-17-90. She smiled as the safe clicked and slowly opened.

Inside, she found more money and items which she dumped into her purse for safe keeping. One of them was a diary with a piece of paper attached. Mercedes found some empty duffle bags and placed a few guns, some more money, and 20 kilos into the bags. She zipped up the bags and left, carefully locking the door behind her. She carried a total of five duffle bags. Luckily, they just looked like clothes so she was hoping no one was suspicious. Although she was concerned, since she knew what the bags contained. She placed the bags into her trunk and made her way back to the city. On the way back, she noticed that she was being tailed by a New Jersey State Trooper. She didn't think anything of it, until the lights flashed behind her.

"Shit!" Mercedes banged on the steering wheel and hesitated to pull over. Once she did, the cop hopped out and stood in front of her window pounding on it with his hand. Mercedes nervously rolled down the window.

"License and registration please." The officer rudely demanded.

Mercedes rolled her eyes as she reached over and grabbed the papers from the glove compartment and handed it to the officer. He snatched it from her and headed back to his vehicle. Mercedes sat there nervously peeking in her side mirrors to see when the cop was coming back to the car. She noticed him walking back to her car and she rolled down the windows.

"Mercedes Carter," he handed her back the paper work and said, "You're Don Carter's daughter right?" He asked, already knowing the answer.

"Yes, I am." Mercedes proudly responded.

"This vehicle is to be seized and towed."

"Excuse me?" Mercedes was astonished.

"Well, I know you know that your father was a big time drug dealer. Everything that he owned was paid for with dirty money. What he did was illegal and this car is in his name." The officer smirked. "I'm going to call in for a tow."

"I live in New York and that's over an hour from here. What am I going to do?" The officer looked at her with an 'I don't give a fuck' look on his face.

"Well, sit tight. You might as well call yourself a ride because you're going to need one." He shook his head and headed back to his cruiser. Mercedes tried not to cry and decided she had to think of something and quick. She was carrying weapons, drugs, and several duffle bags that held millions of dollars in it. That's several federal charges that would have her locked up for many years. Mercedes wouldn't be able to see the rest of her precious life.

She looked back in her rearview mirror and saw the officer getting out of his car to approach hers. As soon as he got close enough to the car, she floored it. The officer quickly ran back to his car and tried to give chase. He quickly caught up to her and was tailgating her with his flashing lights on. He demanded her to pull over on his loud speaker. He didn't know Mercedes was nasty behind the wheel. She maneuvered the car like a race car driver, switching and dipping in and out of lanes. She drove so fast and with such skill, that the officer swerved and almost hit a few cars that were on the road. Ten minutes into the high speed chase, Mercedes noticed two cruisers inching up to her and one tried to sideswipe her. She hit the brakes causing it to hit another car.

Seeing that she had no one following her, she hit the gas once more and was able to be on her way without anyone catching her.

Mercedes sighed in relief as she drove home. She was still a little paranoid, but she was back in the city. She took the back roads to her home in Long Island and parked the car in her garage. She quickly grabbed the bags and headed up the stairs through the back.

She struggled as she carried the bags up the stairs. She opened up her closet and placed the bags with the weapons and drugs inside of a hidden compartment leading to another room.

She didn't need any one finding her stash, not even Emilio. Mercedes plopped on the bed and took in a deep breath. She thanked God that she didn't get caught today. She knew she would have been locked up right now.

She opened up her bag and poured the items she took out her father's safe onto her bed. There was a letter attached to his diary that he had kept, she opened up the letter and it read,

To my Baby Girl, Mercedes Carter,

I was waiting for the day for you to open and read this letter. There's only two ways out, either I'm locked up or dead. I know what I've done in the past will always catch up to me no matter what. Not just me, everyone in life.

Being a drug dealer comes with a lot of consequences, but my father was a Carter. I had no choice but to take after him. This is in my blood. It always will be, now and forever. The Carter family is well-known. Everyone knows where we come from and what we are about. My father Ricardo Carter believed in me and felt I had the heart to run the Carter business. He knew in his heart that I would take it and make something out of it.

When he was murdered by the Colombians, I was devastated. My heart was shattered and I didn't know what to do. All he wanted me to do was to take over and he said that would make him proud. When I turned thirteen-years-old, I inherited everything from my father and put it to work. A few years later, niggas in the street respected me and looked up to me because of all I'd accomplished in a short amount of time. It's all about money, power and respect; Mercedes remember that.

Without power, you have no respect and without money you're broke. The reason I gave you this key to my safe house is because you're the one who holds the Carter future. Maria, your mother, is a very beautiful person, but I know I wouldn't be able to give her this key. She isn't strong enough for this. She's a strong woman to have dealt with my bullshit after all these years, but she's not as strong as you. She already told me if it came down to taking over, she wouldn't do it. Your Uncle Roy is my right hand man. I love him with all my heart but, he isn't a leader. When you were born, there was something different in your eyes that I saw. I saw the eye of the tiger and I shaped you well. You have the heart of a strong person. You literally hold the key to the Carter future in your hands. I want you to take over and make me proud. I want you to have everything you ever wanted and want for nothing. I don't want your kids to starve; if you ever decide to have kids and a family. I want them to grow up how you grew up, living a lavish life. When you were born Mercedes, it changed my life in many ways. I was blessed with a beautiful daughter and I thank your mother for that. There are a lot of secrets in my life that I think you should know about. As you get older, you'll find out many answers that you are seeking. I just hope you make your father proud, I'll see you in heaven someday. I love you Mercedes Carter and remember The Carter family never dies.

Love Always,
    Don Carter

Emilio opened the door, and Mercedes quickly hid the letter and wiped away her tears.

"What's up Babe?" Emilio smiled as he walked in and took off his jacket.

"Nothing, just sitting here chilling you know." Mercedes flashed a smile.

"How was your day with the ladies?" Emilio asked.

"It was alright, we had fun. We just talked and caught up on a few things."

"That's all you did today?" He inquisitively asked.

"Yeah, nothing interesting happened- except that I was being followed by a black Cadillac. It's the same car I saw the day I was with Chino. I've seen it a couple of times."

"Your fine Babe, there's plenty of black Cadillac's roaming around New York City. Just chill out, you've been very paranoid since your father died."

"I don't know babe, it's just weird."

"Chill Baby, relax." Emilio began to massage her shoulders as he kissed on her neck. He always knew how to make her feel better. She allowed him to take control of her body, even though she knew he knew more than he let on. For now, she would have to believe him, until the truth was revealed.

Hidden Secrets

The next morning, Mercedes rolled over and noticed Emilio wasn't in the bed. She looked over at the clock on the nightstand and decided to get up and do a little cleaning around the house. She threw on some casual clothes to begin her day.

As she was cleaning, she heard her cell phone ringing. She ran down the steps and turned down the volume on the stereo. She loved to clean and listen to music; she thought it made the time go by faster. She answered the call and it was Emilio.

"Hello...Hey Babe...where is it? Alright well call me when you get here."

She hung up her cell phone and kept the music low so she would be able to hear him when he came in. He asked her to get his wallet because he left it at home. She ran up the steps to retrieve it. She checked his jacket and found it, but dropped it as she was hanging it back up.

As she picked up the jacket, the wallet fell out causing documents and his ID to fall out onto the floor.

Mercedes quickly picked up the cards and came across an ID. It was Emilio's picture and the name read Francisco Sanchez along with his birthday and it said he was from California. She remembered him telling her he grew up in Cuba. Mercedes was immediately pissed off and realized that the man she's grown to love is a liar. She realized that he's been lying to her about his name and upbringing from the beginning. Mercedes slid his ID back into the wallet and closed it. As she walked downstairs her phone rang and it was Emilio letting her know he was there. She opened the door and stood there looking at him awkwardly, like the stranger he'd quickly become.

"Hey, Babe." He kissed her on the lips and noticed she didn't kiss him back,

"What's wrong Baby?"

"Nothing." Mercedes lied.

"Alright Babe, I'll be back later." Emilio kissed her on the cheek. He knew something was weird with how she was acting, but paid it no mind. Angry with what she just discovered, Mercedes slammed the door and walked up the steps. She decided to call her mother for answers.

"Hey, how you doing Ma?" Mercedes smiled, it was good to hear her mother's voice.

"Hey Baby, I'm doing alright and you?"

"I'm just chilling. How is it living in Queens?"

"It's alright. I'm not use to living like this. They have roaches and shit running around." They both chuckled.

"See Ma, that's why I told you that you can stay with me. You'll have a new place to live soon."

"Yeah, I gotta get up out of here. She tries to borrow everything I own." Maria laughed. "But what's going on with you, how's everything, what's new?"

"Nothing really, I mean Emilio and I started to get serious."

"Emilio? I thought you weren't into him like that?"

"Yes Ma, Emilio. We've been dating for a while now; I guess you could call it that. The thing is he's really feeling me Ma and I'm feeling him but he's...."

"That's good Honey; I can't wait till you get married. That will be a day that makes me proud."

"Oh please Ma, he ain't gonna pop the question-it's too soon for that."

"Please Mercedes. I know Emilio likes you. In due time he will be on his knees with a big ass diamond asking you to marry him, trust me."

"Yeah, I just don't know Ma..."

"Just don't know what?" Maria cut her off.

"If he's the one. There's just something about him that my heart doesn't agree with."

"Babe, I know you're still in love with Chino and all. Of course you're going to be iffy about Emilio, just take your time Babe."

"Ma it's not that..." Maria cut her daughter off.

"Baby I'm sorry, I gotta go. Your auntie needs to use my phone, hers got disconnected today. I'll talk to you later. I love you." The phone call ended while Mercedes still held the phone against her ear.

"Love you too Ma." She threw the phone on the bed and took a nap. Hours into her nap, her phone rang and woke her from her nap. She sluggishly answered it.   "Hello?"

"Hey girl it's Candy."

"Hey Candy, girl what's up?"

"Ain't shit, at home chilling bored as hell, what you doing?"

"I was sleep!"

"Well you need to wake your ass up!" Candy yelled.

"What time is it?" Mercedes wondered.

"It's around eight-thirty and the girls and I were wondering if you wanted to come out and celebrate tonight. We are going to a club in Harlem to celebrate Chino's homeboy's birthday. He invited us."

"Oh, I don't know." Mercedes wasn't sure about going out tonight.

"Come on Mercedes, we all want you to come. It's been a minute since we all went out. It'll be just like old times."

"Alright, I guess I'll go. What time are ya'll trying to dip out?"

"Well ladies are free before eleven. We wanna get there early so we don't have to wait in line." Candy told her.

"Ya'll got a ride, or ya'll want me to scoop you up?"

"That would be a good idea! You can get us from my crib. "

"Alright I'm 'bout to get up and get ready." Mercedes got up to get dressed for a night to remember.

xxxxxxxxxx

Mercedes pulled up in her two toned pink and black Mercedes Benz E350 coupe. She opened her lambo doors and they gently flew in the air allowing her to make her exit. All of her girls were with her, but Mercedes stood out amongst them.

As they bypassed the line, bitches rolled their eyes and gossiped with their girls. They were mad because they had to stand in the line and wait to enter the club. Mercedes just smirked and noticed the tension and hatred that the girls were showing. They knew they couldn't be down with her, so they hated on her. They didn't even get searched and walked up into the club.

They made their way in and the bass from the speakers was pumping. One guy felt on Mercedes' ass while she was dancing; she smacked him in the face. She wasn't going to tolerate any disrespect tonight. She wanted to enjoy herself.

She stood at the bar sipping on her Long Island Ice tea. Her wrist glistened from across the room. She nodded her head to the beat as the music filled the club. Chino's friend Lamar walked over to her as she was at the bar. He was happy to see her smiling and looking beautiful, as usual.

"Happy Birthday, Lamar" Candy cooed.

"Thanks Ma." Lamar said giving her a quick hug. "Hey Mercedes, how you been?" He asked as he looked over at Mercedes and hugged her. "Long time no see."

"Yeah I know; it's been like two years." Mercedes nodded her head.

"I know Ma, I'm sorry for your loss. I heard about your pops and I just want you to know I'm here for you." Lamar consoled her.

"It's cool, thank you. I'm just living, you know shit happens."

"Chino really loved you Ma and I know he's smiling down on us right now." Mercedes got teary-eyed as Jim Jones song came on, "In Love with a Thug." She held back her tears as

Lamar continued talking to her. That was a song that she often heard when she was driving with Chino in the car.

"Yeah I know; we'll meet again one day." Mercedes smiled.

"True, well I'll let you go and enjoy yourself Ma."

"Alright, I will Lamar." Mercedes kissed him on the cheek and he disappeared into the crowd.

"He is so fuckin sexy." Candy said while eyeballing Lamar as he walked away.

"Mhmmm, I think I'm going to have to push up on him." Candy and Mercedes laughed together.

"You're so crazy girl." Mercedes sipped on her drink and jammed to the music. She had a few cups of liquor so she was feeling real nice. Mercedes and the girls were having a great time posted up by the bar dancing. She squinted as she looked across the club and noticed India with her girls.

"Is that India over there?" Mercedes asked.

"Yeah, that's her." Candy eyed India and her crew down. "She's eight months pregnant." Candy sucked her teeth, "Nasty hoe."

"She doesn't even know who the baby's daddy is." Hazel added.

"She already has another baby who's two years old and she's claiming it's Chino's." Shateeya said.

"Yeah right, that baby ain't his! And how the fuck is she pregnant and in the club?" Mercedes screamed.

"Fuck all that, India and I got some business to handle." Mercedes sipped the last of her drink and followed India into the restroom to talk to her.

"Mercedes don't do anything stupid." Mercedes heard her friend Candy say as she grabbed her arm.

"I gotta do this!" She snatched her arm away and headed to the bathroom. Mercedes words were slurred from the drinks. When she got into the ladies bathroom, she noticed India standing there with her protruded belly poking out of her closely fit dress. She stood in front of the mirror smacking her lips together after putting on her lip gloss. Mercedes didn't say anything but began fixing her hair waiting for an opportunity. It came sooner than she hoped.

"Well, well, well! Look who showed up tonight." India sarcastically said.

"Bitch I know you ain't talking to me." Mercedes rolled her eyes.

"Where have you been hiding?" India laughed.

"Bitch please, ain't nobody hiding. Ain't nobody scared of your ass. At least I don't have to jump nobody." Mercedes turned around and stood face to face with India.

"Whatever Mercedes, at least I didn't get Chino killed."

"Bitch what the fuck are you talking about? Him getting killed had nothing to do with me." Mercedes yelled.

"You know what; you're one fucked up bitch. You're probably the one who set his ass up, because you were jealous that I was pregnant with Chino's baby. You wished he had your ugly ass knocked up. That shit that you and your girls did was fucked up. You will pay, trust and believe that shit!" Mercedes retorted. She was drunk and angry after seeing India and she wanted some revenge.

"Whatever, you ain't 'bout shit. That baby ain't deserve to live any damn way. My baby Chelsey is his." India was clearly pushing Mercedes' buttons and wanted her to react. It worked; Mercedes didn't allow India to say anything else. That was her last straw; she turned around charging at her. Mercedes didn't care if she was pregnant or not. She hit her with such force that India fell to the ground.

Mercedes started punching India in the face as hard as she could. India couldn't even keep her eyes straight. She tried to scratch Mercedes in the face, but she was unsuccessful. She was able to scratch Mercedes on her neck.

"You fucking stupid bitch! You killed my baby." Mercedes yelled.

Tears were streaming down her face as she continuously punched India in the face. Mercedes' girls ran in the bathroom and tried to break it up. It took all of them to pull Mercedes off of India.

"Yo Mercedes, she's pregnant chill out." Candy warned her as she pulled her back and stood between them. India held her bloody face.

"I don't give a fuck about her being pregnant." Mercedes pulled out the gun that was in her purse and pointed it at India's stomach. "She didn't give a fuck about me, when I was pregnant with Chino's baby. Her and her little fucking crew jumped me knowing that I was pregnant. They killed my baby! They killed my fucking baby!" Mercedes yelled as she cocked the gun back, ready to shoot.

"Put the gun down, Cedes. How the fuck did you get that in here anyway? You gonna get us arrested." Candy inched towards her trying to get her to put down the gun.

"Fuck that, her baby doesn't deserve to live!" Tears streamed down her face. "She took the only thing that Chino and I beautifully created! Why should I?" Mercedes screamed as her hands shook holding the loaded weapon.

"Come on Mercedes, she ain't worth it B, she'll get hers." Hazel chimed in. "Come on Ma don't do this, you don't want to end up in jail for murder." Hazel walked over and lowered the gun and took it from her. Mercedes stared down at India, looking her in the eyes. "You took away my baby!" India's crew rushed in and wondered what the commotion was, but they received the answer when they spotted India's face and the damage that her face endured. "Bitch-" one of India's girl tried to come at Mercedes, but Hazel pointed the gun in her face. "You better not try anything stupid; shit will go down. I got the gun now." Hazel warned the girl; she backed off and they exited the bathroom.

They left the club and hopped in the car and drove Mercedes home because she was too drunk to drive.

"They killed my baby; I could have been a wonderful mother! But no those bitches did some sucker shit and fucking jumped me and killed my baby." She was drunk and pissed. She let all of her feelings out.

"Yeah we know Mercedes, but life goes on. Don't let that bitch get to you Ma. She'll get hers, trust and believe that." Candy advised. They pulled up to Mercedes' house. She was drunk, but she still worried about her girls and wondered how they were getting home.

"Lamar is going to give us a ride, he's right behind us." Candy assured her as she walked her inside. "We'll be good just go upstairs and get some rest. Mercedes opened the door and walked upstairs to find Emilio sitting on the edge of the bed waiting for her.

"Where were you?"

"Last time I checked, you weren't my fucking Daddy!" Mercedes spat.

"Whoa, whoa, hold up Mercedes." He noticed she was stumbling across the room as she tried to take off her clothes. "Have you been drinking?"

"Why the fuck do you care?"

"Because I care about you Mercedes, I love you." Emilio said with sincerity.

"Please nigga!" Mercedes slurred her words and eyed him viciously. "You don't love me, you're a liar...everything about you is a lie! You lied to me about your name...you said you were from Cuba, but your ID says your from Cali. I don't even know who the fuck you are Emilio or Francisco."

"I can explain Mercedes..." Emilio tried to explain, but she cut him off.

"I don't want to fucking hear it! Mercedes spat. "I want you out of my fucking house and out my life. I don't know who you are. There's something about you that I hate and I don't know what it is. Even though I love you; it's slowly killing me inside." Mercedes broke down to her knees and cried. Emilio tried to console her, but she pushed him off of her.

"Don't you fucking touch me!" Emilio had never seen Mercedes like this. He didn't know how to make it better, so he just grabbed his jacket and left. Mercedes crawled to the bed, while still fully dressed, and cried herself to sleep. Emilio walked outside with his fists balled up.

"I'm going to make her want me even more...I'll do whatever it takes, even if that means being the last person she can lean on." Emilio said as he got in his car and slammed it shut. He had been keeping tabs on Maria for a week now and was waiting for the perfect time to make his next move. The opportunity had presented itself and he was ready for action.

Left for Dead

The next morning Maria found herself home alone. She needed some rest and time to unwind. Brenda was called in to work early and she asked Maria to take the kids to school. She dropped them off and came right back to the empty house. She decided she would put on some music and fumbled through some CD's until she found one of her favorites. It was Stevie Wonder's *Songs in the Key of Life.* She turned it on and proceeded to make some breakfast. She planned to enjoy her 'me' time. She began cooking and heard the doorbell ring.

"Who is it?" She asked before unlocking the door. She wasn't expecting company and only her family members knew where she was.

"Emilio!" Maria was surprised to hear his name and wondered how he knew that she was there. Nonetheless, she opened the door and was met with a gun to her face. Her expression changed drastically when she knew she was in danger.

"What are you doing Emilio?" Maria panicked.

"Shut up and sit the fuck down!" Emilio demanded as he pulled a chair from the table and pushed Maria down in it. He grabbed some duct tape from his pocket and placed it around her hands and feet, preventing her from running.

"What the fuck do you want?" Maria asked.

"You know what I want!" Emilio screamed. "Where's the fucking safe?"

"What safe? I-I don't know what safe you're talking about..." Maria was genuinely clueless to the safe and its' contents. Emilio struck her with the butt of his gun, causing her to fall with the chair. He picked the chair up and dragged her body off the floor. He angrily pushed her back into the chair.

"Stop it, stop fucking lying to me! I know your husband kept a fucking safe with the money and drugs. Where is it?"

"I swear, I don't know." Maria cried. She was telling the truth; her husband never told her anything about a safe. "If I knew I would tell you, but I don't know."

"You're a lying little bitch!" Emilio spat as he pointed the gun at her.

"You ran away from Cuba to be with Don Carter, a notorious drug dealer. It's your fault that your husband got killed. It's your fault that Frank and his other workers died. And last but not least, it's your fault your brother-in-law Roy is dead too."

"What are you talking about?" Maria had no idea what he was referring to.

"Don't play stupid bitch!" Emilio yelled. "You knew this whole time didn't you? You knew your father would come looking for you. You left Cuba without telling your own father and you disobeyed one of his most important rules. Don't ever mess with any of his customers-and you did it anyway! Now look what you created, a bloodbath for the Carter family!"

"I had no choice!" Maria shouted. "I had to leave or my father would have killed me and my baby. You don't know shit! You don't know what love is, even if it showed up and smacked you in the fucking face."

"I love your daughter, and she's falling in love with me too. And I'm not going to have anyone standing in my way...I killed Chino, your husband, and I killed Roy!" Emilio smiled with pride.

"I was sent here by your father to find you and bring you back to Cuba. I honestly don't give a fuck if you live or die. Niggas don't play by the rules out here anymore. I killed them to be with your daughter. I love her and even you can't stop me! I can't allow anyone to ruin what we have and the love that we share. That's why it's your time to go."

"You stay away from my daughter you sick bastard!" Maria spit at Emilio as she tried to get out of the chair, but she was unable to do so. He wiped the spit off his face and rushed towards her. He wrapped his hand around her neck and squeezed.

"You better keep that spit in your mouth before you won't have a tongue anymore. It's time for you to be with your husband and the rest of the Carter family!" Emilio told her. He grabbed and twisted her jaw.

"Fuck you Emilio, go to hell!" Maria still managed to yell with his hand tightly crushing her jaw.

"You're the one who's about to feel like you're in hell, since that's what you put your family through!" Emilio got closer to Maria and placed some duct tape over her mouth to keep her from screaming.

He poured gasoline on the floor and all around the living room. He made sure he poured it all over Maria's arms and legs as well. He laughed callously during this process; he only cared about killing the last person who could come between him and Mercedes. He pulled out a match, lit it and dropped it at her feet. Flames surrounded Maria and jumped onto her fuel soaked skin.

"Say hello to Don Carter for me." He tossed the match and stood there watching her burn for several seconds before turning around and running out of the house. The fire spread quickly; he needed to leave before he was trapped as well. Emilio watched the home erupt in a ball of flames from his car. He knew Maria was dead. He took pride in annihilating the entire Carter family. Emilio beamed with pride that he was able to carry out such a difficult task. He would finally have Mercedes to himself and there was no one who could stop him. He figured with her family dead, her only choice would be to lean on him. He was ready to take care of her in her vulnerable state. Piece by piece, his plan was starting to come together.

xxxxxxxxxx

It had been a few days since Mercedes last saw Emilio. He constantly called her, but she sent his calls straight to voicemail. When she wouldn't accept the calls, he showed up at the house. She pretended she wasn't there. She really cared and had love for Emilio, but she didn't know the real him. She often wondered why he kept secrets from her and hid his true identity. She couldn't be with someone who wasn't truthful.

One day while Mercedes lay across her bed reading, she heard the doorbell ring. She knew it wasn't any of her friends; they always called to let her know they were coming.

"Who is it?" She asked, while waiting for a response. Her heart jumped in her throat when she heard the voice on the other side of the door.

"It's Emilio." He was hoping for a chance to talk with her.

"What do you want Emilio...I mean Francisco." Mercedes mockingly said. She leaned her back against the door.

"Please Mercedes, open the door and let me explain." He begged and pleaded as Mercedes rolled her eyes. She eventually unlocked the front door and folded her arms across her breasts.

"Can I please come in?" Emilio asked. Mercedes looked down and saw he was holding a bouquet of red roses in his hand. He tried to hand them to her, but she ignored them and stepped aside. She was allowing him inside, only for a minute.

"I brought these for you." Emilio presented her with the flowers. They were accompanied by a weak smile.

"Put them on the table." Mercedes rudely responded as she eyed him up and down.

"I'm here to apologize Mercedes. I'm so sorry I lied to you about who I am. I've just been through a lot. I changed my name when I came here. I was born in Cuba, but I moved to California. I didn't like the person I was in Cuba; I wanted to start over. I understand if you don't want to forgive me. I just want you to know I want to be with you. I want you to love me for me and not my past." He grabbed her hands to appear more genuine.

"Okay, are you done?" Mercedes uncompromisingly asked.

"You're so damn arrogant." Emilio smiled. "Please Mercedes, just give me another chance. I need to prove myself to you. I want to show you how much I really love you. You're the woman of my dreams." He gently grabbed her hands and kissed them. "Let me make it up to you, PLEASE!"

"How?" Mercedes was interested to know how he was going to make up to her this time.

"A vacation for two, you and me in the Bahamas for three days. How does that sound?" Emilio pulled out the tickets and flashed them in Mercedes' face. "You know you want to!"

"When are we leaving?" Mercedes smiled and her façade of anger quickly faded. She definitely needed a vacation. She had seen the beauty of the Bahamas in pictures; she was ready to see it up close and personal.

"We can leave today, if you want."

"I'm not packed or prepared to up and leave just like that."

"You have until twelve-thirty, so get ready." Emilio winked at her. He knew he had her under his spell.

"Boy you are so slick. You knew you would get me." She playfully nudged him in the shoulder.

"I'm going to go pack so we can leave." Mercedes ran upstairs to pack her things. She immediately pulled out her pink Louis Vuitton bag and began stuffing clothes and bathing suits inside. After she finished packing, she ran down the steps and found Emilio sitting on the couch reading a XXL magazine. She was ready to head to the airport.

They left in his car. Mercedes was excited and dialed her mother's number. She wasn't able to reach her. She was a bit concerned because it had been a few days since they spoke. They usually spoke daily. Emilio noticed her discomfort and reached over to touch her leg.

"Babe, are you okay?"

"Yeah, I'm fine." Mercedes smiled. She was trying to put the worry out of her head as they arrived at the airport. She smiled and placed her hand on top of his. She wanted to make the best of the situation, but her nerves were telling her otherwise.

You and I

The Bahamas was a dream come true for Mercedes. She had dreamed to visit this place since she was a little girl. They got off the plane and took a cab to their hotel, which happened to be one of the most expensive in Nassau. As they entered their room and settled in, Mercedes walked over to the window. She saw a magnificent view of the waters. It was breathtaking.

"Babe, get ready. We're going out to get something to eat." Emilio said to her. He wanted to show her a good time and help her forget about everything. She did as she was told and proceeded to get ready for dinner.

They entered the dining hall and were escorted to their table. Within minutes, they were enjoying their meal of exotic seafood and pasta. Emilio looked at her in amazement and satisfaction. He raised his glass to her and began to speak with emotion.

"I want to let you know, Mercedes, that I love you. I finally have you to myself and you're all mine. It's just you and me against the world. No one can ever come between us." Emilio smiled as he reached across the table and kissed her. "A toast to you and me."

Mercedes smiled as she raised her glass. After they finished eating their meals, Emilio grabbed her hand and whispered in her ear. "I want to walk around on the beach."

"Alright, let's go."

Mercedes and Emilio took a stroll down the beautiful beach and walked hand in hand. The sun had already set and the light from the restaurants shone onto the sand. They stopped briefly to look at the stars. Mercedes gazed at the sky as she leaned her head back onto Emilio's chest while he embraced her from behind. No matter what happened, she always thought of

Chino when she looked at the stars. A single tear fell from her eyes and landed on her cheek. Through her tears she still smiled, for she knew Chino was looking down on her and protecting her.

"This is beautiful." Mercedes smiled. Emilio stood behind her and kissed her on the neck.

"Not as beautiful as you."

"Oh, is that so?" Mercedes turned around smiling and wrapped her hands around his neck and kissed him on the lips.

"Yes, no one is as beautiful as you Mercedes." Emilio assured her. "Well you're almost as cute as me." Emilio joked.

Mercedes giggled and playfully pushed him in the sand. She hopped on top of him to give him a passionate kiss.

"Emilio," she stopped briefly and looked him square in the eyes.

"Yes Mercedes."

"I just want to apologize for that night when we were arguing. I'm just going through a lot and I don't know what I was thinking..." He cut her off by placing his fingers on her succulent lips.

"Shh, Ma, I understand. I'm not mad." Emilio assured her. "Just make love to me." Mercedes slid her tongue inside of his mouth and they danced to the tune of their beating hearts. She pulled up her skirt and he slid her panties to the side and positioned himself beneath her. He opened his zipper and his erection popped through his boxers. She discreetly sat on his lap and began moving up and down as she rode his dick. This was her first time making love on the beach, and she was enjoying it.

They both moved in unison to the waves crashing ashore. Emilio slipped her breast out of her top, freeing it to roam his lips. Mercedes moaned as his tongue tickled her nipples. She closed her eyes and moaned softly as he ran his fingers through her hair. The speed increased and they both became more aroused.

"Mercedes! Ahhhh, Mami." Emilio yelled her name and held onto her hips as she worked it. Mercedes smirked as she noticed him moaning and groaning. She was putting it on him.

Emilio couldn't take it anymore and flipped her over into the sand. They were under a sand dune and it was dark, but they didn't want to take chances. He straddled her and with every stroke Mercedes scratched his back. He crammed his meat into her body. She looked into the sky and watched the stars dance. She couldn't help but think of Chino. Her heart wanted what it wanted, regardless of who she was with. As much as she wanted to let go, a piece of her always remained with Chino. Her thoughts were invaded by Emilio's voice as he whispered to her softly during climax.

"I love you Ma." He then released his seed in her and they breathlessly collapsed onto the sand.

XXXXXXXXXX

After their midnight rendezvous on the beach, Mercedes woke up in bed with no clue as to how she got there. The sun beamed into her eyes and she looked around in the bed and didn't see Emilio.

"Emilio!" In he walked wearing only boxers and holding breakfast on a tray.

"Good morning Babe." Emilio greeted her and walked over to the bed and placed the tray of food on the bed.

"Morning."

"Damn, Baby something smells good." Mercedes reached over and kissed him on the lips.

Mercedes eyed the tray of food. It was French toast, sausages, eggs and pancakes. She licked her lips as her stomach growled. "You made all of this for me?"

"Yes, all for you. I already ate." Emilio plopped down on the bed and turned on the TV. He relaxed while watching SportsCenter and Mercedes indulged in her breakfast in bed.

"Damn, you were really hungry Baby?"

"Yeah this food was delicious." Mercedes placed the tray on a table and sat back with a pillow behind her back. She lay back on the bed and Emilio made his way between her legs.

"I bet you taste better." Emilio reached over and removed the sheets from her nude body. He began placing kisses on her taut stomach. He explored her mound and traveled down to her clit. He slowly kissed it. He kissed soft and slow and Mercedes moaned as her legs quivered. Climax was imminent and Emilio took it all in. He enjoyed her and cleverly smiled as she looked at the ceiling. She was spent.

"Well, I was right. You do taste better." He said while licking his lips.

"Yes I do, I'm going to get dressed. I don't want to spend all day in bed, although it would be nice." She got off the bed and headed into the shower. She turned the water on and began lathering up. Soon, Emilio came in and wanted to join.

"May I join you?" He asked.

"You're already in here." Mercedes chuckled. Emilio got behind her and caressed her body. They both began to get aroused again.

"Let's stop before we stay in the shower for hours."

Mercedes winked at him and washed up. She left him in the shower and threw on her outfit for the day. She chose to wear a black Gucci bikini and shorts to match. She wanted to relax and maybe swim a little. Her goal was to enjoy this vacation as much as possible.

"Babe, come on. I want to show you around and take you shopping." Emilio yelled out from the bedroom.

"Alright, I'm coming." Mercedes applied her clear lip gloss and walked in to find Emilio just getting dressed.

"You were rushing me and you ain't even ready." Mercedes lightheartedly rolled her eyes.

"My bad Babe, let's roll." Emilio smiled.

Mercedes wrapped her arm in his and they left to spend the day together. They hopped in a cab and explored all the sights. They shopped and ate and enjoyed themselves a great deal. They exited the Versace store and made their way back to the hotel to drop off their bags. After they did, they ventured out to the beach. Reclining in a lounge chair, Mercedes closed her eyes and soaked in the Bahamian sun.

Emilio sat on the edge of the chair. He was chilling and looking as the sun shone on her body. The sun tan lotion she wore made her skin sparkle. Her bikini showed off her sexy body and flat stomach.

"It feels really good out here, doesn't it Babe?" Emilio asked as he looked around and enjoyed the beautiful view.

"Yeah, it really is perfect out here." Mercedes said.

"I've been thinking...what if we could move out here?" Emilio asked.

Mercedes sat up in horror at the thought of leaving her mother behind. Her heart literally began palpitating. She didn't know if the sun was making her hot, but she began sweating profusely.

"I can't leave my mother, she's all that I have left." A tear formed in her eye as she thought of being away from the one person she had left who represented the Carter name.

"Babe, you have to learn that when you grow up you move on from childish things. You have to do things on your own. Your mother won't always be there."

Mercedes looked away and Emilio put his hand on her thigh. "Are you alright Mercedes?" Emilio noticed she was silent for a while.

"Yeah, I'm fine Emilio." She looked at him with a smile and turned away.

"Are you sure? You don't look too sure." Emilio wanted to know what was going through her head. He placed the seed of doubt into her head. He was trying to make her understand that she would be able to survive without her mother. He needed to make sure that his point was well-taken.

"I still haven't heard from my mom. I have a weird feeling that something terrible has happened." Mercedes took a deep breath.

"Maybe she's on a vacation or something." Emilio was trying to make excuses. Mercedes cut him off, she knew better.

"No, that's not like my mother. She would have called. We usually speak daily; she would have wanted to know if I was out of the country."

Mercedes got up from the chair and grabbed her towel. She walked away from Emilio. He called out to her, but she ignored him. She wanted to be left alone. She headed toward the elevator and decided to try once more to reach her mother. After a couple of rings it went to the voicemail. Mercedes decided to leave a message to let her know she was worried.

"Hey Ma, it's Mercedes and I'm really starting to worry about you. Please, can you give me a call to let me know that you're okay? Alright love you Ma." Mercedes hung up the phone and got on the elevator heading up to the room. Once she arrived on her floor, the elevator doors opened. She got off and approached the room. She opened it with the keycard and immediately began stripping into more comfortable clothes. She was overcome with anxiety. She walked out onto the balcony to clear her thoughts. Emilio walked in and interrupted her train of thought. However, he didn't deter her from speaking her mind.

"I want to go back home." Mercedes said.

"Why?" he asked.

"Emilio please, I want to go home!"

Mercedes turned to him and spoke gently with tears in her eyes. "I want to go back home, if that's okay with you." She walked back inside and sat on the edge of the bed.

"Alright Mercedes, we can leave tonight." Emilio sighed. He watched her pack her things. His plan failed and she still wanted to leave. Some things couldn't be avoided; Mercedes would soon have to depend on him for everything.

She continued trying to reach her mother to no avail. Frustration was written on her face and Emilio saw it. The plane ride was a silent one. Neither of them had anything to say. He thought the choices he made on her behalf would make them closer. In actuality, it would tear them apart.

The Hidden Truth

Back in New York, Mercedes felt good to lie in her own bed. Emilio left for a few days to handle some out of town business. She was alone with her thoughts. She was watching the news and eating ice cream, when she saw her aunt's house in Queens burning while firefighters tried to extinguish it.

Her eyes began to fill with tears as she watched.

"Hi, I'm Jessica Richards standing in front of a home that has been burning for two days. Firefighters are here trying to put out the smoldering flames and the police are here collecting evidence. Other residents have been saved, but one resident described as a woman in her mid-thirties is in the hospital clinging to life. Her name has not been released, but if anyone has any information regarding this fire please call.........."

Mercedes looked at the TV and hoped that it wasn't anyone she knew in that house. She hoped everyone made it out safely.

Her cell phone shook her out of her thoughts and Mercedes saw an unknown number on the caller ID. She wasn't going to answer, but figured maybe it was her mother.

"Hello...Hi...yes I'm her daughter...what kind of accident? Oh my God! Oh my God noooo...!"

Mercedes dropped her bowl in horror as the person on the other end shared the news of her mother being the victim in the house fire. She quickly threw on a hoodie and sweatpants, snatched her keys, and ran out the front door on her way to the hospital.

She arrived in no time. She parked the car and dashed inside to the receptionist's desk.

"Excuse   me,   can   you   help   me   please?"

"How may I help you?" The receptionist said with an attitude.

"Hi my mother was rushed to the hospital on um, Tuesday. She was in a bad fire, can you help me?" Mercedes panicked.

"First and last name please?"

"Maria Carter."

"I'm sorry she can't have any visitors right now." The lady informed her.

"What the fuck do you mean? That's my mother?" Mercedes retorted. "I need to see my mother now."

Just then, security walked up to diffuse the situation, but it wasn't necessary. Mercedes was ready to punch the receptionist in the face. Her aunt Brenda stepped up and stopped her in her tracks.

"Mercedes?"

"Hey, is that you Auntie Brenda?" Mercedes eyes were swollen and red after hearing the news. Seeing a family member helped to soften the blow.

"Yes, it's me Baby." Mercedes embraced her and they both cried. "How's my mother, how is she doing?"

"She's still as beautiful as ever. She's a strong woman and the doctor said she'll make it." Brenda smiled as Mercedes sighed. Several tear drops fell from her eyes.

"Yeah she is indeed, what room is she in?"

"She's in room 118. I have to get the kids. They have me in an emergency shelter until they can find me permanent housing."

"Auntie don't worry about it. After Mama gets out the hospital, I'll give you some money and help you find a house."

"Oh, thank you Honey." Brenda hugged her niece. "You're just like your father....well take care I gotta go."

"Take care auntie." Mercedes hugged her one last time and watched her walk away. She made her way to her mother's room. As she approached, she braced herself for what she was going to see. She didn't know what to expect. When she mustered the courage to walk inside, what she saw would surpass anything she ever imagined.

The right side of her mother's face and arm were severely burned. She was covered in bandages and blood seeped through the bandages used to keep her sterile. Maria slept; she was on a cocktail of medication to keep her sedated and to ease the pain.

"Oh my God!" Mercedes said as she examined her mother. "Who would do this to you?" She whispered and pulled a chair beside her mother and sat down. She gently took Maria's hand and held it close to her face. She kissed it. Tears fell onto her wrist. Maria felt the warmth and opened her eyes. She turned to look at her daughter and her emotions took over.

"Hey Baby." Maria whispered.

"Hi Ma, are you okay?" Mercedes stood up over her mother.

"I'm doing fine; your mother is a fighter. I don't ever give up."

"That's good, I'm really glad that you're okay. I can't even imagine losing someone else. You're all I have left. I would be so devastated. I love you Ma." Mercedes kissed her mother on the forehead.

"I'm okay. I'm alive and I need a makeover." Maria forced a smile as a tear trickled from her eye. Mercedes wiped it away.

"Ma, you are beautiful no matter what. Daddy would think you're still the most beautiful woman in the world."

Maria began crying at the thought of her husband seeing her in this state. Mercedes consoled her mother. She could only imagine her pain and what she was feeling.

"Thank you Mercedes, that means a lot to me."

"I'm sorry Ma. I didn't even know you were here. I was in the Bahamas with Emilio. I knew something wasn't right. I felt it within my gut. I was having fun, but I needed to come home. I called you and never got an answer." Mercedes explained.

"Mercedes, I have something to tell you Sweetie." Maria took a deep breath before speaking.

"What Ma? What is it?"

"I want you to listen carefully. You are in danger. All this happened because I opened the door when I shouldn't have. The doorbell rang and I answered. The moment I did, I knew I should've stayed quiet." Maria looked to the ceiling and tried to prevent tears from falling. They escaped anyway and seeped into her ears and neck.

"I sat there and he tortured me, asking me about a safe that I knew nothing about. Then he told me it was my fault that my husband is dead, Chino, and Uncle Roy. He said he didn't care whether I lived or I died...Mercedes I almost died in there..." Maria continued speaking without mentioning the name of her attacker.

"Who did this to you Ma?"

"Emilio." Maria stared at her in the eyes awaiting a reaction.

Mercedes' heart dropped when she heard his name.

"Wait! Hold up!" Mercedes let out a little snicker. "Who did you say?"

"Emilio." Maria repeated.

"Are you trying to tell me that Emilio was the one who did this to you? That set the house on fire and wanted you to burn?" Mercedes got up and began nervously pacing.

"Why would he do this?" Mercedes asked aloud.

"Mercedes, it's a long story. Just know that you need to stay far away from his crazy ass. There's more information that you need to know about him." She told her daughter.

"Pass me my purse." Mercedes gave Maria her purse and watched her as she pulled out a voice recorder. It was slightly scorched, but still able to function. Maria gave it to her daughter and she carefully held it in her hand. She pressed the play button and Mercedes' eyes opened wide. She couldn't believe what she heard. It was true, the proof was right here. He couldn't deny it, even if he wanted to.

"That's why I love your daughter and she's falling in love with me. And I'm not going to have any one standing in my way...I killed Chino, your husband and I killed Roy!"

"I fucking knew it!" Mercedes barked through gritted teeth.

"I didn't want to tell you like this but..." Maria looked at her daughter with remorse. She knew Mercedes was falling in love with Emilio, but to find out he killed so many people close to her was too much to handle.

"It's alright Ma, I just can't believe this motherfucker betrayed me! He's going to pay for what he did." Mercedes took the recorder from her mother and kissed her on the cheek.

"I've got stuff to do Ma. I'm going to call you later to check on you. I love you."

"Mercedes!" Maria called out to stop her. Danger was all around them, but she didn't want it to hit Mercedes. It was too late; Mercedes hopped in her car and zoomed off. Tears blinded her vision as she drove.

She had to pull over to get herself together. She wondered how she could be so ignorant to his deceit. Something about him always felt uncomfortable, but she was blinded by his good looks and hypnotic charm. Mercedes thought how could she be in love with someone that tried to hurt her and her family. Her father always told her to follow her heart and her mind. She didn't listen and now she was dealing with the repercussions.

After gathering her thoughts and coming up with a plan of action, Mercedes ventured home. She would have loved to stay with her mother longer, but she couldn't bear seeing her in that way. She went home and cried herself to sleep. Tomorrow would be a brand new day.

Sweet Revenge

Emilio returned to New York from D.C. the next day. Mercedes decided that she would get up, run some errands and get her hair done. Not only was it a mess, but she needed to feel good. A fresh hairdo always helped.

She drove silently to her mother's salon. Luckily when she arrived, there were only a few heads in there and she was able to be seen without a long wait.

"Hey, how are you Laura?" Mercedes smiled as she greeted one of the hairstylists. Laura was doing a clients hair and turned around to greet Mercedes.

"Hey girl, I'm fine and yourself?"

"I'm doing alright."

"Hey, at least you're making it. Some motherfuckers out here are just barely getting by." The hair salon all started laughing. "What are you getting done today Mama?"

"The usual-just a wash, blow dry and press." Mercedes smiled as she sat down and grabbed one of the magazines from the table.

"Alright after her, I can spice you up." Laura smiled as she continued doing her client's hair. Mercedes browsed through the magazine. Twenty minutes later, it was her turn in the chair.

"Can you handle opening in the morning and supervising everyone else while I tend to my mom?" She asked Laura as she leaned back to be lathered.

"No problem, I did hear about your mother." Laura sympathetically said. "How is she doing?" Laura asked while adding conditioner to Mercedes' scalp.

"She's doing alright. I mean she's still in the hospital, but she's going to make it."

"Yeah that's good to hear, whoever did that shit is fucked up and I hope they rot in prison." Laura said as she massaged her scalp and rinsed it out with water.

"That person is going to rot in hell." Mercedes said. She was beginning to cry.

"It'll be alright Mercedes, just hang in there Mama." Laura rubbed Mercedes' shoulder and smiled at her. Mercedes returned the smile and believed that soon, all would be well. She was going to make sure of it herself.

She had her hair washed, conditioned and sat in the chair to have her hair rollers set. As she sat under the dryer, she perused a magazine. She was oblivious to her surroundings and didn't notice someone staring at her as she read. Finally, she looked up and saw a woman looking at her as if she knew her.

"Mercedes? Is that you?"

"Yes that's me." Mercedes looked at her with a mystified look on her face.

"How are you? You don't remember me?"

Mercedes struggled to place the face, but came up blank.

"It's Milan; I use to work for your father." The woman identified herself. Mercedes laughed; she had so much on her mind these days that she was skeptical of everyone.

"Oh, now I remember who you are. You look so much different with your hair shorter."

"Yeah, I needed a new look...maybe a new identity." Milan chuckled. "I don't live around here anymore, I moved to Brooklyn. I needed to leave Manhattan because the streets were getting ugly out here."

"Yeah, I feel you." Mercedes nodded.

"What's new?" Milan asked placing her purse on her lap and sitting back.

"Same shit, different day. Everyone seems to be dying." Mercedes nonchalantly said.

"Shit is crazy it seems. How is your mom doing? I know it's been hard on y'all with your father and uncle passing." Milan asked.

"Yeah, it is what it is. Some motherfucker tried to kill my mother too. They set my aunt's house on fire and left her to burn to death." Mercedes eyes got watery just thinking about it.

"Oh my God Mercedes, I'm sorry to hear about that." Milan shook her head in disgust. "I'm thinking about moving out of New York, there ain't shit out here for me. I was messing around with Emilio for two years. Around the time your father died he started acting funny. One day he just up and left me and he told me that he had met another young woman who he fell in love with and wanted to marry." Mercedes figured that Milan was talking about her and shifted her eyes as she listened.

"I cried and begged for him not to leave me. I did everything in my power to get him back, but one day he pulled out a gun and threatened to kill me if I didn't leave him alone. Finally he kicked me out of his house." Milan sighed as a few teardrops fell from her eye.

"Oh my God Milan, everything will be alright. Some niggas just ain't shit!" Mercedes replied.

"You got that right." Milan said as she wiped away her tears.

"I feel like going to the house he and his little bitch share in Long Island and blowing that shit up." Mercedes looked at Milan and wanted to tell her that little bitch was her, but she just kept her mouth closed and smiled.

"I thought Emilio was a very sweet guy, but I guess not. I saw him briefly the other day and he told me I needed to retrieve something of my father's, but I lost his address." Milan quickly gave her the whereabouts of Emilio.

"Whoever that little bitch is, she's real lucky because that nigga is definitely packing." Milan smirked. "I ain't gon lie, that nigga got a thick and fat dick."

"I know." Mercedes mumbled.

"Excuse me?" Milan looked at her.

"I said oh really?" Mercedes lied.

"Yeah, but that nigga ain't no good. He's gonna get what's coming to him one day and I hope it's soon. I hope someone knocks his top off one day." Milan said in anger. Mercedes thought that Milan must have loved Emilio a lot for her to still be angry.

"Well it was nice speaking to you girl. Take care and give your mom my condolences."

"Alright I will; thank you Milan." Milan kissed Mercedes on the cheek and left the salon. Mercedes' hair dryer stopped and she sat in Laura's chair so she could have her rollers removed. Since she was at her mother's salon, she got her hair done for free. She always gave Laura a generous tip.

With the information of Emilio's whereabouts, Mercedes got into her car and jetted to the location. She wanted to see where he lived and what he was about. She arrived and parked her car several cars down from the house. She wanted to watch from a distance.

She sat for a while and didn't see anyone, so she walked up to the house and ventured into the garage. She saw a car parked with a white cloth cover. She removed the cover. She was in shock when she realized it was the same black Cadillac with a rusted door that had been following her for years. This was the same car that she saw before Chino was killed. This was the car that she saw at the funeral and the same car that followed her on the highway.

Anger took over her entire being and she began to hate Emilio more than ever. Her thoughts were racing, but she knew no one else could be driving his car.

Mercedes walked up the back stairs and approached a back door. It was already ajar. Inside, she found another door with a lock. Since she didn't have a key, she opened her purse to gain access on her own. She was happy that she carried her gun with her. She shot lock and placed the gun back into her purse.

She looked around to see if anyone noticed the noise. She appeared safe for now.

Once inside, she noticed plain furniture and nothing resembling the life of a baller. From her periphery she noticed a door open and walked towards it. She gently pushed it open and entered a room that resembled a shrine. The walls were plastered with pictures of her and her family. Her mouth dropped, it seemed like she was being followed all of her life. Photos of Don, Maria, Chino and Mercedes were everywhere.

The truth had been finally revealed and the puzzle pieces matched Emilio's betrayal perfectly. Now Mercedes knew that he had everything to do with the death of her father and boyfriend, not to mention the attempted murder of her mother. She ripped off the pictures in fury while screaming and crying. She was so disappointed in herself for believing that he loved her. He only used her.

She left his house and walked to her car with her shoes pounding the pavement. She had never been so angry in her life. She took a deep breath and called Emilio.

"Hey Babe, what's up?"

"Nothing, just thinking about you." Mercedes flirted with him.

"Oh really? You miss Daddy?" Emilio said as he grinned from ear to ear.

"I do miss you Daddy. Do you miss Mami?" Mercedes purred.

"Oh hell yeah, I miss my Mami. When I come home I'm going to spank you; you've been a very bad girl."

"No you've been a very, very, bad boy!" How about I meet you at your house and have a very special surprise waiting for you." Mercedes suggested while putting together her sinister plot.

"How do you know where I live?" Emilio asked. He was thrown for a loop. Mercedes almost got caught up in her lie.

"No Baby I don't, but I was going to ask you." She lied. "I just want to do something really special for you Babe. I want our time together to be memorable as always."

Emilio gave her the address and had no clue what she was planning for him. He also had no idea that she was already sitting in her car on his street, awaiting his arrival.

"There's an extra key under the mat when you first walk in. My house is really messy, but I'll be there soon. Don't snoop around!" He advised her.

"Alright Babe, see ya. It will be a night you won't forget." Mercedes ended the call and grabbed her purse. She got out of her car and walked back up to the house. She replaced the cover on the black car to keep it hidden. She wanted things to be just as they were when he left.

xxxxxxxxxx

Mercedes made herself comfortable inside of Emilio's home. She unwrapped her hair, which was still pinned up from her day of beauty at the hair salon. She wore pink lingerie and kept her high heels on to complete the seductive ensemble. She had a satin robe and tied it under her breasts. It strategically covered the gun she hid in her waist. Emilio was on his way and she soon heard him pull in the driveway. He parked directly behind the car that was covered up in the driveway.

Mercedes prepared a special meal for Emilio. It consisted of Spanish yellow rice, fried chicken, black beans and some mashed potatoes. She removed a vial from her purse and poured a clear liquid into the gravy, potatoes, and all over the chicken. She stirred it well and made sure that it blended together. Mercedes then placed two candles on the table and lit them. Wine glasses finished the décor and she filled them with Moet. Emilio's drink bubbled as she slipped an extacy pill in it.

As soon as she did that, the lock to the front door clicked and Emilio opened the door.

She sat at the table with her hands beneath her chin awaiting his arrival. Emilio walked in and placed a briefcase on the floor. He walked over to the table and kissed Mercedes on the lips.

"Baby, you look and smell great." Emilio complimented her.

"Aww Thank you, Babe." Mercedes smiled.

"Mhmmm this food looks delicious Ma, let me find out." Emilio took off his jacket and placed it behind his seat. He sat down and was preparing to eat.

"I can cook, don't play!" Mercedes snickered and picked up her fork to begin eating dinner.

"I'm just fucking with you Ma." Mercedes watched as he dug into his food. She smiled as she watched him demolish his entire plate. He finished it off by drinking every drop of his Moet. Mercedes had eaten half of her food, when she saw Emilio clutching his chest. Beads of sweat appeared on his forehead and he looked around the room gasping for air. He felt like the room was closing in on him.

"What's wrong Babe? Are you alright?" Mercedes asked while taking another bite of her mashed potatoes.

"Yeah, I'm fine. My throat just feels a little itchy and I feel hot." Emilio cleared his throat as he shook his head trying to shake off the feeling.

"Are you ready for Mami?" Mercedes smiled and sensually kissed him on the neck.

"Hell yeah, I'm ready for Mami. Let's get it on." Emilio yelled. He started acting silly and dancing in a goofy manner. Mercedes looked at him with a peculiar look on her face. She grabbed his hand and led him down the hall. He smacked her ass along the way. The drugs and poison were already working on him.

"You better stop being a naughty boy because naughty boys get punished." Mercedes warned him as they entered the room. She pushed him on the bed and started dancing seductively.

"Do you like what you see?" She asked as she crawled on top of him and purred like a cat. She started kissing him on his neck and made her way down to his shirt and started unbuttoning it. Mercedes licked and kissed all over his chest and sucked on his small nipples. Emilio moaned and grabbed her hair and pulled her up to kiss him. As they kissed, she pulled down his pants and felt that he was hard as a rock. She smiled and grabbed his dick. She yanked it up.

"Damn Mami, why so rough?"

"Because I like it like that, I like it nice and rough." Mercedes smiled and she started jerking his dick up and down causing him to go crazy. She crawled on top of him and started whispering nasty shit in his ear.

"I want you to relax while I ride your dick as fast as I can. I want to you cum all over me and then hit it from the back." Mercedes said as she continued jerking his dick in her hand.

"Damn Mami, you're in full control." Emilio responded. "I want you to do whatever you want to me, whatever you want." He said as he threw his hands up.

"Are you sure about that?" Mercedes asked with a questionable brow.

"I surrender." He said with a huge smile. Mercedes bent over and started sucking all over his neck. She placed soft kisses and left traces on his face and neck as she grabbed the gun.

"I told you before motherfucker. The Carters never die!!! Those around us do." Mercedes said with an enraged tone.

She pulled her gun and aimed it directly at his chest. She jumped off of his lap and let off 4 shots that hit him directly in the chest and stomach area. She enjoyed watching his body jerk up and down. It gave her the same feeling that he had when he took those that she loved.

The smell of gunpowder filled the room and she took a deep breath as it tickled her nose. Mercedes wiped her tears away with the back of her hand. She relaxed her finger on the trigger of the gun. It was then that she noticed Emilio was still moving.

Blood spewed from his mouth as he tried to speak. He was begging for forgiveness. Mercedes had no mercy for him; she put the gun to against his temple and pulled the trigger again.

Moments later, the sounds of sirens grew louder as they approached Emilio's house. Mercedes went to the dining table and sat with the gun next to her plate. She waited for the police to come and take her away. As if in slow motion, she sipped more of her wine and watched the red and blue flashing lights reflect on her face. She was in a daze and had flashbacks of Chino, her father, her uncle and her mother in her mind. She had nothing left to lose. Finally, it was the end for them. For Mercedes, it was only the beginning.

Her revenge was sweet...

About the Author

Out of Boston, Massachusetts comes Ricketta Pryce.

With a passion for writing, Ricketta has been putting pen to paper since junior high school by keeping her journal filled with poems. By 9th grade, Ricketta - or Pinky Dior, as she is fondly called in the literary world - had finished her first manuscript. With the encouragement of a teacher, Pinky was inspired to pursue a career in writing. Now, at age 23, Pinky has several short stories: Hazel Eyes 1 and 2 {DC Bookdiva Publication}, The Diamond Exchange, Valentine's Day Massacre {DC Bookdiva Publications}, "Pink Lipstick & Pistols" short story series. She's also featured in three anthologies, Almighty Dolla, Bitches Ain't Loyal and The Commission {DC Bookdiva Publications}.

She has eight unpublished novels and many more started on her laptop. With more work by Pinky on the way, make sure you keep an eye out for this talented author.

DC Bookdiva Publications

#245 4401-A Connecticut Avenue, NW

Washington, DC 20008

dcbookdiva.com

Name: _____

Inmate ID _____

Address: _____

City/State: _____ **Zip:** _____

QUANTITY	TITLES	PRICE	TOTAL
	Up The Way, Ben		15.00
	Dynasty By Dutch		15.00
	Dynasty 2 By Dutch		15.00
	Trina, Darrell Debrew		15.00
	A Killer'z Ambition, Nathan Welch		15.00
	Lorton Legends, Eyone Williams		15.00
	A Beautiful Satan, RJ Champ		15.00
	The Hustle, Frazier Boy		15.00
	Tina, Darrell Debrew		15.00
	Q, Dutch		15.00
	Secrets Never Die, Eyone Williams		15.00
	Dynasty 3, Dutch		15.00
	A Beautiful Satan 2, RJ Champ		15.00
	Smokin Mirrors, Mike O		15.00
	A Killer'z Ambition 2, Nathan Welch		15.00
	The Commission, Team DCB		15.00

Sub-Total $_____

Shipping/Handling (Via US Media Mail) $3.95 1-2 Books, $7.95 1-3 Books, 4 or more titles-Free Shipping

Shipping $ _____
Total Enclosed $ _____

Certified or government issued checks and money orders, all mail in orders take 5-7 Business days to be delivered. Books can also be purchased on our website at dcbookdiva.com and by credit card at 1866-928-9990. Incarcerated readers receive 25% discount. Please pay $11.25 per book and apply the same shipping terms as stated above

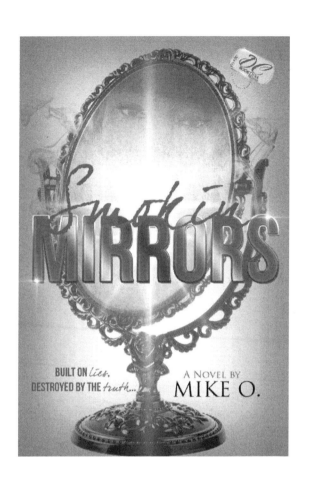

BUILT ON *lies,*
DESTROYED BY THE *truth...*

A NOVEL BY
MIKE O.

In Stock Now!

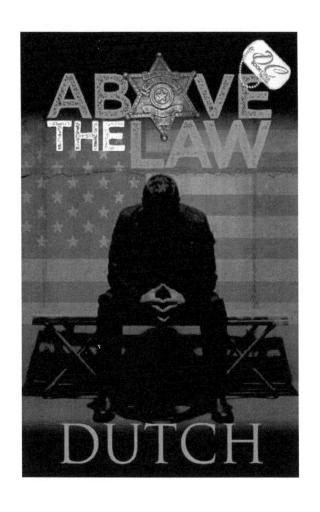

Coming Soon!